AXE'S FALL

AN INSURGENTS MC ROMANCE

CHIAH WILDER

D1715056

I love hearing from my readers. You can email me at chiahwilder@gmail.com.

Make sure you sign up for my newsletter so you can keep up with my new releases, special sales, free short stories, and other treats only available to newsletter readers. When you sign up, you will receive a FREE hot and steamy novella. Sign up at: http://eepurl.com/bACCL1.

Visit me on facebook at www.facebook.com/Chiah-Wilder-1625397261063989

Description

The first time Axe saw her at his friend's wedding, he knew she'd have her long legs wrapped around his waist, moaning and begging for more.

A member of the Insurgents Motorcycle Club, Axe has the tattoos, the ripped body, and the badass attitude. He's great in bed and always leaves women pleading for more. But…

Don't ask him to commit.
Don't ask for a phone call.
Don't expect anything but wild, mind-blowing sex.

That's the way he rolls…
Until he meets her.

It was a one-night stand.
He was gone before she woke up.
Finished. Done. Moved on.

Except he can't stop thinking about her.

What the f*&k?!

Baylee Peters has thrown herself obsessively into her career vying for the brass ring of partnership at one of the most prestigious architecture firms in Denver. Not wanting any distractions, she has shelved romance. Nothing can stand in her way.

Until she meets him.
The dark-haired man with the smoldering eyes and tatted, chiseled body who makes her insides melt.

It was just for one night. So what if the sex was incredible?

Then work takes her to Pinewood Springs. And to him. Her ordered world explodes.

As if she didn't have enough trouble with a sexy, bad boy biker whom she can't stop drooling over, her memory of the night her mother was murdered is coming back, and the killer is waiting to make sure no one knows what she remembers.

Can Baylee trust Axe enough to let him into her life and take control? Can he save her before a determined killer takes away Axe's one chance at happiness?

Axe vows to protect her, and he will stop at nothing until he makes her his woman.

The Insurgents MC series are standalone romance novels. This is Axe and Baylee's love story. This book contains violence, strong language, and steamy/graphic sexual scenes. It describes the life and actions of an outlaw motorcycle club. HEA. No cliffhangers! The book is intended for readers over the age of 18.

Titles in the Series:

Hawk's Property: Insurgents Motorcycle Club Book 1
Jax's Dilemma: Insurgents Motorcycle Club Book 2
Chas's Fervor: Insurgents Motorcycle Club Book 3
Axe's Fall: Insurgents Motorcycle Club Book 4

PROLOGUE

Summer, 1998
Denver, Colorado

THE MAN'S VOICE shattered the quietude. Baylee hugged her stuffed rabbit closer and held her breath. It wasn't her father's voice; he was out on business and wouldn't be back until the morning. She pulled the covers over her head and wished the fear creeping inside her would crawl away.

Silence.

The young girl let out a small breath, closed her eyes, and let sleep replace the fear from a few minutes before.

Crash! Baylee jerked up in her bed, her rabbit clutched to her side, her heart slamming against her chest. Her mother's sobs pierced the veil of normalcy. *Mommy's in trouble.*

Baylee scrambled out of her twin bed and padded to the stairs. From the glow of the fireplace, she saw figures dancing on the walls like shadow puppets. One was tall and gripping, the other was short, curvy, and struggling.

"Please, don't. Leave now. Please," her mother said in a voice laced in panic.

"Give me what you've been teasing me with for a long time. You think you can flirt with me then turn me off? You know you want this."

"I don't. Stop. If you don't stop, I'm going to tell John when he gets back."

"Just one kiss and I'll go. Come on, you know you want it."

The young child quietly descended the stairs until she was more than halfway down. She sat on the carpeted step and clung to the white-painted wooden dowels, peering through them as though they were a looking glass into a world of shadows and fear.

"Stop it! Please," Baylee's mother cried out as she grabbed something on the cabinet next to her.

The scene played out on the walls of the living room: her mother bending her arm and hitting the man's head, his hand grabbing his head then slapping her mother so hard she fell on the floor, the tall outline then pouncing on her mother. Her mother's gasps and muffled screams became weaker, and her body stopped moving.

Baylee leapt up and rushed into the room, screaming, "Mommy! Don't hurt my mommy. Mommy!"

The man, startled, jumped up and approached the young girl, his eyes flashing. She backed up and ran to the front door. Her high-pitched screams rang out through the neighborhood, and neighbors came out on their front porches to see what had punctured the stillness of the night.

A loud *thump* on the door made the man turn and run out of the house through the back.

"What's going on in there?" a deep voice asked on the other side of the door.

"My mommy's hurt. She's not moving," Baylee answered, her voice small. The shrill wail of police sirens echoed eerily in the distance, coming closer.

By the time the cops entered the house, the young girl was kneeling by her lifeless mother—Baylee's eyes unblinking, her body stiff. Even though warm hands touched her, the child had retreated to the world where nightmares lived, where blackness surrounded everything.

From that night on, Baylee Peters's memory would be filled with shadows and darkness.

CHAPTER ONE

Seventeen years later
Summer
Denver, Colorado

*N*ICE ASS. WONDER *what the front of her looks like.* Axe admired the shapely brunette in the pew across the aisle from him in the church. Her celery-green cocktail dress molded over her curvy hips and stopped mid-thigh, revealing long, well-defined tanned legs. Axe's gaze lingered as he imagined them wrapped around his waist while he slammed his cock into her. His body tightened and his fingers itched to dig into her fleshy hips while he spread her "fuck me" legs wide and rammed into her from behind, watching her hot ass jiggle.

Shifting, he readjusted his pants as he raised his eyes to glossy, dark brown hair falling down her back. The setting sun bathed her hair in warm yellow and red hues as it streamed in through the stained glass windows. The impulse to touch it was strong, and he could almost feel the silky strands wrapped around his hand as he pulled her head back while he pounded his dick in her.

The priest said in a clear voice, "I now pronounce you husband and wife."

Axe pulled his eyes away from the luscious creature across from him and watched as Derek, one of his best buddies from childhood, walked down the aisle with his new bride. Axe hadn't wanted to come to Denver for a wedding, of all things, and he'd made up some bullshit about not being able to go, but when Derek called and told him he had to be there, *period*, Axe relented and rode his Harley the three hours to make it.

He and Derek had been buds since they were five years old. They had formed an allegiance early on, Axe beating up the bullies who picked on Derek in the trailer park where they grew up. Right from the start, they'd been tight, their time together meaning less time spent in their not-so-happy homes. Derek's mother was a drunk, and his father was a cruel man who loved to torment anyone who crossed his path. He spent many nights at Axe's trailer, trying to keep out of his dad's way. When someone finally shot the bastard late one summer night, the park rejoiced, and Derek changed forever. He was no longer the kid afraid of his shadow, the one whose blue eyes were sad and haunted most of the time. Derek seemed to relax for the first time in his life.

Axe noticed Derek's mother sitting in the front row of the church, her eyes watery and her face leathered and wrinkled from years of too much sun and booze. Her favorite thing to do most mornings, after she'd woken up hungover, was to stretch out on a cheap, plastic chaise lounge in a tiny bikini, which left little to the imagination, and take in the rays as she sipped her first of many glasses of bourbon.

The first time Axe had seen Mrs. Keary in her skimpy bikini, he'd been around thirteen years old. Watching her breasts swing under a pink top which barely held them in had mesmerized the young boy, and he'd felt something funny grab him in his crotch. The side view of Mrs. Keary had shown white, round flesh spilling out. He'd known he shouldn't have stared, but the sight of it had made him feel weird and excited. Then she'd caught him, and her throaty laugh mocked him.

She'd looked at him, a cigarette dangling from her mouth. "Like what you're seeing?"

He didn't answer, too embarrassed at being caught checking out his best friend's mother's breasts.

"Come on over and touch them, if you like. I'm not gonna tell."

Shaking his head, he'd run away, her raspy laughter following him.

From that day on, Axe had made sure he wasn't around when Mrs. Keary sunbathed.

There, in the church, she looked like a used up, old hag. He hadn't seen her since they all moved from the trailer park many years back.

Derek and his mom moved to Denver during high school, and Axe had joined up with the Insurgents MC when he was seventeen. Even though their paths went in different directions, they'd stayed in touch, seeing each other whenever Derek came to Pinewood Springs. When he'd told Axe he was tying the knot, Axe was happy for him. For such a long time, his buddy had seemed lost. Why he wanted to tie himself down to one pussy was hard for Axe to understand, but it seemed like Derek was happy with the chick who donned his ring, so Axe was cool with that.

As Derek and his new wife walked down the aisle, past Axe, he high-fived Derek, who grinned back. Turning his head around, he searched for the hot woman in the green dress, but she was gone. *What the fuck? Where the hell did she go?* He wanted to see her face, because if she looked anything like the back of her, he was going to have to fuck her before the night was over. Wasn't that supposed to happen at weddings—random sex? If he had to drag his ass to Denver to suffer through a wedding ceremony, he was determined to have some action before he headed back home. He'd definitely be looking for the green-dressed babe at the reception.

THE RECEPTION WAS in one of the large ballrooms at the Excelsior Hotel on 15th Street. Through the large windows, the skyscrapers looked as if they could touch the clouds. The lights of the surrounding buildings winked and sparkled as night descended.

Large, round tables dotted the ballroom, and silver and blue crepe paper streamed down from the chandeliers. Large, tissue wedding bells dangled from the ceiling, and a large paper-flower backdrop covered the wall behind the wedding party table.

"May I help you, sir?" a woman dressed in black pants and a starched white shirt asked him.

"Trying to find my table," Axe replied.

The waitperson searched the guest list and directed Axe to table number eight. Looking around, he spotted the bar on the other side of the room and made his way over to grab a beer. A group of three women in their early twenties giggled and raked their gazes over his muscular body. His normal attire of blue jeans, black t-shirt, and his Insurgents' leather cut had been replaced by dress clothes: white dress shirt molded over his ripped chest and sculpted biceps, and black pants fitting snug across his firm ass and bulge.

Axe checked out the women openly; they were dressed in silk and satin cocktail dresses. They all had the same hairstyle, were blondes, and teetered on very high heels. One of the women, the one with the cherry-red strapless dress, had nice tits, but he wasn't interested. He was looking for a woman in a celery-green dress.

Knowing the women were going to approach him, he threw them a charming smile, winked at them, and headed back toward his table. The high-pitched giggling from the group grated on his nerves.

As he walked, he saw Mrs. Keary scrambling toward him. Pretending not to see her, he changed his direction, but his friend's mother caught up to him, clutching his arm with her bony hand.

"Hello, Michael. It's been a long time." She moved her eyes up and down his body, lingering a little too long on his crotch. "You're looking good. You're all grown up now, aren't you?"

"Hey."

"When was the last time I saw you?"

Axe shrugged.

"It was right before you and your mother moved from Evergreen Lane. How old were you? About fifteen?"

"Sounds 'bout right."

"How is your mother doing?"

Axe didn't want to answer any more questions, especially about his self-absorbed mom. All she ever cared about was finding a man. If she could keep one, Axe would be shocked. It was like his mom fed off male attention. After his dad had ditched the family when he was nine years old, Axe had been taking care of his mom and fending for himself.

Strung out on prescription drugs most days, and lamenting over her sad life, she didn't have the time or energy to include her son.

"Fine." Axe yanked his arm from Mrs. Keary's grip. "Gotta go."

"Promise me you're going to dance with me. Just one dance." She batted her cheap, false eyelashes.

"I don't dance."

"I can show you. It'd be for old times' sake, you know?"

"No, I don't."

"You're not being very friendly. You're hurting my feelings."

Axe narrowed his dark eyes. "That's too bad, but I don't give a fuck." He smiled thinly when her eyes widened in surprise. "See ya." He turned around and went in search of his table.

Before he reached table eight, he heard the ringing of the dinner bell telling the guests to take their seats. Axe plopped down on his chair at the table for ten and stared at the tissue paper flowers and bells in the centerpiece. A basket of rolls, small packets of butter, and two silver gravy bowls containing salad dressing were on the table. Not giving a damn whether it was proper or not, Axe grabbed a roll, buttered it, and took a large bite out of it. As he chewed, his table filled up. People introduced themselves to him, and he cursed Derek for making him a part of this hokey shit.

The wait staff placed plates of mixed greens in front of the guests, and Axe drenched his salad in creamy Italian dressing. As he placed a forkful in his mouth, *she* slipped in the empty chair across from him. Seeing *her* in front of him in all her beauty and ripeness took Axe by surprise. His throat tightened, making him cough.

"Are you all right?" one of the guests at his table asked.

Nodding, he tried to stop choking. *I must look like a fuckin' idiot with watering eyes and red face.*

After gulping down some water, his throat finally stopped seizing, and he looked at her from under hooded lids. Her gaze met his as he took in her beautiful hazel eyes. For a few seconds, he gaped, losing himself in her stare and feeling like a fucking teenager. She smiled at him—perfect white teeth with a tiny glimpse of pink tongue. How he wanted that tongue on his body, her Cupid's bow lips fitting perfectly around his cock.

"Hi," she said in a smoky voice.

Fuck! "Hey," he replied, still unable to take his eyes off her.

"It was a nice ceremony, don't you think?" She brought her wine glass to her lips and took a sip.

Not as nice as the image of your lips parted open and moaning as I lick your pussy. "Yeah. It was cool." Axe continued to hold her gaze until she shifted her eyes to the centerpiece, a light red blush staining her cheeks.

"Who do you know? The groom or the bride?"

Axe threw her a half-smile. "Groom. You?"

"Bride." Her laughter was sultry, even though he could tell she was nervous by the way she kept smoothing down the tablecloth.

"You're very pretty." His eyes moved to her mouth, then slowly made their way down to her peek of cleavage.

"Oh. Thanks." The woman turned to the older gentlemen beside her. "Can you please pass the pepper?"

Before the man could react, Axe stood up, leaned across the table, and handed her the pepper shaker, his hand touching hers. A spark lit and blazed through him, and he raised his eyebrows as she gasped, staring boldly into his dark gaze. *Fuck me. What was that?*

"Thanks," she mumbled, then averted her eyes, breaking the intensity of the moment.

"No problem." He smiled, loving the way she absentmindedly doused her salad with pepper then choked when she took a bite. Yeah, he was making her nervous. The way she bit her lower lip was sexy as fuck, and the perpetual blush on her neck and cheeks was turning him way on. Before the night was over, he'd have to have his cock in her pussy, which he bet would be wet and sweet.

Throughout the rest of dinner, they checked each other out. By the time the table was cleared, Axe sported a rock-hard dick, straining against his zipper. He was ready to grab the vixen by her hair, slam her down on the table and fuck her like a wild animal in front of all the wedding guests. Never had he experienced such an urge to bang one particular woman.

Fucking women was as much a part of Axe as breathing was. His first fuck had been in the woods behind the trailer park when he was fourteen. Sadie had a reputation for being easy, and she was three years older than Axe, but she took him by the hand one late, summer afternoon and showed him what to do to a woman. After that, he was hooked. He fucked his way through half of the girls in his high school then proceeded to do the same in community college.

Since joining the Insurgents, he'd come to love easy pussy from the club whores and hoodrats whenever he was horny, which was most of the time. Axe didn't want the drama dating involved, or the constraints of being tied down to one woman, so he fucked them and walked away. He always made sure he left the woman purring, though, and he'd never had any complaints.

The woman who made his dick throb intrigued him. She wasn't like the club whores or hoodrats. Something about the way her body was covered up by her sexy dress made him hornier than he'd been in a long time.

The music started, bringing Axe out of his daydreaming. He hated dancing, but he'd make an exception and ask her—at least he'd be able to hold her. Before he could scoot his chair back, however, a lanky man in his early thirties approached her and whispered something in her ear. She laughed, placing a small hand on his. Axe growled. *What a flirty bitch. She checks me out all through dinner, and now she's making a play for this nerd? Fuck that.*

She stood up, and the wedding guest led her out to the dance floor. She was tall, her four-inch heels adding even more height. Axe wanted to feel her heels digging into his ass as he banged her hard against the wall. Why didn't he forget about her and pick another woman? Several had been giving him the once-over, and he still had the giggling threesome from earlier in the evening. Axe liked fucking two and three women at once, and he knew the airheads would be more than willing, but he wasn't interested. All he wanted was to screw the woman who moved so seductively on the dance floor.

He watched as they danced. The nerdy guy kept trying to look down her dress, and the way he pressed her in to him told Axe that he wanted to feel her tits against him. Axe couldn't blame him for wanting that, but he wasn't going to let it happen. The jerk's dick was probably semi-hard. And why was she allowing him to hold her like that? *Fuck, she's so close to this guy, they'd need a crowbar to pry them apart.* Axe was going to stop it. Immediately. He sauntered over, making a bee line for the couple.

"I'm cutting in," Axe stated, his eyes focused on her mouth.

"Well, I—" the man began, then stopped when Axe's death stare froze him. Her dance partner dropped her hand and backed up, allowing Axe to take over.

Her hand was silky, and he curled his arm around her waist, tugging her closer to him until her tits were pressed against *his* hard chest.

"Are you always this pushy?" she asked in a soft, lilting voice which skimmed over him, hitting him right in his cock.

"Only when I want something."

Her eyes widened. "What do you want?"

"You."

The woman's lips parted, and Axe wanted to slip his tongue inside her warm mouth.

"Excuse me?"

"You heard me. We can play it like you don't know what I'm talking about and I'll keep feeding you lines, or we can be honest. I want you, and you want me." Axe placed his fingers against her lips. "Don't deny it. You've been eye-fucking me since you sat down at the table."

She gasped. "What kind of woman do you think I am?"

Axe leaned down and whispered in her ear. "I don't know, but I'm aiming to find out." When he took her earlobe gently between his teeth for a second, he felt her shiver.

"You're pretty sure of yourself, aren't you?"

"Yeah, and I'm pretty sure you're gonna be screaming and begging me for more after I'm finished with you."

The woman cocked her head, scrutinizing his face. It was as if she were battling with some internal voice. Axe knew she was intrigued, but she was fighting with her goody-two-shoes persona. He hoped like hell her naughty girl beat the shit out of the good girl so he could have some fun.

"I don't do this sort of thing," she said softly against his ear, her breath tickling his neck. She was too sexy.

"I'm not judging you, sweetheart."

"If—and I'm not sure I'm going to do this—but *if* I decide to throw caution to the wind, this will be a one-night stand only. No names, no phone numbers, no personal information at all. Okay?"

Axe kissed her neck, murmuring, "You're my kind of woman. Nothing but a good time. No strings attached. I'm totally on board."

"I've got a room in the hotel."

"What're we waiting for?"

"Shouldn't we stay until they cut the cake?"

"I'm sure we can find something to eat besides cake." He winked at her, and she blushed. It had been a long time since he'd made a woman blush. *This is gonna be more fun than I thought.*

Discreetly, they walked out of the ballroom and entered the elevator. When the shiny brass doors closed, Axe crushed his lips against hers, pulling her close while he squeezed her ass. Stiff at first, she eventually relaxed and opened her mouth, his tongue diving in. During the entire elevator ride to the twentieth floor, they groped, panted, and kissed until the bell dinged and the doors opened.

"I'm in room 2032," she said between breaths as Axe continued to kiss her.

"Lead the way, sweetheart."

CHAPTER TWO

A S BAYLEE INSERTED her key card, her thoughts spun out of control. *What the hell am I doing? I don't even know this guy, and I'm taking him up to my room for a one-night stand. Am I nuts?*

The door swung open, and a nicely decorated room greeted them. The king-sized bed looked like a beacon guiding the lovers to it. Baylee knew she was beyond insane; in all her years, she'd never done anything like a one-night stand before. Yes, she'd been going through a dry spell because her career was so demanding, but the last thing she wanted was the complication of a relationship. Before she came to the wedding, she'd told herself that if she found someone interesting she'd have a no-strings attached liaison for one night. But *telling* herself and *doing* it were two different things. She didn't think she'd go through with it.

Baylee had noticed him in the church, out of the corner of her eye as his stare bored into her. His chiseled good looks stood out among the wedding guests. The way he looked at her made her stomach flutter. Later, at the reception when she'd walked up to the table, Baylee noticed it was *him*: the sexy, dark-haired man whose stormy eyes locked with hers, and she took it as a sign that her one-night stand was meant to be. Even then she didn't think she'd have the nerve to actually go through with it. Yet lo and behold, she was now in her room with this gorgeous stranger.

From where she'd sat, she could see how ripped his chest and arms were, and she had to force herself to turn away for fear she'd start to drool. His mop of hair fell down over his forehead, and she wanted to lean over and brush away the strands. When he'd sneak glances at her, a slow throb pulsed through her center, and she'd pictured his hands and mouth stroking every inch of her body.

Then he took her in his arms on the dance floor, and she'd melted. But in her hotel room, standing before him and his rock-hard bulge, she began to have second thoughts. *Baylee, you need this. Let this hot guy fuck your brains out, get rid of all your pent-up tension, and go on with your life. An opportunity like this doesn't come around every day.*

"Whatcha thinkin' about, sweetheart? Not changing your mind, are you?" Axe stood back, his dark gaze roaming up and down her body. "I bet you're beautiful under all your clothes."

Baylee twirled a strand of her hair around her finger, staring back at Axe. He was gorgeous and at six-foot-three, he was just the perfect size for her five-nine height. Even with her high heels, he still stood taller than she. Licking her lips, she took in his strong jaw and broad nose, which looked like it may have been broken more than one time. His full lips exposed straight, white teeth when he smiled. His face had a hard edge to it, and she was sure he'd show her a night to remember. The guy was clearly dark, dangerous, and rough around the edges. A perfect person to give her the release she craved without the fear of falling for him. She'd bet he was a dirty talker, and she hoped he was, because she loved a filthy-mouthed man. It was one of her secrets she didn't share with anyone—not even the men she'd been involved with.

As she stood there, staring at him, he walked over and yanked her against him, his mouth covering hers. He kissed her with such ferocity it took her breath away. Her stomach was doing a samba, and she chided herself for reacting so foolishly to a stranger she'd never see again.

"You taste delicious. I have a lot of plans for your luscious lips." Axe's breath on her made her shiver, and she clasped her arms around his neck tightly, throwing her head back further so he could bury his tongue deeper in her mouth. "Fuck yeah, baby. I like that," he said huskily when he broke away from her.

"I like the way you kiss me."

"Oh, I'll be doing a lot more than that. By the time the sun rises, you're gonna be hoarse from all the screaming I'm gonna make you do."

Axe led her over to the bed then whirled her around and unfastened her cocktail dress.

As he slipped the dress off her, she heard him suck in his breath. "Hot-as-fuck ink job." He kissed around her delicate branch tattoo with pink and white flowers running down her spine. Axe then moved his mouth to her neck and shoulders, bringing it back to her tattoo. Each kiss was wet, warm, and sensuous, and by the time he made it to her lower back, her dress lay on the floor, pooled around her ankles.

A low, breathy whistle tingled her skin. "Fuck, you're gorgeous. Love your lace panties. Your ass is so sweet and soft," he said as he grabbed two handfuls of her cheeks and squeezed them. His breath became heavier as his hands trailed up her back, landing on her rounded breasts. He cupped them firmly and she moaned, leaning against his hard chest.

"Mmm, feels good," she whispered.

In one movement, he'd unfastened her lace bra, her breasts spilling out. Her dusky rose nipples were quickly stiffening as he pinched and pulled them while his tongue traced a scorching trail from her earlobe down past her neck, settling on her delicate shoulder. He sank his teeth into her tingling skin.

"You like a little pain with your pleasure?" Axe's lips on her skin fed the dull throb between her legs.

"Maybe," she panted.

"I guess you're gonna have to find out if that's your thing." He licked and tenderly kissed the area he'd just bitten.

"Is it yours?" Baylee held her breath in anticipation of his reply.

"Oh, yeah, baby."

She swallowed hard, trying to digest what he'd just told her. Baylee had always had fantasies of being tied up and having a man take charge in the bedroom. She worked in a man's world, and had to fight twice as hard and produce two times as much as any of the men in her company, just to prove she was as good as they were. It was tiring.

Each time she hooked up with a man, she wished he'd take charge in the bedroom. But she always ended up with a sensitive man who was awkward when he tried to talk dirty, and who'd ask so many questions when she'd tell him to tie her up that by the time she was finally secured, all her desire had waned.

The dark-haired man had awakened her senses from the moment she'd laid eyes on him, had watched her with such fire and lust that all her senses were in overdrive. The way his mouth moved over her skin electrified her, and when he bit her, the pain mixed with the pleasure that followed as he caressed the soreness blew her mind.

Turning her head toward him, he possessed her mouth again, one hand tucked under her chin while the other tweaked and pulled her nipple. It was exquisite. Axe guided her to the bed, his lips never leaving hers, his fingers flicking her stiff nipples causing her pussy to clench and throb like mad.

He broke contact with her only to push her down on the bed. Then he loomed over her, his hair falling down over his forehead, his dark-chocolate eyes reflecting a voracious fire. Once again, his lips seized hers, and his tongue plundered the depths of her mouth. Eagerly, she sucked on it as her arms circled his neck, drawing him closer to her. Baylee moaned as his mouth continued ravaging her while his hand glided down her body, landing on her inner thigh. She squirmed under him, twisting her legs as encouragement for his hand to explore further, to touch her pulsing, wet mound. Axe kept his hand dormant on her thigh, though, the heat from it on her skin made her crave his touch even more. Taking her knee, she rubbed it against his hand, nudging it toward her engorged sex, but he didn't move it—not one fucking inch.

Breaking away from his mouth, she whispered, "Touch me."

"What the fuck do you think I'm doing, babe?"

She turned her head away. Axe's penetrating stare unnerved her, making her feel embarrassed. "No, I mean *really* touch me."

A hint of a smile played on his lips. Grasping her chin, he forced her to look at him. "Tell me what you want."

"You know." Redness spread across her cheeks.

With the tip of his warm, delicious tongue, he licked across her lips then traced over her cheeks and jawline. "Like this?" he rasped, his words vibrating against her skin.

"That feels good, but I want you to touch somewhere lower," she said in a barely audible voice.

"Where?" His tongue flicked her earlobe sending tingles over her body.

"My pussy." There, she'd said it. She'd said it many times in her sexual fantasies in her head, but she rarely said it aloud. The men she'd dated were not the kind who wanted a woman to say "pussy" during sex. But something about the way the handsome, dark man acted told her he'd love a woman to say it.

"Well, babe, I have plans to touch and do a lot of nasty things to your pussy, but *I* will decide when that happens."

But you're driving me fucking crazy! Baylee ran her fingers down his back as he blazed a wet trail from her neck to her collarbone. She slipped her hand between her legs, needing to touch her aching mound to relieve some of the pressure. But before she could even graze her swollen lips, Axe grabbed her hand and brought it up.

"You'll touch yourself when I tell you to. For now, I'm the only one who gets to touch your pussy. Is it aching to be touched?" His finger circled the skin around her nipples.

Nodding, Baylee squirmed again, trying to reposition herself so his thigh would hit it. No such luck; he was unmovable, his legs like steel rods. And what the hell was he doing to her chest? His finger kept coming so close to her hardened nipples, but he just missed them as he played with her breasts. Axe's tongue scorched her skin as it traced her collarbone, and that damn hand of his teased as it rested on her inner thigh, millimeters away from her shuddering mound. Baylee's body was in a state of agitation. It was like every nerve was a livewire, ready to short-circuit at any second.

Then he grasped her arms and put them above her head. He drew back and stared at her quivering flesh: her hardened, dusky buds, her glistening pussy, her slightly parted and trembling legs. His dark glance started from her hazel eyes then moved slowly over her body down to her feet before heading up again, lingering for a few seconds on her sex and tits. As he assessed her, she swept her look over his chiseled chest, noticing a large cobra tattoo spread over it, the evil eyes boring into her. Axe's stomach was flat, a sprinkling of dark hair disappearing beneath the waistband of his pants, which clearly showed he had a raging hard-on. From the way his pants bulged, she suspected his dick was a big one, and her mouth watered from just thinking about how it would taste and feel in her mouth.

"Liking what you see?" His rough voice brought her eyes to his face. He smirked. "That's good, 'cause I'm lovin' what I'm seeing."

In one movement, he slid his belt out of its loops. "You want to be tied up, baby?"

His question went straight between her legs and she swiveled her hips, trying in vain to clench her thighs together to relieve some of the ache.

A small chuckle. "I'll take that as a yes."

He held her wrists together and looped the belt around them. Raising her arms above her head, he secured the belt through the slats on the headboard, tying it in place. She pulled down and realized she really *was* tied up and couldn't get undone without his help. Her body was on fire, but her mind kept screaming what a fool she was. *I'm letting a stranger tie me up. I'm helpless with a man I know nothing about. But the way he makes me feel is like nothing I've ever felt before.*

He loomed over her, his face inches from hers, his voice breaking in on her thoughts. "If you want me to untie you, just say 'Harley.' Cool?"

"Like the motorcycle?"

"Yeah."

"Okay." *Crazy or not, I'm going to let this hunk take me on the ride of my life.*

"Good girl." He leaned down and took her bottom lip in his mouth, sucking it before his tongue moved inside.

Baylee kissed him back with such hunger it startled her. It was like she was a starving woman. And in a sense, she guessed she was. She hadn't had sex in over a year, and the few men she'd slept with in the previous four years didn't stir even one ounce of the passion this stranger had in the short time they'd been together. What was it with him? He was a sex god, and it was her lucky night. Being tied up made her feel so out of control, and she loved every second of her erotic vulnerability.

Axe pulled away from her mouth then kissed her cheek, trailing kisses down to the sensitive stretch of skin along the side of Baylee's body. Her creamy flesh was taut due to her bondage, and she sucked in her breath when Axe's tongue skimmed over her. The way he licked and scratched sent a rush of goosebumps in its wake. Moaning softly, she twisted and turned, her restraints heightening the sexual experience.

"Keep your legs open and don't close them. Understand?" he growled as his nipped her sensitive flesh.

She spread her legs wide, the touch of air cooling her dripping mound. She looked down at Axe and met his hungry eyes. Her stomach flip-flopped. *Remember, Baylee, this is a one-night stand. Nothing more. You just lucked out and got a guy who knows how to fuck.*

"You got a great body, darlin'."

"Thanks. I try to stay fit."

He chuckled and moved his mouth to her tits. While he gently bit her breasts, his hand continued lightly tickling the sides of her body. The delicate skin under her arms purred each time he caressed it. It was official—her whole body, even her scalp, was burning.

Each time he neared her nipples, he'd back away and play with the sides and underside of her breasts instead. Her rock-hard beads were aching for his touch, but he kept them at bay. After several minutes of sweet, tormented teasing, he sucked one hard bud into his mouth while he pinched the other one between his fingers. She bucked from the sheer ecstasy of it as jolts of intense pleasure zig-zagged from her head to her curling toes. Never had the feel of a man's mouth on her nipples been so exquisite.

"You want it a little harder? I love to bite, and your nipples look so tasty."

"Not too hard."

"I'll bite, and you tell me if you want it harder or not."

She nodded, then closed her eyes to experience the sensation without distraction. The first nip on her buds tingled. "Harder," she moaned.

Axe obliged.

"Harder."

Axe's teeth clamped down on her nipple while his fingers tweaked her other one. *Oh, yeah.* That was the sweet pain she was looking for. It was so good she thought she was going to come. Axe must have suspected as much because he said in a harsh voice, "Don't fuckin' come."

She willed herself to stop the waves beginning to roll deep in her core, but it was damn difficult with the way he was touching her, running his fabulous tongue over every inch of her skin. She was dying for his mouth on her pussy and his dick in her mouth. Just thinking about it had her wet and ready.

Axe slipped his hand under one of her firm ass cheeks and dug his fingers in, squeezing hard while his wicked tongue trailed the insides of her thighs. Pulling on the belt and twisting her torso, pleasure and anticipation whirled through her like a Tasmanian devil. If he didn't touch her soon, she'd lose it.

Blowing softly against her skin, Axe crept his way toward her engorged, shiny pussy. As she watched him, he shot her a lust-filled gaze from under hooded eyes. Baylee sucked in her breath and held it as his soft lips neared her sex. Sighing, she closed her eyes and waited for the release she needed. Nothing.

What the hell?

She opened her eyes just as he zipped down his pants and threw them off, his thick, long shaft pulsing in front of her.

"Open up, sweetheart." Holding his dick, he straddled her, then bent over and seized her face roughly. "I want your sexy lips wrapped around my cock."

When he rubbed his dick across her lips, his pre-come dampened them. When she licked her lips, saltiness played on her tongue. He slowly guided his hardness in her mouth, first putting the crown of the head in to give her a chance to swirl her tongue around its smoothness. It was sinfully delicious. Axe leaned in closer, pushing his cock further into her mouth. Baylee slid her tongue up, down, and around his thickness, paying special attention to the underside of the head. She could see her hunger and passion reflected in his gaze as their eyes met.

Placing his hands on each side of her face, he held her head still as he thrust his rod in and out of her welcoming mouth.

"Fuck, my cock loves fucking your mouth. Wrap those sweet lips tighter around it. That's good, baby. Real good."

As his passion heightened, he threw his head back and closed his eyes, thrusting his hips forward and back as he pummeled her mouth with his cock. She expected him to come any second, waiting for his warm seed to fill her mouth and throat. Instead he pulled out, brought his mouth over her nipples, and sucked them hard. Then, with both hands, he spread her legs wider and placed his mouth over her clit.

Holy fuck! When his hot mouth covered it, her insides twisted in pleasure. From the bottom of her sex to the top of her hood, his tongue stroked her over and over in long, trembling moves. It was more than she had ever dreamed of. Spreading her open with his fingers, he flicked the tip of his tongue over her sweet spot.

"You like that?" he growled.

"Oh, yes. It feels so good."

"I know it does. And look how fuckin' wet you're getting." Axe kept flicking her clit with his tongue, watching as she writhed beneath him.

Each stroke to her arousal pushed her further toward the cliff of abandoned ecstasy, and his wicked tongue kept up its assault at a frenzied pace. "I'm real close to coming. I don't think I can hold it anymore," she gasped.

Before she could get lost in the feeling, he shoved two fingers in her pussy.

"Oh, fuck!" she cried.

As he played with her clit and finger-fucked her, the wave she had pushed back crashed through her body, filling her from her toes to her head, then pulling her further into a sphere of pleasure and contentment like she had never experienced. Opening her eyes, Axe came into focus, a cocky smile on his lips.

"It was good?" he asked.

"No. It was fuckin' great." She knew she was feeding into what she had seen as a huge ego, but she didn't care. He deserved a pat on his back—or better yet, a pat on his ass—for making her come so hard, harder than she'd ever come before.

"Do you like big cocks?" he asked as he trailed his fingertips over her stomach.

Shivering, she said, "You have a big one."

"Yeah…?"

"You know you do. I'm sure the women love it."

"Haven't gotten any complaints. You want my big cock in your tight pussy?"

Nodding, Baylee licked her lips.

Axe kissed her stomach and murmured against it, "I aim to please."

He leaned over and undid the belt, freeing her wrists. Running his finger over her nails, he said, "I want to feel *these* digging into my back and ass as I fuck you." Then he hoisted her legs up over his shoulders and spread her wide. Smacking his lips, he bent down and swiped his tongue over her wetness several times. "You taste delicious."

Baylee moaned and grasped his shoulders, her fingers digging into his flesh.

"That's it, baby," Axe groaned. "Harder. Draw some blood." He winked at her then reached over and grabbed his pants next to them. After securing the condom over his shaft, he moved his cock to her heated slit, slowly pushing in.

"Oh. Mmm, that feels good," she whispered as she dug her nails in deeper.

"I'm sure it does. I'm gonna fuck your pussy hard and rough, 'cause I'm betting you like it that way. Am I right?"

"You know you are."

She watched him as he looked at his cock entering her, a smile of pure joy spreading over his face. Then he was in, and his dick made her feel full.

"Damn, you're tight. When's the last time you fucked?"

Embarrassed, she lied, "A few nights ago."

"Is that right? You've got a tight cunt, sweetheart."

The headboard slammed against the wall as Axe pummeled her over and over, his feral grunts and her deep moans filling the room. Baylee balled the sheets as she turned her head sideways and closed her eyes, her nerves tingling and on high alert as her pleasure rose steadily. Before she could savor her building orgasm, Axe flipped her over on her knees, pushed her head and tits against the mattress, spread her thighs wide, and shoved his delicious dick back inside. As he pounded her, he grabbed her long, brown hair and pulled it back, making her scalp burn and her eyes water. She stuffed the sheet in her mouth to help quiet the screams threatening to erupt from her.

When he rubbed the side of her engorged clit, she lost it, and her screams came out as low, guttural rasps against the sheet. A thousand jolts of intense ecstasy coursed through her body as she bucked and trembled, her legs spastic, threatening to collapse. He groaned and thrust a few more times before he pulled out and collapsed next to her, panting and heaving, his magnificent chest rising and falling.

Baylee rolled over onto her back and covered her forehead with her arm.

"Oh, my God. That was intense," she said between breaths.

He reached over and squeezed her tit. "Glad it was good for you."

"Was it for you?" she asked tentatively.

"Fuck yeah." He stood up and padded to the bathroom, his firm ass flexing with each step.

Baylee remained in bed wondering what the protocol was for a one-night stand. Did she thank him and show him the door? Did she ask him if he wanted to spend the night? What the hell was she supposed to do? She sat up and finger-combed her hair.

"Ready for another round?" Baylee looked over her shoulder and saw that Axe's wonderful dick was erect once more. *How can he be hard again so quickly? The guy is amazing.*

"Sure, why not?" She flashed him a devilish grin.

A crooked half-smile crossed his face. Standing next to the bed, he dragged her toward him. "Yeah. Why the fuck not? The fun is just beginning."

CHAPTER THREE

THE MORNING SUN streaming in through the picture window woke Baylee up. As she squinted through sleep-bleary eyes, she brought her slender fingers to her temples and pressed hard, trying to quell the incessant pounding. She groaned and covered her eyes with her hands. *Damn, my head hurts. It feels like a freight train is running through it. Fuck.* Pushing herself up, she staggered toward the bathroom in search of some aspirin.

After swallowing a couple of pills, she shuffled back to the room, the sunbeams stabbing her eyes. Closing the curtains, she welcomed the darkness of the cool room. *What a night. I drank too much and fucked too much.* Her cheeks burned brightly, and a funny squiggle seized her stomach when she thought of the dirty deeds she and her one-night stand had engaged in the previous night. But in that moment, with a pounding head and sore muscles, she realized they may have been a bit overzealous.

Baylee glanced at the empty spot next to where she'd slept. He was gone. She had no idea when he left; she hadn't heard him leave. After hours of sex in various positions, she'd finally collapsed, sated and exhausted, sleep quickly overtaking her. Scanning the room, she noticed he didn't leave anything like a phone number or a note telling her how wonderful she was, or that he was so smitten he wanted to see her again.

Okay, Baylee, just stop. You had a one-night stand with a gorgeous stud, but it was all about the sex. Don't make anything more of this. It was obvious he hadn't. She was sure he probably did this type of thing on a regular basis. She was just another fun night for him. But wasn't that what she wanted? Hadn't she been the one who said she didn't want to know any personal information, not even his name? He'd complied with her wishes, so why was she miffed? Why did she feel slighted that he hadn't left her a note, hadn't woken her before he left?

He'd just slipped away, like a thief in the night, after robbing her of her humdrum sex life. *How in the hell am I ever going to enjoy sex again after last night?*

Baylee sighed then lay back down, trying to shut out the memories of Axe's soft, warm lips on her body. It was a one-night stand. She'd never see him again, and that was fine; she was too busy for anything that involved any emotion other than lust anyway. Her sexual rendezvous was mind-blowing and should last her for quite a while. Thinking she'd take advantage of the quiet of the room, she closed her eyes and fell fast asleep.

MONDAY MORNING BLUES affected a lot of people, but not Baylee. She loved Mondays and greeted them with a spring in her step, ready to finish old projects so she could start new ones.

At twenty-five years old, Baylee had her professional life mapped out. She was a junior associate at Derry, Decker, and Vale Architecture Firm. She was the only female architect in the office, expected to do twice as good a job as the male associates just to break even, but she didn't care because she could run circles around them. The other two associates, Kirk and Logan, resented that she worked so hard. They thought she was trying to outshine them—and in a way, they were right—but making partner was important to her. It was a validation of her abilities but, more importantly, it was a tribute to her mother.

Baylee's mother had been an architect too, and she'd inspired Baylee to follow in her footsteps. Some of Baylee's earliest memories were of the two of them building neighborhoods and towns out of Legos. Baylee was happy she had those memories, because her world went dark the night her mother was murdered. As hard as she tried over the years to remember what had happened that night, what the man had looked like who'd killed her mother, she couldn't. Though recently, the dark shadows that lurked out of focus in the corners of her mind had begun to take on some more distinctive shapes. *Maybe it'll come back to me eventually.*

That was what her therapist had told her would happen. Dr. Scott said that as time went by, the shadows would become clearer, and she'd start to remember small things. He'd explained that something, anything really—a scent, a sight, a taste, a sound—could trigger the memories, and then they would come quickly. He'd done his best to prepare her for that, but even after all these years, her recollections of that night were still pretty fuzzy. She wished she could remember so justice for her mother could be served. The killer was never found, and he continued to roam about, a free man who was probably killing other women.

The thought made her shudder.

The phone rang, breaking into her thoughts.

"Good morning, Katie," she greeted her secretary.

"Good morning, Ms. Peters. Mr. Decker would like you to bring the blueprints for the strip mall project."

"Tell him I'll be there in ten."

Baylee looked out her office window at the tall buildings, the Front Range of the Rocky Mountains reflected in their mirrored windows. She was so grateful to Gary Decker for giving her this job. After college, Baylee had applied to many firms around the Denver metro area, but none of them had called her back. As a last resort, she asked her dad to speak with Gary and Bob Derry. They had started the architectural firm with her mother twenty-five years before, and over the years, her dad and the two men had become good friends.

Two days after he'd spoken with them, they'd hired her. And for the past two years, she'd worked her ass off to prove to them that they hadn't made a mistake. Gary and Bob were more than pleased, and the newest partner, Warner Vale, couldn't say enough good things about her. She was one of the two they were considering for partner next year. Baylee couldn't be happier. She just wished her mother had lived to see this day. Baylee knew she would have been proud.

After grabbing her laptop, the blueprints, and her cup of coffee, she shuffled over to Gary's office. When she entered, she was surprised to see the other two partners and Logan.

"Was there a meeting I forgot about?" she asked while setting down her laptop on Gary's desk.

"Nothing planned. We wanted to get you and Logan together to discuss the new strip mall project we're designing in Pinewood Springs," Warner Vale said.

"I've already come up with some very innovative designs I can share." Logan plastered on his charming-executive smile.

Baylee thought she was going to puke.

"We can look at them. The important thing is pleasing the client." Warner loosened his tie a bit then cleared his voice. "Our client is a motorcycle club. The members are a bit rough and colorful, but we'll treat them like any other client."

Logan leaned forward on his chair. "You mean like a Hell's Angels-type of club?"

Warner laughed nervously. "I hope not."

"What Warner means is that it really doesn't matter who they are. The point is we've been hired to design and build a strip mall in west Pinewood Springs, and we're getting paid a whole lot of money to do it." Gary sipped his steaming coffee.

"How involved is this club going to be? I mean, do we have to deal with all of them or is there a leader?" Baylee asked.

"Not sure. Right now, we're working with the president of the club. Banger is his name," Gary said.

Snickers whispered around the room.

"What the hell kind of name is *that*?" Bob asked.

"I guess it's a road name. I've been reading up on motorcycle clubs since we were awarded the project. Most of the guys have road names. But never mind that; we have a job to do. I think we'll mostly be working with the president, and maybe his VP."

"If it's in Pinewood Springs, how are we supposed to oversee the project?" Baylee said.

"I'm going to need you and Logan to stay there until the project is complete. I'm putting you both on it. Gary, Warner, and I will take turns going to Pinewood Springs to make sure everything is okay, but this is your project." Bob looked at the two junior associates. "I'm sure you'll enjoy small-town living for a few months."

Baylee's mind whirled. She had to work with Logan every day on this project *and* be stuck in a small town? How was she ever going to survive? She knew Logan would do anything to make her look bad, so she'd have to be especially diligent in her work. If she did a good job with this project, she could finally achieve her dreams.

The only kink in the plan was working with this motorcycle club. She really didn't have a clue about them, except what she saw in the movies or TV documentaries. Sighing, she knew the next few nights would be filled with biker research so she could grasp what kind of client she'd be working for.

"What's the name of the club who hired us?" she asked.

Warner flipped through some sheets in a folder on his lap. "Let's see… Here it is. The name is Insurgents."

"Thanks." Baylee wrote down the name so she wouldn't forget. Before she arrived in Pinewood Springs, she'd make sure she knew everything there was to know about the Insurgents MC.

★   ★   ★

BAYLEE SPED HER car toward Jalisco's, the Mexican restaurant where she was meeting her close friend, Claudia. Every Monday night, they'd have a couple of margaritas and talk about men, mostly.

Elated to find parking right in front, Baylee maneuvered her two-seater Mercedes into the space. As she walked into the restaurant, she was aware of a group of business men seated to her right, checking her out and whispering comments about her as she passed.

Their eyes are probably glued to my breasts. Ugh! What I wouldn't do to have smaller ones.

Baylee was in a minority when it came to her feelings about her ample chest. Claudia kept telling Baylee to give her some, and most of her female friends had gotten breast implants to give them what nature had provided for Baylee.

Since she'd started developing, male eyes had been ogling her, rarely looking at her face first. She hated being judged by her cup size, and it drove her crazy whenever she entered a room. Many of the men would gawk at her, and that made her feel like less of a person.

Turning her head to the group, she asked, "Didn't your mothers teach you that it's rude to stare?" Before allowing them to answer, she tossed her long, brown hair and searched for Claudia's smiling face.

Claudia had found them a small booth in the corner by a window, looking out over the parking lot.

"Sorry I'm late," Baylee said as she slipped into the booth. "I really need a drink. Crazy day."

"All your days are crazy," Claudia countered as she placed the menu down on the table.

Neither woman had to look at the menu—they knew it by heart. Coming practically every week for the past three years made them experts on what was available.

"How was your day?" Baylee asked as she picked up a tortilla chip and dipped it in the salsa.

"Okay. I mean, how exciting is it to clean people's teeth all day? Just glad Dr. Jacques pays well."

"I hear you." Baylee wrinkled her nose. "I don't know how you do it. I couldn't."

Claudia shrugged. "It's really not so bad. I couldn't figure out all the diagrams and math shit you have to do. I guess we're even."

The women placed their drink orders—a mango margarita for Baylee, and a regular one for Claudia.

"How's Logan doing? Did he get a girlfriend yet?"

Baylee groaned. "I still can't believe you have the hots for my nemesis. I doubt he has a girlfriend. He and his buds go out a lot for happy hours, and I'm always hearing him brag to Kirk about how many women he picks up." She popped another chip in her mouth. "These are really good tonight."

The waitress returned to the table and set their drinks down. Baylee picked hers up and took a big sip. After she licked the sugar off her lips, she said, "And get this: I have to be stuck with *stud-man* in Pinewood Springs for who knows how long. Talk about bad luck!"

"Really? Damn. How did that come about?"

"I suspect it's because we're the two single ones in the office. Kirk is married with a couple of small kids, so I don't think they'd send him on an out-of-town assignment. I guess they figure we don't have a life." She smiled wryly.

"This is the first time you've had to go out of town on a job, huh?"

"Yeah. I mean, the firm has been hired out to do some jobs in Las Vegas, San Francisco, and even Boston, but I never went on those. No, I get to go to the swinging town of Pinewood Springs, which probably has a population of about five hundred." She shook her head in dismay.

Claudia laughed. "I think it's bigger than that. I used to go there a lot when I was a kid. They have a large natural pool and all these cool hot springs spas."

"Oh, great, I'll sweat off my boredom. But the worst thing is I have to work with Logan. Not too pleased, but if I do a great job—which I plan to—then I'm a shoo-in for partner next year."

"Never know. Working so closely together in a small town with not much to do? Maybe you and Logan will hook up."

"Bite your tongue!" Baylee took another swig of her drink.

"Speaking of hooking up, did you go through with finding someone for a one-night stand at Deidre's wedding?"

Baylee nodded.

"Oh, shit!" Claudia covered her mouth. "I never thought you were going to do it. Never."

Baylee sighed. "I didn't think I was, either, but then this drop-dead gorgeous guy hit on me and I just had to go through with it. He looked like he'd be great in bed. You know, he was the dark, smoldering type."

"Did he deliver? Sometimes good-looking guys are shit in bed. How was your stud?"

"Awesome. Fucking awesome. It was amazing, and the guy didn't stop. He was like a sex machine. Damn, we were at it like rabbits most of the night. I was so damn sore the next morning."

Claudia chuckled. "You going to hook up again?"

"No. I don't even know his name. It was strictly a one-night stand. Just pure sex, and it felt good avoiding all the chains of a relationship. Each of us could just walk away without any expectations. That's what I wanted."

"You don't think about him or wish you could see him?"

Pausing, Baylee brushed her fingers across her lips. "I wouldn't complain about having another romp with him, but I'm so busy with my career right now, I can't think about being with anyone. And then there's this project in Pinewood Springs. How could I start anything with anyone *now* when I'll probably be gone for a few months? Anyway, like I said, I don't even know his name."

"You can come to Denver on the weekends. It isn't all that far."

"True, but I don't trust Logan. I know he'll try and sabotage me whenever he gets a chance. Nope, right now, the only thing that fits in my 'love' life is casual sex. The way this guy pleased me, I can go months before I'll be feeling dry."

"I hope making partner is worth giving up your chance of finding a great guy. Maybe this guy would've worked out. You don't know."

"I don't think so. I mean, he didn't ask for us to get together again. From the way he acted, I got the impression that one-night stands are kinda his thing."

They both laughed, and then Baylee changed the subject to Claudia. As she filled her in on her latest dating escapades, Baylee couldn't help but remember how incredible it felt with the sexy stud inside her, or how he licked and traced her tattoo with his tongue. *Stop, Baylee.* Maybe getting away from the city for a few months would be a good thing. At least in Pinewood Springs, she wouldn't be wondering every time she came into a restaurant or walked down the street if his face would be among the crowd. Pinewood Springs looked like it was the perfect distance she needed for the memory of his hands and mouth on her body to fade away.

CHAPTER FOUR

Pinewood Springs

AXE SAT AT the bar in the clubhouse's great room, rubbing his finger up and down the neck of his beer bottle. To his right sat Rosie, one of the Insurgents' club whores, a perplexed look on her face.

"What's happening?" Jerry asked as he clamped his hand on Axe's shoulder.

"Nothing much. Just came in to grab a cold one. Fuck, it's sweltering outside." Axe took a long pull on his beer.

Jerry glanced at Rosie then turned back to Axe. "What's up with Rosie? She's giving you the evil eye."

Axe shrugged.

"He doesn't wanna have any fun," Rosie said.

Jerry raised his eyebrows. "Really? Now that's a surprise. You gonna leave poor Rosie high and dry?"

"Guess so. Why don't you take care of her?"

"I think I will." Jerry grabbed Rosie's wrist and yanked her to him. "Come on. I'll have some fun with you."

Rosie pressed in to Jerry and ran her long fingers down his side.

"Later," Jerry called out as he and Rosie walked toward the small rooms down the hall.

Axe jerked his chin and grunted. *Fuck, there goes some prime pussy, and I'm just sitting here drinking a beer. What the fuck?* He kicked the bar stool next to him, knocking it down. Blade, one of the prospects, rushed over and picked it up. Axe narrowed his eyes. What the hell was going on with him? He'd been acting like a fucking idiot ever since he returned to Pinewood Springs the previous week.

It was true he was working more hours than ever in the bike repair shop, and for the past week, it'd been hotter than Hell. He never liked the heat all that much; he'd take a snowstorm over a heat wave any day. Maybe that was it.

But maybe not.

Motioning to Blade for another beer, Axe looked around the room. It was pretty quiet at the clubhouse, but then Wednesday afternoons tended to be dead. Most of the brothers were at work, and the few who were at the clubhouse were either watching the races on the big-screen TV hanging on the back wall, passed out drunk, or screwing one of the club whores or mamas.

Damn. I should be fuckin' one of the whores. For reasons he couldn't explain, Axe wasn't in the mood for any of them, hadn't been since he fucked his brains out with that hottie at Derek's wedding. Why *that* should make a difference, he didn't know, but he was pretty sick and tired of thinking about her while watching other brothers having a good time.

Axe never thought twice about a woman after he banged her. A few minutes after fucking, he'd push the bitch out of his bed to put as much distance as possible between him and her. That was just the way he rolled. He wasn't the settling-down type. And if the way he treated the women bothered them, they never said; they simply left with a gigantic smile and the afterglow of several mind-blowing orgasms on their faces.

The citizen women he sometimes hooked up with would write their phone numbers on his hands or his chest, their eyes gleaming in expectation of another encounter with him. After he left, Axe couldn't rub the numbers off his skin fast enough, and he never saw them again, at least not in the way they craved. He'd bump into them at the grocery store, or at biker rallies, and they'd rush over with hope in their eyes that maybe he'd end up between their legs for one more romp, the memories of his hot tongue on their wet mounds too much to bear.

Axe, being the sonofabitch he was, would flirt like hell with them, making them believe they were special and he may spend the night with them, but then he'd disappear, go to the clubhouse and fuck a few of the club whores at the same time. He preferred to do his main screwing with the club women or the hoodrats; there was less drama and little to no expectation that his coupling with them would mean anything more than pleasure for that moment in time. Once he was done satisfying himself, he'd tell them to high-tail it out of his room. Axe hated entanglements.

The club whores and the hoodrats knew the score. They were at the clubhouse as property of the Insurgents, and that was the way they wanted it. In exchange for keeping the clubhouse clean, fixing some of the meals, and servicing the brothers whenever any of them wanted, the women had the protection of the club, all the pot they could smoke and booze they could drink, and the kind of freedom they craved. The hoodrats knew the score as well, and even though they weren't Insurgents' property, they willingly came to the club's parties to lose themselves in drink, drugs, and sex for a short while.

Axe loved the easy sex without pressure. Yeah, that was how he rolled, and it suited him just fine.

Until now. What the fuck?

He couldn't get the woman in the celery-green dress out of his mind. The night they'd spent together had been absolutely wild. It was like she couldn't get enough, like she was starving, and he was there to feed her cravings.

Her long, silky hair swishing across his body as she rode him drove him crazy. As he replayed the way her heavy tits jiggled as he slammed into her tight pussy from behind, and the feel of her incredibly soft lips peppering his taut skin with kisses, his cock hardened and strained against his blue jeans. The dark-haired sweetie did a fucking number on him, but he was still surprised that he couldn't get her out of his mind, off his skin, or away from his dick.

"Feeling lonely?" a sultry voice purred. Long nails raked down his back.

He turned around and saw Lola, one of the club whores. Her green bikini top barely held in her tits, and her short skirt showed a glimpse of her curved ass cheeks.

"Hey, Lola." Axe swiveled back to face the bar, his elbows on the counter.

"Hey, yourself. What are you doing all alone? Want some company?"

"Nah. I was just taking a break. It's hot as Hell in the shop. Getting ready to go back."

"I'm surprised you're not with Rosie. She seems to be your favorite for the past few months. You haven't been with me unless Rosie is there, too. I miss being alone with you." Leaning in, she brushed her lips against his cheek and her tits against his arm.

Axe pushed her away. "I told you I have to get back to work." Swinging his arm around, he added, "Find yourself another brother."

Lola looked startled. He couldn't blame her—he was startled, too. Did he *really* say that? He was turning down a good fucking with Lola? Something was definitely wrong with him.

Axe tossed back the rest of the beer in his bottle and stood up. "See you around." He padded across the floor then walked out into the white heat of the day.

CHAPTER FIVE

A N OPPRESSIVE HEAT pushed in on Baylee as she left the cool confines of her car. The colorful flowers in large, mosaic planters and the elm trees surrounding the hotel stood still in the July heat. The dry, mountain air—thin and scorching—made her feel claustrophobic, like a mouse trapped in a shoe box. She hurried up the steps, seeking refuge inside the hotel lobby.

The cold AC slapped her face as soon as she flung open the glass doors, stealing her breath. If not for that, the first thing Baylee would have noticed was the four-story chandelier dangling over the atrium of the elegant hotel. Stained glass windows from when the Palace Hotel was first built in the late 1800s reflected their patterns on the marble floor, a kaleidoscope of color and brilliance.

Okay—maybe Pinewood Springs wouldn't be so bad…

After registering, Baylee picked up her tote bag and headed toward the elevators. Glancing around the bustling lobby, she scanned the crowd to see if Logan's face would be among them. She was sure he was staying at the same hotel, although she secretly prayed the firm had put them in different ones.

"Baylee." Logan's chipper voice bounced off the marble walls.

Damn. "Logan." She turned around and greeted him with a thin smile.

"What room number do you have?"

"I'm on the fifth floor." She turned the keycard over. "Number five thirty-seven. I didn't notice you when I checked in."

"I've been here for about an hour. I came up a little early. I had to wait for my room to be ready, so I was hanging out in the bar." He ran his hand through his short, brown hair. "I think we're neighbors. My room is five thirty-eight." He smiled.

Damnit. "Great. Well, that'll make it convenient if we have to work after hours."

He nodded. An awkward silence ensued as Logan stared at Baylee while she brushed imaginary lint off her cotton knit top.

Picking up her tote, she said, "I'm going to head upstairs. I want to settle in. See you around." She turned to the elevators and pushed the button, praying the door would open quickly.

"Do you want to have dinner together? We could go over our plan of action when we have to present the blueprints tomorrow."

My plan to avoid Logan socially isn't panning out at all.

"Thanks, Logan, but you know, I'm really bushed. I'm going to order room service and turn in early."

He pursed his lips, nodding his acceptance. "We can have dinner another time. It's not like we're leaving any time soon. Maybe tomorrow night? We can go over what happens at the meeting."

The elevator doors opened. All Baylee wanted to do was go to her room, close her curtains, and lay on the bed. A dull throbbing in her head threatened to turn into something nasty if she didn't take a couple of aspirins soon.

Before she could walk inside the elevator, Logan grasped her arm. She turned.

"So, dinner tomorrow night?"

"That's fine." She had to get away.

"Excellent." He let go of her arm. "I'm going to have one more beer. I'll catch up with you later."

"Whatever," she mumbled as the door trundled shut.

Trudging down the hall, Baylee wondered what in the hell she was going to do in Pinewood Springs for three or four months. If the pace of small-town living didn't drive her insane, she knew spending her time with Logan would push her over the edge.

After tipping the bellhop, Baylee kicked off her shoes and shuffled over to the window, squinting against the blaring sun. She sighed as she took in the blue skyline broken by the jagged peaks of the Rocky Mountains, dotted with dark green foliage. *Maybe I can get back into hiking. It's been a while.* When Baylee was at the University of Colorado in Boulder, she and a group of her friends hiked many of the mountain trails that circled the university town. Once she graduated and moved back to Denver, her whole focus had been on her career.

Looking out the window at the beauty of the landscape, Baylee realized how much she missed doing some of the things she used to before she became a crazed career woman. It seemed that ever since she had her one-night stand, she'd begun to question if she were making a mistake to be so single-minded in her pursuits.

Logan's smug face flashed in her mind. She couldn't lose to him. She was the better architect; vanity wasn't telling her that, only the facts. Baylee had bailed Logan out more than a few times over the past two years for simple mistakes he'd made on projects they worked on. She never told Gary, Bob, or Warren, and she was positive Logan wouldn't have been as discreet if she were the one who'd screwed up—he'd be chomping at the bit like an impatient race horse at the starting line.

Once I make partner, I'll slow down a bit. Maybe I'll meet a nice, sexy man. Who knows? Who the hell was she kidding? The only man she'd love to have in her life *and* her bed was the brooding stranger she spent the night with the previous week. Baylee couldn't get him out of her mind. Even though her common sense told her she was crazy fantasizing over something that would never happen—she didn't even know his name, for God's sake—her body craved his touch, his wickedly delicious tongue which made her come over and over that night.

Damn. When would he leave her mind? Probably not until she found a living, breathing replacement, and her purple vibrator wasn't it. She heaved another sigh. At least she was far away from Denver, and she'd be so busy with the big construction project that by the time she returned home, her sexy one-nighter would be a very distant memory.

Baylee zipped open her tote bag, taking out a couple of aspirins and a bottled water. She pulled the curtains closed, replacing the brightness with a cool, comforting darkness. She downed the tablets, stripped down to her underwear, pulled down the bedspread on the king-sized bed, slipped under the sheets, and covered her eyes with her arm. As the low hum of the air conditioner began to lull her to sleep, she prayed the shadows from the past wouldn't creep into her dreams, turning them into nightmares as they often did. *I need to sleep without the past clawing at my present.* Baylee tugged the soft blanket around her, then let sleep overtake her.

AXE STRETCHED HIS long legs in front of him and cursed under his breath about the malfunctioning air conditioner. It seemed that each time the temperatures hovered around one hundred degrees, the damn thing went out. His wet, gray muscle shirt clung to his chest, and his ripped biceps glistened with perspiration. After he guzzled down a bottle of ice-cold water, he twisted the cap of another and poured the chilly liquid over his head, bringing momentary relief.

A persistent fly buzzed around his face, and each time Axe tried to catch it in his large hand, the fly zipped away. The elusive insect pissed him off big-time, and he made it his mission to nail the fucker by the time church wrapped up.

Banger pounded the gavel on the old, scratched wooden table the members crowded around for their weekly meeting. The table couldn't accommodate all thirty members, so metal folding chairs lined the concrete walls of the room. On hot days—even when the cooling system was working—the room was suffocating, but when the air conditioner fizzled, it was a sauna replete with the pungent scent of sweat.

"I know it's hotter than Hell in here. The fuckin' AC crapped out again. We got a repair man looking at it, but it's happening too often. Seems like a good time to take a vote on replacing the unit. It's gonna be expensive, though, 'cause the repair guys are telling me that if we replace one, we gotta replace the other two that cool the building."

"We got the money, let's get rid of this fucker and get a new one. This fuckin' sucks," Bear said as he wiped his brow with the palm of his hand. Bear was large and stocky and didn't tolerate the heat too well. He was always bitching how hot it was during the summer, and when the first snowfall came, he'd be out in the parking lot, laughing and doing wheelies with his Harley.

"Yeah, we got the money. Let's vote. Seems like it's gonna be unanimous, especially since it's so fuckin' hot in here." Banger looked around the room. "All in favor of purchasing a new cooling system, say 'aye.' "

The wave of "ayes" bounced off the walls, and Banger motioned to Jerry to come up front.

"Jerry, go tell that repairman we want to replace the whole system. Tell him I want to talk to him, so he's to wait here until we're done. Say, in 'bout thirty minutes or so."

As Jerry slipped out of the room, Banger addressed the members. "We got a problem in our county, and we gotta take action right away or it's gonna be a mess."

A loud bang on the table brought the eyes of the membership to Axe. He shrugged then motioned Banger to continue. When Axe lifted his hand up, he saw the fucking fly had dodged his fist. *Fuck!* He swatted the air as its buzzing filled his ears.

"As I was sayin', we got a problem." Banger looked toward Hawk, who stood up.

"Yeah, word is meth is being sold in this county." He wiped the trickles of sweat running down his tanned face. "I know it's been a long time since this shit has come up, but it was bound to happen. You know we have an implicit deal with the Feds to keep hard shit outta here, and they leave us and our dispensaries the fuck alone because of it. So we have to act fast, before they catch wind of it."

"I'll bet it's those sonsofbitches Dustin and Shack. They've been trying to get back at us ever since we put them outta business. We shoulda killed them when we had the chance," Jax said, his hot face made redder from anger.

The membership emitted sounds of fury, and Banger had to hit the gavel three times before the room calmed down. Hawk shook his head. "It's not those guys." He held his hands up, silencing the protests from a few members. "My old lady and I went down to southern Colorado last week for her friend's wedding. While we were in Puebla, I stopped by the Night Rebels' clubhouse, and Steel told me the meth was coming from a new MC who're calling themselves Skull Crushers. The prez said the shit wasn't coming from the Deadly Demons or the Demon Riders, who we know Dustin and Shack are riding with now, only these punks who've started the MC."

"They wearing a bottom rocker that says *Colorado*?" Throttle asked, his voice hard as iron.

"Steel says no. If they had that shit on their cut, we'd be talking about a turf war right now. Seems like they're a group of Neo-Nazi punks who ride rice burners, don't get what respect is, and think they're invincible. Fuckin' assholes who need to be dealt with. Of course, I'm getting confirmation on all that, but once I find out it's them, they're dead."

The membership whistled and held their arms in the air, waving their fists in support of the club's solidarity. Each and every member would die for the other. The Insurgents were brothers, they were family, and they were loyal to the end. No one messed with them.

Banger stood up, and everyone quieted down. "I'll take *that* as a unanimous vote that we stomp on whoever is responsible for bringing shit into our county."

The guys whistled.

"Okay. Let's hear from Hawk on the treasury report."

Hawk opened his laptop and gave a stack of papers to Chas to hand out. Axe glanced at the numbers on his copy, but he zoned out when Hawk started going over them. His mind wandered to the same thoughts it always did since his one-night stand at his friend's wedding—to the seductress in the celery-green dress. As hard as he tried, he couldn't rid his mind of the luscious woman who made him come harder than he ever had. Her kisses were the perfect combination of sweet and nasty, and her tits? They were so soft and perfect. He couldn't get enough of touching her skin; it was like velvet.

Axe glanced up and saw Hawk holding the ledger sheet and pointing to some column. Instead of paying attention, Axe debated whether to call his friend Derek on his honeymoon so he could ask his wife who her friend was. The thought of his perfect lay, the memory of the way she moaned and screamed as he made her come, sparked a fire so intense in Axe that it took him by surprise. He *had* to know who she was. He needed to see her again, and have his cock inside her once more. Axe had no idea why this woman grabbed him that way, but she did and seeing her again was imperative.

His hand flew up as he closed it over the annoying fly. Opening his fist slowly, he cursed when it was empty, his focus immediately going back to the woman. Axe was sure once they fucked a few more times, her pussy would be familiar and he'd grow bored and move on. Screwing the same woman became tiresome quickly for Axe. He usually was a one-time guy, so the fact that he wanted to hook up again with the mystery woman surprised the shit out of him. He had to admit that she was hotter than most; no wonder he wanted another taste. Once he had it, he could walk away. No problem. But until it happened, thinking about her all the time was driving him fucking insane. The only way he could stop the automatic replay his mind was stuck on since their one-night stand was to fuck her again.

When Banger yelled out Axe's name, he was in the land of the tall, dark-haired woman, had her toned legs wrapped around him as he pummeled her tight cunt with his big dick.

Rock, who was standing behind Axe, nudged his shoulder. Axe blinked and focused on a not-too-happy Banger.

"Sorry. Did I miss something?"

Banger's brow creased. "Get your goddamned head outta your ass. What goes on during church is important. What the fuck is wrong with you?"

"It's the heat, that's all." Axe looked down at the fly resting on the table, taunting him. He didn't think Banger would understand if he gave more attention to the fly than to his president.

"Bullshit! You've been acting strange for the past week. I don't know what's wrong with you, but you need to get over whatever the fuck it is. Now."

Diverting his eyes away from the fly, Axe glanced at Banger. "Okay."

Banger rubbed his hand over his face. "What the fuck is going on with the strip mall project?" Irritation laced his voice.

"Oh, yeah. Well, nothing much. I'm meeting with the architects from Denver tomorrow morning, and I'll go over the blueprints. The structural engineers will be there, as well. Unless there's a major problem, we should break ground in a week."

Banger nodded. "Good. You let me know how it goes every step of the way." He took a big gulp of his ice-cold beer. "Don't fuck up. Got it?"

Axe clenched his jaw and threw a hard look at Banger. "I'm on it."

As Banger picked up the gavel, Axe jerked his hand out with lightning speed and crushed the fly. "Fuck you. Nothing messes with me," he muttered under his breath as the gavel hit the table.

"Church over," Banger boomed.

Axe scooted onto one of the bar stools lining the bar. Before he opened his mouth, the prospect placed a cold bottle of Coors in front of him. Axe drained it in one long pull. As the empty bottle hit the counter, another one sat in front of him. Axe wrapped his hand around the bottle.

"What's up with you?" Jax asked as he swung onto the stool next to him.

Axe shrugged. "Nothing much. Same shit."

Jerry leaned over and grabbed the shot the prospect placed on the bar. "No, he means what was that shit about in church?"

"Nothing. I was so damn hot, I couldn't concentrate."

"That's fair," Jax commented before he popped two green olives in

44

his mouth. After swallowing, he said, "Why've you been avoiding the club girls?"

Axe slammed his beer on the bar. "I haven't, and why the fuck is what I do any of your goddamned business?"

"Just wondering why a horn dog like you suddenly doesn't want any club pussy. Getting it somewhere else?"

"Back the fuck off, okay? I've got this mall project on my mind, I'm helping out at the bike repair shop, and I don't need to explain myself to any of you assholes."

"Having a lot of shit to do never stopped you before," Jax ribbed.

Jerry laughed.

Axe sulked. He was pissed because they were right. He wasn't interested in club pussy, not when he had the image of the silkiest legs wrapped around him, and the best night of fucking he could ever remember.

"Hey," Chas said as he slid next to Jax.

Axe, expression glum, stared straight ahead.

Tilting his chin to Axe, Chas asked, "What's the matter with him?"

Jax popped some more olives in his mouth. "Got pussy—or, I should say, *lack* of pussy—on the brain."

Chas chuckled. "Yo, brother, you do seem like you're going through a dry spell, especially since you got back from Denver. Banger even noticed you've been weird."

"We think he may have met someone there, and he's getting prime pussy and doesn't want to share." Jerry laughed then motioned to the prospect for another shot.

Axe sat silent as he tried to quell the rage building inside him. If he didn't temper it, he'd end up bashing some heads, and then Banger would be really pissed at him. *Damn, they're right.*

"So, did you meet someone?" Chas prodded.

Axe clenched his jaw and continued to stare ahead. *Fuck yeah, I met someone, but I don't know who she is.*

"You gonna tell us who?" Jax asked.

"More importantly, are you gonna share her? Not with these two, of course." Jerry pointed to Jax and Chas. "They're tied down already. But with me?"

Axe narrowed his eyes. *When I find her, I'm not sharing her with anyone. What the fuck is wrong with me? Jerry and I, and sometimes Throttle, love sharing women. Threesomes and foursomes is the way I usually roll around the club. What is it about this woman? Fuck, I don't even know her name!*

"Nope, Jerry, I don't think he's gonna share. She must be something real special for our buddy to keep her all to himself." Jax clapped Axe on the shoulder.

Axe knocked Jax's hand off him and downed his beer. He pushed away from the bar and looked at them. "Fuck the hell off."

As he sauntered out, their guffaws surrounded him. Axe held up his middle finger high in the air and exited the clubhouse.

The Harley jumped to life as he switched on the engine. Sitting on his humming bike, Axe took out his phone and stared at the blank screen for a minute. The magenta-tinted clouds bathed the biker in a warm glow, the heat of the day dissipating as the coolness of the night crept in. Axe put his phone away, then took it back out and sent a text to Derek. He *had* to fucking know. Shifting gears, he left the compound and rode out into the open space.

Chapter Six

*K*NOCK. KNOCK. KNOCK. Baylee covered her head with the pillow. *Knock. Knock. Knock.* Louder that time.

"Ugh…" Baylee threw her pillow on the floor and propelled herself out of bed, padding to the door bleary-eyed. Opening it a crack, she groaned when she saw the broad smile on Logan's face.

"Why in the hell would you be knocking at my door at seven in the morning?" she asked as she tried to finger-comb her bed-hair.

"I thought you'd be up. We have an important job to do, and you're always so early and eager to get started."

"We don't have to be at the firm until nine o'clock. That's like, in two hours."

"Thought you might want to grab some breakfast. We can go over our strategy."

"I don't do breakfast. A strong cup of coffee, black, is all I need. Oh, and before you get any ideas, I don't do lunch, either."

"Wow. How do you function?"

Baylee shrugged.

"Get dressed and I'll meet you in the restaurant for coffee. Say, in thirty minutes?"

"I'll meet you at the firm at nine. Go away, Logan."

"You're cranky in the morning, aren't you?"

Sighing, Baylee closed the door and trudged back to bed. What was Logan up to? They'd worked together for a little more than two years— she knew him, knew he wasn't being solicitous for the hell of it. Perhaps he was awkward being in a new place and not knowing anyone but her, but Baylee was sure he was up to something. Maybe he was cozying up to her to find out what her ideas were, then he'd steal them from her and claim them as his own. It wouldn't be the first time he did something devious like that on his climb up the firm ladder.

Baylee tried to get another hour of shut-eye before she had to start her day, but sleep eluded her; she tossed and turned, mashing her pillow to re-fluff it. Cursing Logan, she shuffled to the bathroom to take a shower.

An hour later, she slipped on a sleeveless, light gray pencil dress with a hemline that rose slightly above her knee. The dress hugged her in all the right places, showing off her curves in a subtle and professional manner. Light gunmetal four-inch pumps completed her look. Checking herself in the mirror, she swiped peach lip gloss over her nude lipstick. With her black leather briefcase and matching clutch bag in hand, she left her room.

Driving around Pinewood Springs was a breeze. That was one thing she hated about Denver—the constant traffic. It took forever to traverse the big city, but in less than ten minutes, she pulled her car in the firm's parking lot. *Small-town living has its perks.*

She was early. A smug smile whispered across her lips. *How's that, Logan?* He was probably still stuffing his face with a ton of carbs. The man could eat. The first time they went out for lunch, she'd been amazed how much he could pack away. He was lean, so she figured he worked out a lot. Baylee didn't know too much about Logan, and she wanted to keep it that way. Since they were on the same career path, it wasn't a good idea to become too friendly, especially when it came to promotions and the like. Logan was very competitive, as was she, and they often clashed.

Baylee just didn't trust Logan, and she presumed he didn't trust her, either. The next few months in Pinewood Springs would prove to be more than challenging for her. She had to watch Logan, make sure he couldn't sabotage her efforts. Claudia, who kept begging her to arrange a "meeting" with Logan, thought she was paranoid, but Baylee knew how cutthroat the corporate world could be, and Logan gave off slimier-than-average vibes.

"May I help you?" a pleasant-looking woman in her mid-fifties asked as she walked through the door.

"I'm Baylee Peters. I'm the architect from Denver, and I'm having a meeting with Stanley Danesk."

"Yes, Ms. Peters. You are expected. You're the only one here so far. Let me show you to the conference room."

Baylee followed the secretary down a long hall lined with generic paintings of mountain scenes, boats, and ocean landscapes. The woman opened a door and invited Baylee into a medium-sized room with a long table and eight plush chairs covered in a burnt orange, geometric pattern.

"Would you like something to drink? Water, coffee, tea, or a soft drink?"

Baylee smiled warmly at the woman. "A cup of black coffee sounds great."

"I'll be right back with your coffee, Ms. Peters."

After she left the room, Baylee took in the spectacular views outside. Pinches of green, purple, indigo, yellow, and pink carpeted the base of the sky-piercing mountains. Below the rock skyscrapers, the town thrived. Iron streetlights and elm trees dotted the sidewalks on the streets around the firm. A small park with a white-wood gazebo lent a nostalgic feel, and Baylee half-expected a brass band to start playing.

"Here you are."

Baylee turned around and saw the secretary placing her coffee down on a coaster on the table.

"Thank you. What is your name?" she asked.

The woman smiled. "Tina Lambert. Is there anything else I can get you?"

"No, I'm fine. Thanks, Tina."

At a couple of minutes to nine, Logan entered the conference room with three gentlemen. "That's a good one, Stan." Logan's loud laugh grated her nerves.

Can always count on Logan to be the first one with lips puckered to kiss ass. Baylee grinned to herself, standing as the men entered the room. Logan gave her a quick glance, disappointment registering on his face.

"Good morning, Logan." She smiled sweetly. *That's right. I'm not late, jerk.*

"So, you made it okay."

"Of course." Baylee turned away from Logan and greeted the three gentlemen who were at various stages of checking her out. She extended her hand. "I'm Baylee Peters, an architect with Derry, Decker, and Vale."

A man in his late thirties with short, blond hair and brown eyes grasped her hand and shook it. "I'm Stan Danesk. I'm a partner with Machol, Greenberg, Norton, & Danesk Engineering Firm. It's a pleasure to meet you." His eyes scanned back down to her bust.

"I'm James, lead engineer," a bearded man with twinkling blue eyes said as he shook her hand.

"And I'm Fred. I'll be working with Stan and James. I'm a newer addition to the firm." A man about twenty-eight with red hair and big, brown eyes smiled and took her hand.

After a few minutes of small conversation, Stan said, "Everyone, take a seat. The client should be here shortly."

Baylee chose the seat facing the magnificent view, her back to the door. She opened her briefcase, spread out her notebooks, pens, bottle water, and laptop, and took a sip of her still-hot coffee. As she turned on the laptop, she heard the jingle of chains behind her.

Stan stood up and cleared his throat. "Ah. Here he is. Come on in and have a seat, sir."

From the corner of her eye, Baylee observed black biker boots and denim pass by her, and the glimmers from dangling chains pricked her field of vision.

"Good, everyone is here. Since we'll be working on the strip mall project as a team, I'd like to go around the room and have everyone say something about themselves. It's important that we have a human aspect to all the metal and steel." He laughed as though he'd said something clever. Logan practically guffawed while James and Fred chuckled.

"I'll start," James volunteered.

Baylee logged in to her computer. *This is totally lame. Why do people do this touchy-feely shit?*

"My name is James McKnight, and I went to M.I.T. to study engineering. I joined with…"

Baylee tuned him out as she checked the temperature. *Holy shit. It's one hundred and one degrees out. Maybe I'll take a dip in the pool when I get home from work.* She looked up from her computer as James rambled on. Her gaze snagged on the dark eyes of her one-night stand. His surprised look was quickly replaced by an impassive one.

Baylee sucked in her breath, her eyes widening. Everything in the room went blank. The only sound she heard was the beating of her heart. What the fuck was *he* doing at the meeting? The room spun around her, and she couldn't wrap her head around the fact that he was in her space, staring intently at her. His lips barely concealed the beginnings of a smirk. *What the hell is going on? How can he be* here, *of all places?*

Then he spoke with the mouth that did so many wicked things to her the previous week.

"Name is Axe." His eyes never left her face.

Axe? Who names their kid Axe?

All of a sudden, she was aware that the room was silent. Baylee glanced around. All eyes were on her.

"Did I miss something?" she asked in a soft voice.

"We're sharing something about ourselves," Logan said.

Pink streaks colored her cheeks, and she saw Axe smile at her discomfort.

"I'm Baylee. Baylee Peters." Her voice was raspy, and she wished she could disappear.

"Hello, Baylee," Axe said in a husky tone, making her name sound dirty.

She swallowed hard, nodded, and stared at her computer screen.

"Is that all you're gonna share, Baylee?" Axe licked his lips.

He's mocking me. "Yep." She stared at him defiantly.

"That's no fun." He leaned forward on his elbows, then said, "Do you like to have fun, Baylee?" His deep, smooth voice caressed her while small shivers shimmied down her spine.

"I think we should move on to discussing the project," Stan said, breaking through the sexual tension.

She ripped her eyes away from Axe's and pretended to concentrate on what Stan was saying, grateful he'd turned out the lights so they could see the PowerPoint presentation better. *At least I can't see Axe's eyes on me. I can't believe he's on the project. Of all the people in this damn world, he is the one I have to work with. What are the odds of that? And what the hell is he doing in Pinewood Springs? I thought he lived in Denver. And a biker? Shit.*

Stan spoke of structural issues, possible construction problems and how they could be remedied, and all Baylee could do was remember how big Axe was, how delicious he tasted. She crossed and uncrossed her legs as she remembered how his lips, his tongue, and his fingers felt on her skin. She had come so hard so many times under his expert and sinful moves. *Damn, I'm getting turned on just by thinking about how awesome our time together was.*

Even though it was dark, she didn't dare glance over at him; she could feel his stare boring a hole in her. His nearness was driving her insane. So much so that, by the time the meeting was over, she had to hold herself back from yanking him across the conference table and riding him right in front of all of them. *Damnit! Get a grip.* She reached for her bottle of water, hoping the coolness would extinguish the heat that had been building inside her for the past hour.

How was she supposed to make it through the summer with Axe on the project? Having him that close—the man she'd been dreaming and fantasizing about—would be pure torture. It also made it impossible for her to connect with him, since it was against firm policy to date a client.

But even if office policy was lax, she could never date him because he made her panties damp, and her body tingle. He was danger in leather. She already knew what he could do to her, and she couldn't risk her heart to a leather-clad Casanova.

After the meeting ended, Baylee jumped up, gathered all her belongings, and zipped out of the conference room. She didn't stop until she found herself in a small café across the street, a few storefronts down from the firm. The aroma of freshly baked muffins hung heavy in the air, and Baylee flopped down on a red-painted wooden chair. She brushed her hair from her face and stared out the windows. The last thing she wanted was for Axe to see her if he came out looking for her.

"Are you ready to order?" a college-aged woman asked.

Baylee craned her head to read the menu board. "Bring me a lemon poppy seed muffin and a cup of coffee—black."

She couldn't believe any of it was real. It was like she was still in the comfy bed at the hotel, and any minute now, Logan's annoying knocks would wake her up. It couldn't be true. Axe didn't look like a biker at the wedding. She sighed. Not only was he a biker, but he was an *outlaw* biker. When she'd found out the Insurgents MC was the client for the strip mall project, she'd read up on them, and the reputation they had made the hairs on her nape stand up.

The young waitress placed the muffin and coffee in front of Baylee. As she sipped, unwanted images of Axe's mouth on hers made her stomach lurch and twist. *His mouth and hands were all over my body. How can I go back? How can I work with him?* Remembering his touches and his hardness plowing into her, she squirmed in the chair as a sweet sensation formed in her pussy. *Damnit! This is a mess.* Axe was nowhere in sight yet her body was misbehaving. How would she control it when they worked together? *Damn, damn, damn!*

How could she go back? What would she say to him? "Uh… what have you been up to since we last saw each other? You remember, the night we fucked each other's brains out?" It was beyond awkward—it was downright embarrassing. When he was a nameless sex god, it'd been fun, titillating, and exciting. There was now a name to her sex god, and it was enough to make her give up her chance at partnership to Logan. She should call Gary and tell him she wasn't feeling well, that she had to quit the project.

What I ought to do is high-tail it back to Denver and hide out until all of this is nothing but a bad memory.

But then Logan's sneer flitted through her mind when she thought of how he'd react if he made partner. He'd be insufferable. No, she'd worked too hard to let a sexy biker dash her chances of securing a place around the partners' table, even if he had given her a night to remember. She could do this. She was a levelheaded professional, and even though the situation was not ideal, in time, everything would work itself out.

It had been a shock seeing him at the meeting—that was all. She was already becoming used to the idea of *him* being there. Anyway, it wasn't like they were working together in the same office like she was with Logan. She and Axe didn't have to see each other every day.

Baylee took a deep breath. *It's going to all right.*

She jumped when a thunderous rumble diverted her attention. She noticed Axe revving the motor of an electric yellow Harley, the chrome pipes, handlebars, and tire rims gleaming under the sun's rays. She watched as he put on his sunglasses, swung his corded legs out, and made a small U-turn. The glistening straight pipes roared as he blasted past the café. Just when she'd convinced herself she had it together, he had to ride past her on his Harley, exuding sex from every pore of his perfectly sculpted body. *This is going to be way harder than I thought.*

Back at the office, Baylee forced herself to put Axe out of her mind and concentrate on her work. She was relieved to see him go. Now she could work without any worries of running into him.

After thirty minutes, Logan came by her office and poked his head in. "Are you okay?" he asked.

"Yeah."

"Why'd you run out of the meeting this morning?"

"I didn't feel well. I needed to get some fresh air. I feel much better now. Thanks for asking." She turned back to her computer.

"Do you know the client?"

Baylee bit her inner cheek then feigned surprise. "No. Why do you ask?"

"It looked like you may have recognized him, or something. And the way he stared at you throughout the whole meeting made me think he knew you."

Her laughter was too shrill. "Well, he is a man, and a biker at that, so I kind of expected him to act without much decorum."

Logan chuckled. "I see what you mean. I can't say I blame him, though. You're a beautiful woman. If I ever stared at you like that, you'd probably slap my face."

Red tinged her cheeks. She wasn't sure what to say. An awkward silence settled around them, and when Stan walked into her office, relief spread over her once again.

"How are things going? Are you settled in?"

"Pretty much. Thanks for giving me an office with a view."

"You're welcome. If you need any help, Tina Lambert will be your secretary. She's great, and she said you two had already met."

"Yes, we did. Thanks, Stan."

"Give me a shout if you need anything."

Baylee nodded and watched as Logan and Stan headed down the hall. Leaning back in her desk chair, she sighed. She couldn't get Axe on his bike out of her mind. It was going to be a long afternoon.

CHAPTER SEVEN

*W*HAT IN THE *fuck is* she *doing on the strip mall project?* The hottest one-night stand he'd ever had was the club's architect? A wide smile broke out over Axe's face as he raced his Harley toward the clubhouse. The slight gasoline fumes, waves of heat coming up from the engine, and the rush of the wind all made his heart pump. There was nothing like riding a Harley, hugging the curves and swallowing up the asphalt.

Having the hot piece of ass who had taken his mind and dick hostage for the past week might make this one of the better summers he'd ever had. Remembering the look on her face when she recognized him made him laugh. *Bet she never expected to see* me *in the conference room. Too fuckin' funny.*

The Harley rolled into the clubhouse's parking lot. Axe entered the club through the back door, making his way to Banger's office.

"How did the meeting go?" Banger asked as he shoved some papers on his desk to the side.

"Not bad." Axe then told him what had transpired earlier that morning, but he left out his acquaintance with the sexy architect. He didn't think Banger would see the humor in it, especially since he was still pissed off at him for zoning out at church the previous day.

"Keep an eye on those suits. Make sure they do what they're supposed to do and they don't pad the bill. They all think we're dumb biker fucks. I know their kind. Watch 'em."

"I'll watch over the project real good," Axe answered with a smirk.

After leaving Banger's office, Axe went to his room in the basement. The clubhouse had several club members living there. The third floor rooms were reserved for board members, but the basement had rooms for members who lived there as well as extras for visiting members or brothers who drank too much or just wanted to crash.

Axe had lived at the clubhouse since he'd patched in eight years before. He loved being in the middle of all the action and camaraderie. There was always something going on: a pool game, the fights on TV, or a party. Being able to walk up a flight of stairs and get good pussy with one, two, or three club whores was his idea of living. Up until recently, Rosie had been his favorite fuck; she knew how to give a blowjob, and her cunt was real tight considering she'd been with many of the brothers.

Axe knew he was one of her favorites, and she'd always come up to him whenever she saw him, hoping to have a little fun. All the women—club whores and citizens alike—were crazy about Axe and his sexual prowess. He knew the club whores appreciated that, especially. Some of the brothers just banged into them—like the women were draining holes—until they jerked off. Then they were done before the women were even heated up.

Not Axe. He was into pleasing a woman for the time he was with her, and he did a damn good job of it. But once he was done, he'd push them away. Yeah, he was a bastard, but he didn't pretend to be anything else. Every woman knew what they were getting before he stuck his dick in them—a great fuck, but nothing more.

His motto with citizens was to never fuck them more than once. He found out the hard way that they read way too much into anything more. Club whores knew their place. They were there to please the brothers, no risk of any complications. But sometimes, club pussy was too familiar, boring. Then Axe would venture out into the citizens' world and hook up with a hot-looking chick. Right up front, he'd make it perfectly clear it was a one-fuck deal. They always agreed then they'd pout or throw him attitude whenever he walked away without a backward glance. Axe hated that shit. It wasn't like he wasn't honest with them.

Citizen women always thought they could change him, and that one night of fucking would blow his mind and make him bend his rules. Well, it didn't... until he pulled a one-night stand with Baylee.

Baylee. Her name fit her. He liked it. Axe's brow creased; Baylee was making him bend his rule. He wanted to fuck her again in the worst way. The way she pretended everything was cool that morning, even though he saw her eyelids twitching, told him she was bothered by him, and *that* made him hornier than hell.

A soft knock on his door broke in on his thoughts.

"Come in."

Rosie entered, wearing short-shorts and a crop top that revealed the underside of her ample tits.

"Hiya. You been doin' okay? You haven't been paying any attention to me." She jutted out her lower lip in a sensual pout.

"Been busy, that's all." He looked at her hot body, a jolt of arousal shooting through him.

"Need some company?" Rosie sat down next to him, her hand moving up his arm. "Looks like you need me to help you out a bit." She smiled broadly as her eyes lingered on his dick.

Fuck, I'm pitching a tent. He turned sideways and took in her earnest face, thinking he should have her kneel in front of him and suck him off. He had a willing, hot woman wanting to have sex with him, and he was sitting on the edge of the bed trying to rationalize it. What the hell was the matter with him?

"Nah. I'm good."

Perplexed, Rosie licked her lips as she stared at him. "Did I do something to make you mad at me?"

He laughed. "No. It's nothing personal. I still think you're hot and all that, it's just that I got a lot on my mind right now." He rubbed his palms against his jeans. *Like wishing Baylee were here instead of you, begging me to fuck her. Damn, just remembering her hands tied and my mouth on her taut, soft skin makes me want to blow my load. Fuck!*

"So, we're still good?"

"If you're asking if I still want to fuck you, then yeah, we're still good. I just don't wanna do it now." *At least not with you.*

"Why not?"

"Shit, Rosie, I just don't. Get outta my room and find a brother to cool down your horny ass. Stop asking me questions. Go on, get outta here."

Rosie stood, then ran her hand through his dark hair. He inhaled sharply.

"Sure you don't want something, baby? Tonight's gonna get crazy with some of the out-of-state members. I'm gonna be real busy." She raked her nails down his neck. "Right now, you got me all to yourself. I don't have to be anywhere for at least a few hours."

"I'm sure." He pushed her hand away. *What in the hell am I saying?* "I gotta get back downtown."

He rose from the bed, pulled down his t-shirt, and walked toward the bathroom. "Close the door on your way out," he said.

In the bathroom, he stared at his reflection. His dick was impossibly hard, and he'd have to get it down before he went back to confront Baylee. "You coulda fixed your dick with Rosie. She was a sure thing," he said to his reflection. Running his hand through his hair, he turned on the shower. Baylee was a sure thing, too. She was different, and unlike anyone he'd been with, but women didn't say no to him.

A couple more fuck sessions oughta do it for him. She was worth bending his rules. When he was finished, he'd leave her satisfied and ruined for any other man.

With a grin on his face, he stepped into the shower.

BAYLEE GLANCED AT the clock on the wall above her desk. It was already five o'clock. The time had flown by so fast. Once she got over the shock of seeing *him*, the knot in her stomach untied, especially as the day progressed and there was still no sign of Axe. The night they'd spent together, she'd pegged him right—he was definitely a one-time deal with women. She'd bet he never went out with the same woman twice. He hadn't even attempted to follow her when she'd rushed out after the meeting. She'd worried herself sick for most of the day. *How silly.* They were two people whose worlds happened to collide for a work project. Nothing more. No big deal.

"So, your name's Baylee," a deep voice said.

She whirled toward the doorway and saw him filling it, in all his muscular splendor—*Axe.* His dark hair looked damp, a few tendrils curled and stuck to his jawline, making her fingers ache to brush them aside just as they had back in Denver at the wedding. His fierce gaze held danger and lust, causing her breath to hitch. His t-shirt molded sinfully over his toned chest, the ripples of his muscles showing through. And his tattoos danced whenever he moved his arms. She knew every one of the tats on his arms, and she could see in her mind's eye the ones hidden under his t-shirt. Baylee had traced each and every one of them with her tongue.

Her cheeks flushed a rosy pink. *If only he wasn't so sexy.* Her wide eyes lingered on his full, sensual lips. *I know what that mouth can do to my body.*

No! Focus, Baylee. Focus!

"That's right, and your name is Axe?"

"Uh-huh." A half-smile tugged at his lips.

She smiled, exuding a confidence she didn't feel. "It's nice to formally meet you." She laughed, but it was a little too high, too strained. She averted her gaze back to her desk. "I was just finishing up. Is there something I can help you with?"

His eyes lingered on her mouth as he slowly nodded. "Let's start with you taking care of the hard-on I've had since I saw you this morning." He walked into her office and closed the door behind him.

Baylee swallowed. "What?"

Before she could ask another question, he silenced her with his mouth on hers, nipping and licking it.

A current of pleasure shimmied down from her lips to her dampening panties. *This is insane! It was a one-night stand. Nothing ever comes out of those.* Pushing him back, she cleared her throat and said, "Please, don't do that again. I'm at work and not in the habit of kissing men I don't know at my desk."

His hot breath scorched her neck as he leaned in and whispered in her ear, "You know me very well."

"Not really. I didn't even know your name or where you lived, until today."

"Those are fillers, babe. *This*—" he cupped his thick dick "—is all that matters. It's what we feel that matters, not fuckin' facts." He tugged her to him.

"I need a little more than *that*. Anyway, it was a one-night stand. Remember our agreement—no names, no strings attached? We weren't supposed to see each other again."

"And here we are. I'd call that fate, or some fuckin' good karma." He placed his hand on the back of her head, leaned down and kissed her, gently at first, then more demanding.

A thousand sparks pricked her skin and her toes curled as she met his deep kisses, her arms snaking around his neck, fingers running through his silky hair.

"Fuck, I never thought I'd see you again. I want to fuck your pussy. I know how sweet it is." He placed his leg between hers and gently pushed her backward, walking her to her desk.

Her thighs bumped into it, and Axe began to guide her back. But then reality set in and she shoved him away from her.

"Are you crazy? I'm at work. I can't do this."

"It'd be awesome, but if you'd rather fuck at your hotel, I get that. Let's go." He curled his arm around her waist and drew her close.

Baylee's body relaxed against him, her mind calling it a traitor. *I can't do this.* Uncurling herself from him, she rushed to the door, cracking it open. "*We're* not going anywhere. I'm going to my hotel, and you're going to wherever it is you go. We had a one-night stand. It was great, but it was for only one night. It's too bad we have to be in each other's lives for a short period of time, but we're both adults. I'm sure we can deal with it."

Axe narrowed his eyes. "Are you going to tell me that you never thought about me or what we did, not even once, since we fucked?"

"That's hardly the point."

"I thought so, and that's *exactly* the point. We already know we enjoy pleasuring each other, so what the fuck's the problem?"

"The problem is the night ended a week ago. I'm simply not interested." Her stomach twisted and turned at the lie. "I really have to go. Perhaps I'll see you tomorrow. Goodbye."

Axe stood motionless before her, his bulging eyes indicating he was shocked that she wasn't just going to let him take her on her desk. What would happen if Stan walked by and heard them? Axe was crazier than she'd thought.

She walked down the hall and out the lobby door. When she got off the elevator, she practically ran to her car, fearing he'd come after her and she'd weaken. It felt so good being in his arms again, having his mouth on hers, his tongue inside. And the filthy way he spoke to her made her mound quake. She had to make sure to never be alone with him again; she knew she wouldn't be so strong next time.

In her hotel room, the red message button flashed on the phone on the nightstand. She picked it up and listened to the message. It was from Logan, asking if she wanted to meet for dinner. The last thing she wanted to do was go out with him and listen to him brag about how invaluable he was to the firm. She'd call him and tell him she was beat and was going to order room service, then go to bed. For a split second, she wished Axe was with her in her room, doing all the delicious things he'd done at the wedding.

You're hopeless, Baylee. Just hopeless.

CHAPTER EIGHT

BAYLEE WOKE UP, her yellow nightshirt drenched in sweat and her chest heaving as she desperately gulped air into her lungs. Tears rolled down her cheeks as her heart slammed over and over against her ribcage. *It's only a nightmare. You're safe. Calm down and breathe.*

After several minutes of trembling and gasping for air, her body unraveled nerve by nerve. She glanced at the blue numbers on the clock radio next to her bed. Three o'clock glowed eerily. Shaking her head, Baylee scooted out of bed and went to the bathroom to splash some water on her face. Her reflection revealed a white pallor with a sheen of tears and sweat. Her hair was tangled and unruly. After drying her face, she brushed out her hair then slipped on something dry.

The nightmare was especially brutal this time. Usually, she'd wake up panting when the menacing shadow began creeping toward her, but this time the dark shape had loomed over her, sunken eyes boring into her as hands wrapped around her neck while she cowered on the steps of her childhood home. It was always the same nightmare, a throwback to the night when her mother's life ended in violence. In her dreams, Baylee was the scared child watching a hulking shadow snuff out her beloved mother. Her cries drew the killer's attention, and he began walking toward her, but then she'd always wake up, panicked. He'd never come close to her, but this time, he'd put his hands on her neck.

She felt them. They were cold, like death.

As she sat on her bed, she shivered, her arms wrapped around her drawn-up knees. As the terror of her nightmare subsided, a flash of the man's arms pierced her brain. Something was different; the shadow was clearer, and she'd seen a large scar running up his arm from above his wrist to his elbow. Did the killer have a scar, or was that just an image in her nightmare, in the world of dreams and illusions?

Dr. Scott had warned her to be prepared for the memories, because they could set off a major panic attack. Over the course of the previous year, she'd been recalling several details: the way the man's shoes squeaked on the hardwood floor when he rushed up to her, the hatred emanating from him as he raised his hand ready to strike her, the loud knock on the front door, and the overwhelming scent of something sweet and pungent. She couldn't remember what it was, but he reeked of it, and she remembered she didn't like it.

Baylee knew as long as her mother's murder remained unsolved, the nightmares would continue. After all these years, there were no clues, no suspects—nothing. She cringed every time she thought of the killer, wondering how many more women he'd murdered. She needed closure in the worst way, but she'd also been making enormous progress in moving on. She was grateful she'd found Dr. Scott, and credited him for coaxing forth the memories locked away in the recesses of her mind.

By that point, her body had calmed down, and she was all right. The nighttime didn't appear to be as scary as it had an hour before. But when she lay down again, she tossed and turned. Each time she closed her eyes, the scar on the man's arm and his light eyes consumed her mind. Sighing, she reached over, turned on the reading lamp, and opened her book. The words danced in front of her, but she couldn't focus enough on what she was reading. It was so quiet in the room, and Baylee wished she had someone to talk to. She was desperate enough to call Logan, but she knew he would be fast asleep. Claudia would also be asleep, and Baylee didn't want to wake her up, especially since Claudia was up at five in the morning to workout.

Axe's smug face flitted across her mind, and she grabbed her phone on impulse to text him. *Wait, what the hell am I thinking?* When Stan handed out the numbers for Axe, Banger, and Hawk—she couldn't believe the names of these guys—it was for Baylee and Logan to get ahold of them for *business* reasons, not to pass the time or flirt.

Oh, well.

Before she could talk herself out of it, she sent him a text.

Baylee: *What do you do for fun around here?*

She waited a few minutes, looking at the words in her book, but not understanding them.

Axe: *Fuck.*

She stared at the screen for a few seconds, debating whether she should respond.

Axe: *Want me to come over?*

Yeah, I do.

Baylee: *No. Just wondered. Now I know.*
Axe: *Now you know.*
Baylee: *Nite.*

Her phone pinged again.

Axe: *What're u wearing?*

Baylee knew she should turn off her phone, but for reasons she couldn't articulate, texting Axe in the middle of the night made her feel safe and less lonely.

It kept the shadows away.

Baylee: *Short nightshirt.*
Axe: *U got panties on?*

This was going out of control fast. She had to nix this. He was her firm's contract, and she knew better.

Baylee: *Maybe.*
Axe: *Ur killing me.*

Baylee: Am I?

Axe: U know it. U wet?

Her eyes widened. He was so brazen, so sexual, so dirty, and she absolutely *loved* it. She was acting like such a slut with him, giving him the wrong impression. She couldn't have sex with him again, could she?

Baylee: I can't tell u all my secrets…

Axe: I'm hard. U wanna tell me what u'd do to me if u were here?

He wanted her to text dirty, like phone sex, but she couldn't do it. She'd gone too far with the game.

Baylee: Not in my job description.

Axe: It's one of the perks of ur contract.

Baylee: Another time. Gotta go. Too late. Nite.

She turned off her phone, not trusting herself to be good if he responded again. She had no business teasing him. A man like that wanted action, not words. She may have unleashed a monster she'd have to tame, or at least douse with a bucket of cold water.

She switched off the lights, the little "conversation" she'd had with Axe relaxing her. She closed her eyes, and in barely five minutes, she was fast asleep.

★ ★ ★

"I WAS PLANNING on working through lunch," Baylee said to Logan as he sat across from her in her office.

"You have to eat. Anyway, we have some things we need to go over. Stan said the president of the motorcycle club wanted five storefronts instead of six. The club wants to have a burger joint and needs the extra space for that. We have to tweak the design."

"Can't we do that now?"

"I can't think on an empty stomach, and I'm too busy this afternoon. We could do it tonight in your room, if you'd like?"

A night spent with Logan was not her idea of a good time. "That won't work. All right, let's go over the change at lunch. Let me grab my purse and iPad."

Logan beamed. "I found a good restaurant next door. They make the best Monte Cristos."

"Sounds good. I'll let you lead the way."

The Broker Restaurant catered mainly to the business crowd for lunch. The décor was sleek and modern, muted shades of brown adorning the walls and seating while bronze abstract sculptures decorated the built-in shelves which lined the walls. Small spotlights focused on the local sculptures and other artistic creations, and each item was available for sale. Low lighting created an intimate ambiance.

When Baylee and Logan entered The Broker, the cool air wrapped around them.

"It's nice in here," Baylee said as she followed the hostess to their table. "I didn't think it'd be this hot in Pinewood Springs since we're so high up, but damn." The bronze chair was heavy and Logan helped to push her closer to the table.

"I know what you mean. It's miserable, but Stan told me it's unusual for it to be like this."

After giving their order to the waiter, they discussed possible changes for the strip mall. The waiter set down a melted turkey, avocado, and Swiss sandwich in front of Baylee, and Logan had the piping-hot Monte Cristo with a mountain of fries.

"Yum, the turkey sandwich is really good. Nice choice in restaurants." Baylee savored the flavor as she sipped her iced tea.

"It's nice having lunch with you. I'm liking getting to know you better. We've worked together for over two years, and I think this is the second time we've had lunch. We should do this more regularly when we get back to Denver."

Baylee nodded, but the last thing she wanted to do was become friends with Logan. She didn't trust him at all, and all this bonding he was foisting on her didn't deter her assessment of him.

"The two architects at play," a deep voice snarled.

Baylee cocked her head and locked eyes with Axe.

"Hi." She dabbed the corners of her mouth with her napkin.

"How're you doing?" Logan chimed in.

Turning his back to him, Axe ran his eyes over Baylee's face, lingering on her mouth. "What the fuck? You have time to spend with this asshole, but not me?"

Baylee stopped breathing at the same moment Logan sputtered and choked. She met Axe's hard eyes and silently pleaded with him to stop. No chance—he was on a roll.

"I've been calling you all morning. Why haven't you picked up?"

"I didn't receive any calls from you." She took out her phone then froze, realizing she'd forgotten to turn it back on after their late-night texting. "My phone is off. Sorry, I forgot to turn it back on."

"You turned it off after so you couldn't get any of my texts, right? What the fuck kind of game are you playing here?"

Panic seized her. Logan was at the table, and she couldn't let him know she was texting Axe in the middle of the night. He'd have a field day with that one.

Discreetly, she slipped her hand from her lap, reached out and touched Axe's thigh. He shook under her fingers. In a low voice, she said, "Please, stop. We can discuss this later. Not now." She mouthed, "Not with him," tilting her head in Logan's direction.

Axe jutted out his jaw then looked at Logan for the first time. "You're done here. Get a take-out box and finish up at the office. I need to speak with Baylee alone."

Logan's eyes widened and his lips parted. "What? Are you joking?"

"Do I look like I'm fuckin' joking?" Axe crossed his arms, his ripped biceps flexing. Logan caught Baylee's gaze. "Baylee...?"

Clearing her throat, she said, "Axe, this is rude. Logan and I are having a business lunch. We're going over design changes Banger wants. You and I can speak later."

For the first time since he came up to their table, Axe looked at the notebooks and electronic devices spread over the tablecloth. Baylee saw his eyes soften when it seemed to dawn on him that she and Logan were not having a social lunch.

"That's cool." He pointed his finger at Logan. "I changed my mind. You can stay."

The color came back to Logan's face and Baylee released her breath, relieved that a near catastrophe had been averted.

"We'll talk soon. See you," she said cheerfully to Axe.

Axe pulled out a chair, sat down, then crossed his denim-clad leg over his knee.

"What're you doing?" Baylee asked.

"Sitting. I wanna hear how you're gonna handle the changes so I can report to Banger."

"I was going to call him later today and go over everything."

"Now you don't have to."

Logan straightened his tie. "I think it's great that you're joining us. Maybe you can give us some input?"

Axe quirked his lips, ran his glinting eyes over Logan's earnest face, and snorted. He placed his hand over Baylee's. "Show me what you got. I wanna see *all* of it." He winked.

A perfectly good sandwich was ruined; there was no way she could swallow another bite. When the waiter came by to give Axe his beer, Baylee told him to take away her plate.

"Would you like a box to take it home?" the waiter asked.

She shook her head.

"You hardly ate anything, babe. That can't be good." Axe smirked.

"I lost my appetite."

"Is that so? Funny thing is, I'm starving." He leaned over, picked up the other half of her sandwich, and took a big bite. "Fuck, that's good."

The waiter began to walk away when Logan said, "You can take mine. I'm finished."

"Do you want a take-out box?" The waiter then glanced at Axe.

Axe laughed. "Fuck, no. I'm good." He took another large bite of Baylee's sandwich.

The waiter cleared away Logan's plate, hastening back to the kitchen.

"You weren't hungry, either?" Axe asked as he wiped his mouth with the napkin.

"Guess not," Logan responded flatly.

"If neither of you were hungry, then why the fuck didn't you stay at the office and work on the changes? You professionals don't use common sense." He took a swig of beer.

Logan sat up straight. "We better go. Stan doesn't like us taking too long for lunch. Ready, Baylee?"

Baylee pushed her chair back, but Axe whipped out his hand. In one fluid movement, he had her back against the table.

"Baylee will join you later. We have some stuff we need to talk about."

"Is it business?"

"It's none of *your* fuckin' business. You tell Stan that Baylee is with me, and she'll be running late. If he has a problem with it, he can call me. He has my number." Axe motioned for the waiter to come over.

"Yes, sir?"

"Another beer, and give the check to him." Axe gave Logan a half-smile.

After Logan paid the bill, he said, "I'll see you at the office, Baylee."

When he was out of earshot, Baylee, bristling for the past ten minutes, hissed, "You are the rudest asshole I have ever met."

Axe leaned back in his chair. "Yeah. What's your point?"

"You're impossible. Logan and I were having a business lunch, then you come barging in, tossing all your fucking testosterone around, and now you want to *talk*? No fucking way." Baylee picked up her purse, but Axe's strong grip on her arm held her in place.

"I don't like him. He's an ass-kisser, and I fuckin' hate them. I thought you had a date or something. Now I know it was for business, so I'm cool with that."

She shook her head. "What are you talking about? What if it *were* a date? How is that any of your business? You act like we're going out or something. We had a one-night stand. It's done. Get over it."

Several people turned their heads as her voice escalated. Axe watched her in amusement.

"Stop looking at me with that annoying smirk on your face. You don't understand that Logan and I are in competition for partnership. He'll use anything against me. It is against firm policy for an employee to go out with a client, so you just made Logan a happy man. Now, he has some shit he can take to Gary, Bob, or Warren, and I'll be on the fucking radar. Thanks a lot."

Nodding, Axe pursed his lips. "You want me to take the asshole out?"

She threw her head back and emitted a frustrated moan. "Is that all you got out of what I said?"

"Basically, you want something, and that asshole is keeping you from getting it. I can eliminate the competition. It's not a big deal. I can take care of it."

"I can't believe you're serious."

"Damn straight. Just give me the word."

"Are you crazy? I don't want you to do anything to Logan. This is bizarre."

He shrugged.

He has to be joking.

"Enough about him," Axe said. "I'm coming by tonight."

"Not tonight. Stan is taking Logan and me out for dinner."

"Again with the asshole?"

"Stan's trying to be nice since we're new to Pinewood Springs."

"I'm trying to be nice with you, too, but you're making it difficult." Axe brushed his fingers up and down her forearm.

Baylee shivered as goosebumps carpeted her skin. *Feels so good. He has the gentlest touch, but it can be rough and intense, too… Focus, Baylee!*

"Another time, okay? I need to go. I don't want Stan and the others to think I'm a slacker."

"You're not, are you?"

"Of course not. I work my butt off."

"Then why do you care what others think? You know who you are, so fuck the rest of them."

"It's not that easy. What your boss thinks about you affects promotions, raises, and a whole bunch of other things. It's important to keep up good appearances."

"Fuck that. I don't give a damn what anyone thinks about me. I know who I am. Fuck the world."

"That's charming." She scanned his face—he was so incredibly handsome. "Don't fool yourself about appearances. Everyone cares, to some extent. Take your biker world, for example. You have to show rival clubs you're rough and tough, so you exude a certain appearance. You do it without thinking. You just did it earlier to Logan. You're not immune to it, and neither is 'your world,' "

Axe gave her a hard look. "I gathered you were feisty and witty the night we fucked, but I didn't know you were a smartass."

"The truth hurts, huh?" She smiled. "I really have to go." She slid her arm away from his touch and pushed her chair back. "It was interesting… All of it."

Axe rose to his feet, his tight jeans and t-shirt not leaving much to the imagination. Baylee noticed several women checking him out. For a split second, she felt very possessive of him and, without thinking, she leaned in to him and brushed her lips lightly against his. When she pulled back, hunger brimmed in his dark-chocolate eyes.

"I'll see you tonight," he rasped.

"I told you, I'm going out to dinner."

"I'll wait for you until you return." As he whispered in her ear, his hot breath tickled her neck. "Your texting stunt made it impossible for me to sleep last night, sweetheart."

Baylee swallowed hard and pulled away. She had to get away from him before her body gave her away. Axe ignited a fire in her like no other man ever had; if she wasn't careful, he'd burn her alive.

"I'm sorry about the texting. I don't know why I did it. It shouldn't have happened," she said as she walked through the restaurant.

"I'm not complaining. You were lonely, and you reached out for me. I like that."

"Anyway, I can't meet up with you." She stopped in front of the hostess's podium, fern trees in large, brushed-nickel planters decorating the area. The glass entry doors were coated with a brown film, cutting down on the afternoon glare.

Baylee turned to Axe and said in a low voice, "I don't mean this in a cruel way, but I'm not interested—in *any* guy. I'm committed to my career, and being involved in any way is not in my plans. The one-night stand was my way of blowing off some steam. It was nothing more. I'm sorry."

Before Baylee could take a step forward, Axe dragged her behind the tall fern trees and crushed her against his steel chest. With his hand tangled in her hair, he pulled her head back and covered her mouth with his. A small gasp escaped from her lips, and his tongue dove in. The kiss was deep, hard, and hot. Her body melted into his as she circled her arms around him, running her hands up and down his back. A powerful leg pried open her legs and he slipped it in-between, rubbing her pulsing mound with his knee. When she moaned, he broke away. Baylee looked at him, her eyebrows raised.

Burying his face in the space between her ear and neck, he nibbled her soft skin, whispering, "Yeah, keep telling yourself you don't want me." He patted her ass lightly, turned away, and waved. "Later, babe."

Coming out from behind the ferns, Baylee watched Axe swagger to his Harley as her heart pounded against her chest. How could she act like such a hussy, and in a nice restaurant of all places? Every time she came into contact with Axe, it ended with their lips pressed together.

Taking out her compact mirror, she was horrified to see her swollen lips, flushed face, and the messy hair strands on her cheeks. Shaking her head, she ambled to the ladies room to fix herself up before returning to the office.

ALL THROUGH DINNER, she pretended to listen to the conversation and laugh at Stan's jokes, but her mind was on a tall, built, rugged sex god. At various times throughout the evening, she'd wished she'd taken Axe up on his offer.

Stan told another engineer joke. *Right about now, Axe would be eating me out.*

"That's a good one, isn't it, Baylee?" Logan asked, his ass-kissing at its all-time high.

She forced a laugh. "Sorry to break up all the gaiety, but I'm pretty tired. I'm going to call it a night."

"It *is* getting late. I was enjoying myself so much, I lost track of the time," Stan said.

After the bill was paid, she and Logan drove back to the hotel. Logan headed toward the bar. "Want a nightcap?" he asked.

"Nope. I didn't sleep so well last night. I'm exhausted."

As they stood there talking, the hairs on the back of Baylee's neck crept up. An ominous feeling enveloped her. She glanced around quickly, but nothing seemed out of the ordinary.

"Well, I'm going in. See you in the morning," Logan said.

"Night," Baylee replied.

Logan disappeared into the bar, and again, she sensed someone watching her. Trying to shrug off the uneasy feeling weaving its way through her body, she scanned the lobby again, her blood pumping fiercely. Over to the right, behind the thick marble pillar, a flash of khaki caught her eye. Someone was hiding behind the pillar. She *knew* it, *felt* it—she wasn't imagining it. A group of people came into the lobby, chattering and laughing while they headed to the elevators. Baylee rushed to follow and blend in with them.

As they waited for the elevator, from the corner of her eye, Baylee noticed someone come from behind the pillar. She turned her head enough so she could see him. He was a tall, lean man in his late forties, wearing khaki pants and a long-sleeved shirt. He walked slowly toward the elevators.

Right before the door opened, one of the women in the group said, "It's too damn early to turn in. Let's get a drink in the bar."

Her other companions readily agreed. Then they were gone, and Baylee, who seconds before was surrounded by people, was completely alone, exposed and vulnerable. The elevator door opened and she jumped in, pushing the number for her floor then the "close door" button frantically. Her pulse raced. *The door has to close. Now.*

The elevator started closing, and Baylee leaned against the cool, smoky-colored mirrored wall, letting out a relieved breath. She was safe. The door nearly shut, a hand slipped in, and it bounced open once more. The piercing gaze of the man behind the pillar locked on to hers.

"Oh," she said aloud as her heart fell into the pit of her stomach.

The man stepped inside.

CHAPTER NINE

A BURST OF adrenaline kicked in, and Baylee sprung past the man. Before he could react, the elevator door shut. She stood frozen, fixated on the closed shiny door. Was the man meaning to harm her, or did she overreact? Her instincts told her he was following her, watching her. The thought of someone targeting her scared the hell out of her.

She debated taking the stairwell, but decided against it. Tears stung her eyes as she stood motionless, not knowing what to do. The elevator bell rang, and her racing heart felt as though it would explode right out of her chest. Her leg muscles tightened, and she sprinted away before the doors opened and the man came out.

Dashing into the bar, she searched the room for a place to hide.

"Baylee," Logan called as he waved her over to his table.

For the first time since she'd worked with him, she was happy to see him. She walked over to his table and took the seat across from him, so she could see the lobby. The waitress took her order and, in less than a minute, the scorching warmth of brandy burned down Baylee's throat.

"Did you change your mind about having a drink?"

She placed the brandy snifter on the wood table. "Yes." Scanning the bar, she said, "It's nice in here. Looks very rustic and inviting. I bet the stone fireplace gives a lot of heat in the winter. It's huge." She stared at the massive fireplace that filled the entire back wall.

Logan agreed, then began rambling about the project and what they needed to do. As he droned on, Baylee tuned him out, her pulse racing each time the elevator doors opened. Then she spotted him, coming out of the elevator, moving his head all around. He was looking for her. A chill snaked its way down her back, and she shifted in her chair so Logan blocked her. She silently prayed that the man wouldn't come into the bar.

Her prayer went unanswered.

When he entered, Baylee bent down, pretending to pick something off the floor. She watched his brown loafers as they took a few steps, hesitated, then retreated. Slowly, she sat up, observing him as he left the hotel, his cell phone next to his ear and his mouth moving. A sigh of relief washed over her.

"Are you okay? You look real pale, all of a sudden," Logan said.

She laughed nervously. "It must be the brandy. Alcohol and exhaustion never mix well for me." The back of her neck ached, and she rubbed it.

Logan finished his drink. "Are you ready to go up?"

"Yes. Are you coming?"

"Yeah, I'll go with you."

They rode up the elevator in silence, and when he walked her to her room, she was grateful. "Thanks for seeing me to my door. Goodnight."

"No worries. Are you sure everything's okay?"

"I'm sure. Thanks again. See you at work in the morning."

After she secured the third lock, Baylee exhaled. She'd been on edge ever since she sensed someone watching her. When she noticed the man in the lobby, her fears were confirmed. Maybe he was just a pervert, but she had a gut feeling it was more. Her inner voice told her it was somehow related to her mother's murder, but her voice of reason argued she was being paranoid and ridiculous. The murder had happened so many years before, and in Denver, not Pinewood Springs. Only a few people knew she was in town for a few months. She was acting like a scared little girl. Or was she?

Many times over the years, she'd felt someone watching her. She'd never seen anyone, and couldn't prove it with hard evidence, but she knew *he* was there, lurking in the dark corners of her life. Watching. Waiting for her memory to come back so he could silence her forever. The niggling feeling shrouded her life, but how could it happen in

Pinewood Springs? She'd never been to the town before, and she knew her mother never had, so why did she experience the same fear and dread of being watched?

Maybe it's all in my mind. Am I crazy? Baylee had read that sometimes a person thought someone was stalking him only to find out that what the person perceived to be real was all in his mind. Was the sense of danger, the fear someone was watching and following her, and the man in the lobby all a coincidence?

She massaged her throbbing temples. *Damnit! I wish all this would stop.* With a shaky hand, she placed two white tablets in her palm. Dr. Scott had prescribed the sleeping pills only when the nightmares became too much, when the shadows overtook her body and mind. She didn't take them very often, but when she did, they were her slice of oblivion for eight hours.

After swallowing the tablets, she turned on the TV, lay on the bed, and waited for the pills to work their magic.

BAYLEE STRETCHED LIKE a cat before rolling out of bed. She opened the curtains and sunshine streamed into the room. A night of uninterrupted sleep had done wonders for her psyche.

After gulping down a lukewarm cup of coffee, she dressed in her favorite outfit: a soft rose pencil skirt, a white mid-sleeve blouse with ruffle detailing, and peep-toe pumps. A chunky necklace and a wristful of silver bangles completed her look.

The drive to the office was smooth, and she arrived with five minutes to spare. When she settled into her desk chair, eager to start the day, Stan walked in.

"We're meeting in the conference room in about fifteen minutes. A problem has developed on the strip mall project, and we need to find a solution."

"All right. Does the problem have anything to do with my designs?"

"No. By the way, I loved what you did with expanding the restaurant. I took a look at both your ideas and Logan's, and I'm going to go with yours. Fine job, Baylee."

"Thank you." *Yes! Score one for me.*

When she entered the conference room, Axe sat at the table. His gaze traveled up her body, caressing every inch of her. She fidgeted under his stare; it felt like fingers against her skin. Sliding into the seat across from him, she avoided his dark eyes lingering on her mouth.

"Looks like we're all here. I called this meeting because we have a problem with the zoning permit. As in, there isn't one." Stan paused for effect. "Axe, I thought the club had the permits in order."

Axe shrugged. "It should be fine. I'll get back to you after the club meets later today."

"Okay. Let's talk about the design of the extra square footage and the structural impact."

Each time Baylee offered her input, Logan interrupted her. She was about ready to walk over and sucker-punch him when her phone pinged. She opened the text.

Axe: U look hot in ur skirt.

Baylee looked up and met Axe's hungry glance. Quickly, she turned her eyes away and focused her attention back on Stan. Another ping. She glanced at Axe, but he watched Stan.

Axe: Are u wearing those sexy lace panties u had on the night we fucked?

She choked then began coughing.

Peering at her, Stan asked, "Are you okay?"

Axe slid a glass of water to her, a wry smile painted on his face.

After she took a sip, she moved the glass away. "I'm fine. Go ahead. I'm okay, really." Baylee switched her phone to vibrate then stared straight ahead, intent on Stan.

Her phone pulsated. She willed herself not to look at it, not to look at him. Out of the corner of her eye, she saw him watching her, his amused expression mocking her.

Another vibration. She was tense beyond belief. Even though she didn't want to encourage him, she *had* to read his texts. Wishing she were stronger, she opened the messages.

Axe: *I'll take ur reaction as a yes on the panties.*

Axe: *Glad ur so bothered by me.*

She had to put a stop to this.

Baylee: *We're in a meeting. I'm sure u need to know what's going on so u can tell your club.*

Axe: *I'm only sure of one thing. I want to lick ur pussy. I miss ur taste.*

Baylee's widened eyes shot over to him. He licked his lips, his tongue bringing back delicious memories. *Focus.* James was in front of the group with another engineer Baylee did not recognize. Charts and diagrams covered the two easels, James pointing to them as he spoke.

Another pulse.

Axe: *Ur scent is amazing. Fuck, u've given me a hard-on.*

She discreetly typed under the table.

Baylee: *Do u want to get me fired? Stop. Please.*

Axe: *Having too much fun.*

Baylee: *Please.*

She looked at Axe, her eyes pleading.

Axe: *Only if u promise to have dinner with me tonite.*

She squirmed in her chair, pushed her hair behind her ears then chewed on the end of her pen.

Axe: *Are u wearing a bra?*

She sighed loudly.

Baylee: *K. I'll go out to dinner with u. Only as business colleagues.*
Axe: *Sure, no problem. My thoughts exactly.*

Yeah, right.

When she looked up, her eyes met his briefly before he diverted his attention to the two engineers at the head of the table.

For the next hour, Axe gave the team his undivided attention, but Baylee could only think about him. His closeness was driving her crazy, and his leather and citrus scent embraced her. The whole situation was insane. They'd already had sex, so what was the harm in having a casual sex arrangement? It would only be for the summer. No strings attached. She'd be going back to Denver in a few months, so why not have a good time while she was in Pinewood Springs?

The truth was she couldn't resist him anymore. She had tasted the forbidden fruit, and she wanted more—a whole lot more. Axe seemed to be eager for it, and it was becoming harder to stave him off, to play like she was the good girl. She wasn't. She desired to have dirty, nasty things done to her by him. And the fact that he was a filthy talker excited her even more.

Axe wasn't even a real client. The club was but, ultimately, he didn't call the shots—Banger did. *Get a grip, Baylee. Think about what you're doing.* She would have to tread carefully because desire, ambition, and treachery were everywhere. Her desire for Axe was overwhelming, but she badly wanted the partner position with her firm, and she wouldn't put it past Logan to stab her in the back when her defenses were down. If she decided to have a summer fling with the sex god, they'd have to be discreet.

"If there aren't any questions, we're all done here," Stan said as he helped James fold up his charts.

Baylee gathered her office things, preparing to leave. The team shuffled out the door and she followed, head down, reading an email from Claudia. *Bang!* She slammed into something hard. Rubbing her head, she looked up and stared into Axe's muscular chest.

"Sorry," she muttered.

Axe pulled her close and said huskily, "I'll pick you up at seven o'clock." His teeth grazed across her ear.

"I'll meet you. Since you like texting so much, send me the name and address of the restaurant."

"I said I'll pick you up."

Stubbornness shone in her gaze. "I'll meet you, or I won't go."

Axe's face grew tight and he gripped her arm. "I'll let you have your way *this time*, but next time, I call the shots."

He swaggered down the hall. *He's such a chauvinist.* But she knew she was in trouble. The whole time his fingers touched her skin, she was burning up, and the way his breath caressed her neck made her panties damp.

Yep, I'm in big trouble.

CHAPTER TEN

"MCFAHEY FUCKED US over big-time. I'm glad I killed the sonofabitch!" Jax pounded his fist on the table after hearing Axe tell the members there wasn't a zoning permit issued for the strip mall.

"If we'd known the piece of shit double-crossed us, we'd have made him die a slow and painful death," Rock, the Sergeant-At-Arms, said as he ran his finger over his hunting knife. "I'd have peeled the fucker's skin off then gutted him."

Angry voices tried to one-up each other as they described the terrors they would've subjected the crooked councilman to had they known of his treachery. At that moment, McFahey was a lucky sonofabitch to be rotting in a deep grave on the side of the mountain.

Double-crossing an outlaw club was a stupid thing to do, and the perpetrators never lived to tell others not to do it. Death was a welcome gift after hours of slow torture before a brother made sure the betraying sack of shit breathed no more. Much to the chagrin of the Insurgents, a bullet through the back of McFahey's head was no punishment.

"The fuckin' asshole screwed the club over, and it makes us look like dumb shits in front of the professionals. Like we don't know what the fuck we're doing," Axe said bitterly. He was so pissed off that his stomach was doing weird shit, like twitching whenever he thought about having dinner later on with Baylee. That woman did something to him; his blood pumped and his dick woke up just by thinking of her.

She'd looked so hot in her tight skirt and blouse, and the way her cheeks had burned red when he'd teased her made him want to leap across the table and kiss her hard, deep, and wet. During the team meeting, she'd driven him fuckin' insane. The suits had blabbed on and on, and all Axe had wanted to do was fuck Baylee. He knew how good it could be; after all, he'd had all of her deliciously sweet body for a night, one taste of her making him crave her even more. She was like a drug he couldn't get enough of. He was even willing to make a fool of himself to his buddy Derek by calling and asking about her so he could track her down. He was ready to act like a pussy just to contact her again. *And now she's here, on my turf.*

"Axe, can you fuckin' pay attention? Are we interrupting a wet dream, or somethin'?" Banger asked.

The men whistled and hooted.

Straightening in his chair, Axe scowled. "No, I was thinkin' about the strip mall, that's all."

"Bullshit, you were thinking about fucking someone. I know that look," Jax joked.

Guffaws echoed throughout the room.

"All right. Keep it down. What's going on with getting the zoning permit secured?"

"I told them we'd talk about that at church."

"We're not gonna be able to get shit from the city if we go alone. I thought this was taken care of." Banger rubbed his hand over his face.

"McFahey swore he passed it through. One of the architects is gonna meet with the zoning director and see what the problem is. The architecture firm has the preliminary blueprints. The engineers wanted to know why this became a problem so late in the game," Axe explained.

"How the fuck do we know? Something's not right here," Hawk said as Banger nodded. "We gotta get to the bottom of this."

"I'll let you know once the architects meet with the city." Axe leaned back in his chair. There was no way he was leaking out the fact that one of the architect's was hotter than fuck. No way. Baylee was his plaything for the project, and no one was getting near her—he'd make sure of that.

He frowned when he thought of the fucking suit. Logan. He had shifty eyes, and Axe didn't like him at all. He didn't trust him, and he couldn't figure out if Logan was trying to get into Baylee's panties or was trying to fuck her over. The suit was a snake in the grass, and Axe had to keep his eyes on him. No one was getting near her, and no one was hurting her. He'd pound them to the ground if anyone tried anything with her.

After church, Axe joined his brothers for a beer and a shot of Jack. He had a few hours to kill.

"So, who's the bitch you're fucked-up over?" Jax asked.

"No one."

Throttle came over and clapped Axe on the shoulder. "You think we believe your bullshit? You haven't fucked a whore in almost two weeks. Who's the bitch?"

"Why the hell are you keeping score on who I fuck and when?"

" 'Cause I can't let you turn into a pussy like Chas, Jax, and Hawk."

"Who's a pussy?" Hawk said as he joined them at the bar.

"You. You've had that dreamy-eyed shit look going on since you and Cara met. Now you're going to the mall to pick out china. Fuck." Throttle threw back his Jack.

"I draw the line on china and shit." Hawk laughed. "Cara and Sherrie are doing all that, and not lovin' a woman is being a pussy."

"What the hell does that mean?" Throttle grumbled.

"Gotta go back to the shop. Ask Chas and Jax, they know." He stopped at the doorway and said over his shoulder, "Go ahead and ask Axe, too. He's been bitten."

"What the fuck?" Axe swung around on his bar stool, but Hawk had left, the roar of his Harley blaring through the open doors.

"Well, Axe?" Throttle poked.

"I'm outta here. Later." He drained his beer and walked out into the sun.

NAUSEA MIXED WITH the butterflies fluttering in her stomach. Why was she so nervous about going out with Axe? It was ridiculous. Two weeks before, she'd let a complete stranger do very intimate things to her, and she'd relished every moment, passion electrifying every part of her body. But she was scared to go out with Axe, the very same man who'd brought her to mind-blowing orgasms. All of a sudden, she was shy? What the hell was going on with her?

After slipping on a simple black dress, nothing too revealing, Baylee checked herself out in the mirror and frowned. Her ample breasts made it impossible for her to hide any cleavage, but it was the best she could do. Before leaving her room, she swiped on clear lip gloss over her raspberry-colored lips then walked out to meet the sex god.

THE RESTAURANT AXE chose was located on the outskirts of town, nestled in a valley. Baylee spotted the name of the eatery, Le Crystal, on an unassuming sign partially hidden by a weeping willow.

When she pulled into the small parking lot, she noticed Axe's electric-yellow Harley. She parked in the space next to it. Up close, his bike looked massive, powerful, and gorgeous—just like the owner—and the chrome reflected the sun's fading rays.

Inside, she greeted Axe with a big smile. "I checked out your bike. It's awesome." *Like you.* Her gaze skimmed over him, taking in his tanned skin and chiseled cheeks.

Axe snagged her around the waist and nuzzled his face against her soft hair. "Thanks." He kissed her on the cheek. "You look gorgeous, as always."

The hostess showed them to their table, a small one tucked into a dark corner.

"I read that your club owns a restaurant. Is this it?"

"No."

She surveyed the place, noticing the intimate lighting, the couples at small booths and tables holding hands and kissing. "This place is not easily seen from the road. I missed it twice. It's secluded."

"Never noticed."

"Are you hiding me?"

Axe smiled as he shook his head.

"Are you married?"

He burst out laughing. "Fuck no. Why'd you think that?"

"I don't know. This place seems like somewhere a husband would take his mistress."

"It does have a reputation for that. The food is good, though, and I wanted to get away from the brothers. I didn't wanna bump into any of them tonight."

"I guess being with the same group of people all the time would be too much. You live at the club, don't you?"

"Yeah, but I've been thinking about getting my own place. Do you live alone in Denver?"

"Yes. I live in a high-rise downtown, and I love it."

When the waitress came over, they both ordered sirloin steaks, loaded baked potatoes, and green beans with cherry tomatoes.

Baylee, sipping her third glass of red wine, gazed into Axe's dark eyes. The way he spoke, the way his shirt clung to his upper torso, and his cute, crooked smile exuded so much sexiness that Baylee was ready to forgo dinner and drag him straight to her hotel room. Maybe it was the wine, but her body was tingling, every nerve on fire.

"Do you have a girlfriend?" The question popped out of her mouth before she could stop it.

"No. Do you have a boyfriend?"

She shook her head. "Too busy." She motioned the waitress to bring her another glass of wine. "Why don't you have a girlfriend? You're handsome. I'm surprised some woman hasn't snatched you up."

"I don't wanna be snatched up."

"Never?"

"That's right. I'm a one-night type of guy. Don't go in so much for repeat performances."

"You could've fooled me. You keep pushing me for an encore." She giggled. *I'm getting smashed.*

A bemused smile brushed across his lips as he scooted his chair closer to hers. "You're different. I most definitely want a repeat performance with you."

The waitress set down another glass of red wine in front of Baylee.

Axe kissed Baylee's cheek, his hand resting on her upper thigh. "You're my spicy minx." He nipped and kissed a trail to her earlobe, taking it into his mouth and sucking it gently.

She demurely pulled away.

"Why're you being so shy, sweetheart? It isn't like I've never done *that* to you before."

"That was different. I didn't know you. You were nameless—no information. Now, you've morphed into someone real. You're not a fantasy anymore."

"Isn't reality better than fantasy? You can't fuck a fantasy."

"I did." She giggled again.

He sat back, a wide grin on his face. "I like you tipsy."

"I hope you like me drunk, because that's where I'm going."

The waitress brought their steak dinners, and Axe ate all of his and most of hers. Blame it on nerves or stress, but Baylee had decided to drink her dinner, and by the time she and Axe were in the parking lot, she was in no shape to drive.

"You're riding with me. We'll come back tomorrow and pick up your car. Have you ever ridden on a bike?"

"Only my ten-speed." She laughed.

"Cute. A Harley?"

"Nope."

"You gotta hold on real tight, okay? Just feel the movement and let it guide you. Don't worry, I know what I'm doing."

Baylee wrapped her arms around his waist and crushed her body against his back. The bike jumped forward, the roar deafening. Before she could think about her fear, the powerful machine blasted out of the parking lot and down the road.

The rush of wind revived her and her foggy brain cleared. The aspen and pine trees were just shapes in the dark as the Harley zoomed past them. Baylee rested her cheek against the soft leather of Axe's cut, breathing in his familiar scent of citrus. She could get used to being on the back of his bike.

The ride was too short, the iron horse coming to a stop much too quickly for her liking. Axe jumped off then helped her, the alcohol making her wobbly legs worse. She crumpled in his arms.

"Whoa. You okay? Can you walk?"

"I'm fine. Thanks for a nice evening."

"I'm gonna make sure you make it to your room. Come on."

They crossed the lobby and stepped into the waiting elevator. Silence pooled around them as they rode up to the fifth floor. Axe walked her to her room, and she opened the door and leaned against it. He bent down and kissed her, deep and wet.

"I'll call you tomorrow," Axe said.

He turned away, but Baylee tugged him back, guiding him into her room.

He grinned and kicked the door shut. "This feels familiar, sweetheart. And this time, I know what to expect."

CHAPTER ELEVEN

THE MOMENT THE door closed behind him, Axe had Baylee in his arms, his mouth hungrily covering hers as his tongue delved in, pushing deep. She moaned as he grabbed a fistful of her hair and twisted it, pulling her head back so he could plunge further into her mouth. Moving his hand down, he placed it on her ass, kneading it roughly, her large breasts brushing against him with each breath she took.

"I'm on fire. How the fuck do you get me so worked up?" he murmured against her lips.

"I want you, too," she said breathlessly.

He walked forward, guiding her, still devouring her lips as he pinched her nice, firm ass. When her calves hit the bed, she lost her balance and fell, yanking him on top of her. She wrapped her arms around his neck, pulling his lips closer to hers until there was no space left between them. His deep, thrusting kisses sent chills down her spine and ignited a burn inside her.

He broke away and stood up, removing his shirt and kicking off his boots. Leaning over her, he placed his hands under her arms and lifted her toward the top of the bed, then lay beside her, jerking her in to him again. Shivers raced across her body as he traced his tongue over the curve of her neck, pausing to suck and nip at the tender skin. The hairs at her nape stood up as he skimmed his fingers over her bare arms, tickling them and licking her sensitive flesh. Each touch sent jolts of desire straight to her aching pussy, and she spread her legs, inviting him to touch.

He chuckled, trailing his tongue up her arms, then to her neck and earlobe.

"Anxious?" he whispered in her ear, his hot breath scorching her skin.

"I want you."

She grabbed his hand and placed it over her dampened, throbbing sex. He slid it away before catching her eyes, hunger reflected in his dark orbs.

"I decide when I touch your pussy. I'm calling the shots."

He bit her lip and she cried out, the copper taste of blood on her tongue. Then he licked her lip gently, and pleasure skated to the tips of her hardening nipples.

"Take your dress off," he ordered as he pulled away from her.

Baylee rose from the bed and slipped her black dress over her head then tossed it on the nearby chair. Axe looked into her eyes before his gaze moved down to her breasts, then her hips, lingering for a few seconds before it moved back to her tits.

"You're gorgeous," he rasped, his eyes locking with hers. "Fuck."

Her cheeks reddened, and she felt exposed under the feral, predatory look in his eyes. Instinctively, she crossed her arms over her chest, avoiding his gaze.

"Come here." He patted the mattress.

She padded over to the bed, her arms still in its place. Reaching out, he clutched her wrist and pulled her to him until she was flush against him. He nuzzled his face in the crook of her neck then nibbled her soft skin, his hands quickly unfastening her bra.

"You are so fuckin' soft. I can't get enough of tasting you," he whispered.

The flaming touch of his mouth ignited every part of her tingling skin.

"I love the way you touch me," she murmured as she ran her hands through his dark hair.

"I'm glad, 'cause I plan to touch you all over. I love the way you feel."

In one move, he slid down and sucked her cherry-red nipple in his mouth, intense pleasure dancing inside her walls. As he sucked, he moved his hand down to the crotch of her damp panties, rubbing and twisting his palm against her pulsing heat. The sweet sensation drove her body to buck and grind against his unrelenting hand. He removed it suddenly, his trimmed nails scratching up her side, landing on her beaded nipples, pinching and tweaking them.

"As I remember, you like it rough."

With her head to the side, her eyes squeezed shut, she groaned, "Yes, hard."

He bit down on her nipples then proceeded to bite and suck her tits, leaving red marks.

"You've got great tits. I've been thinking about playing with them since we fucked."

The intensity of the sweet pain made her body flush with sensitivity, and she was overcome, pleasure lancing all her nerves. *He makes me feel so hot and alive. I've been searching for this for a long time.*

Gliding her hand down, she unzipped Axe's jeans, wrapping her hand around his hot and pulsing dick. She didn't recall it being that big, but she remembered how he filled her up. Her mouth watered as she saw the glistening head, a couple of beads of pre-come still clinging to it. Pushing up and shoving Axe backward, she bent over, licking the salty beads off his soft crown. A guttural moan ripped past his lips.

"Fuck, baby. That's it. Suck my cock."

She pulled the hard shaft out all the way and ran her tongue over its length, grasping the base of it tightly. Swirling her tongue over the smooth crown and the underside, she opened wide and wrapped her lips around his dick, pulling it in and out of her mouth, sucking him hard and deep.

"Oh, yeah."

Baylee moaned as she sucked him, her bright eyes looking into his as she took him deeper.

He said huskily, "My cock looks so good in your mouth."

"It tastes and feels good in my mouth."

He reached to the side and kneaded her ass, then shoved his finger inside her wet slit.

"Oh, God. That feels so good," she breathed against his shaft.

"I love how wet you are for me," he grunted as he shoved his finger in and out of her.

As she felt her pussy quiver, he pulled out and moved her off him. Startled, she asked, "What's wrong? Was I too rough?"

"No, you were perfect. You want to kick this up a notch?"

The wicked gleam in his eye made her body tremble in pleasurable anticipation.

"Yeah."

"You got a scarf or some nylons?"

She jumped up and ran to the dresser, taking out a pair of thigh-highs. Turning around, she met his smoldering gaze.

"Love watching your ass move. Fuck, you got an ass that brings men to their knees."

She crawled toward him and he caught her arms, dragging her closer before crushing his mouth to hers. Each touch from him shifted her body into overdrive.

"Lie down," he ordered.

Baylee lay on her back and he grasped each wrist and tied it with the nylons, pulling her spread-eagle until her skin was taut. Her body hummed with excitement as his intense gaze roamed over her.

He whistled softly. "Fuckin' hot. You turn me on so bad, babe. Look how hard I am."

Axe moved his dick to her face and rubbed it all over. Her drenched pussy throbbed and she closed her legs. He leaned back, his dick still inches from her mouth, and pushed her legs apart.

"No fuckin' way. Keep your legs open," he demanded.

He rolled away, and peeled his jeans down his legs, revealing the muscles in his thighs. As he stepped out of his pants, his boxers crept down, giving away the curve of his ass as he took out a condom wrapper from the pocket of his jeans. Discarding his boxers, he climbed back on the bed, placing his knees right above her shoulders.

"Open that sexy mouth and take my cock."

She opened wide, and he shoved it in her mouth then held the sides of her face as he thrust back and forth.

"You like that? You love fucking my cock with your mouth, don't you?"

His filthy mouth almost sent her over the edge. She loved it; every fantasy she had contained a dirty-talking bad boy. She couldn't get enough of him.

He pulled out then kissed her neck, trailing his hands and tongue down the sensitive stretch of skin along the side of her body. The way she was tied, the skin was pulled tight; when Axe scratched and grazed it, her body trembled. It was like she was on sensory overload.

Each time Axe bit her, she'd wince and tug at her restraints, and then he'd follow it with a lick and a kiss. Sometimes he'd blow his hot breath over her breasts, her ribcage, her belly, leaving a trail of goosebumps. There wasn't a part of her body he didn't touch, scratch, kiss, or lick, and by the time he flicked his tongue softly on her inner thighs, she was ready to explode.

He pushed her knees up and wide, exposing all of her to him, and she saw the savage desire in his eyes as he took her in. Burying his face in her pussy, he breathed her arousal in deep then, with the tip of his tongue, he flicked her clit. Fire burned inside her as she squirmed and twisted.

With his fingers, he pulled open her swollen lips and licked her from the bottom of her hot opening to right above her clit. He took his finger and rubbed her nub quickly.

"Look how wet you're getting."

He stroked her clit while his other hand held her lips wide open. He pushed his tongue up her hot pussy, her ass flexing and wiggling on the mattress. Thrusting several times, he swept it over her fully once more, all while his finger stroked her sweet spot.

"Love it, babe. You're getting so wet now."

More rubbing and licking.

"Look at it, it's coming right out for me. It feels good, doesn't it, babe?"

He replaced his finger with his tongue and rubbed around her sweet spot while he inserted two fingers in her, twisting them around, driving them in and out. Baylee was beside herself. Her body was flushed with heat and her nipples were swollen as she writhed and moaned, twisting against the restraints.

With urgency, Axe ripped the foil packet with his teeth, covered his pulsing cock, and spread her knees further apart. He placed his hand under her ass cheek, lifting her higher. When he pushed in her soaking pussy, Baylee screamed out from the sheer ecstasy of it.

"Fuck, you're tight. My cock feels good in your pussy. You like it?"

"I love the way it feels. Harder. I want it harder."

A big grin broke out over his face. "You sure?"

"Harder," she gritted, thrashing her head from side to side.

He lifted her higher and slammed into her, each time harder than the last. As he pounded in and out of her, her hips bucked up and down amid loud moans and gasps of pleasure. When Axe brought his finger to her slick clit, she lost it, shattering into a million pieces as deep, scorching pleasure raged through her. It wasn't anything she'd ever experienced before. And as Axe grunted and panted, she felt him burst inside her, her silky walls encasing him. It was glorious.

He collapsed on top of her, his chest heaving. She wanted to caress him so much, but she couldn't because her hands were still tied. Plus, this was a casual sexual thing, something that didn't involve cuddling and caressing each other. This was fantastic sex—the best she'd ever had, but it was just sex.

Axe turned sideways and kissed her jaw. "Fuckin' intense, babe. Awesome. Shit, let me untie you." He retrieved a knife from his rag then cut the stockings. "I'll have to come better prepared next time."

He rolled next to her and drew her to him, and she pillowed her head on his shoulder.

Wait! What are we doing?"

"Umm, you have to go."

"What?" He pushed himself up with his elbow.

"I mean, what we have is casual sex. It was the best, but it's done, so you have to go. Anyway, I can't risk Logan seeing you coming out of my room."

"Are you fuckin' serious?"

"Yeah. Cuddling and sleeping over is too intimate. What we have is casual. We have to keep it that way."

Axe bristled. "Casual's the way I want it, too." He rolled out of bed then dressed. At the door, he looked over his shoulder. "I'll be back in the morning to take you to your car."

All of a sudden, he was gone, and the room seemed too quiet. *This is what you wanted.* Axe was taking his cue from her; he appeared to be content holding her. It was nice, but she couldn't go there. Casual sex was perfect, and he'd left like she asked him to. So, why did a part of her heart ache? Ridiculous. Axe was perfect for casual sex, especially since he had women at his disposal twenty-four-seven. When she told him he had to leave, he hadn't even argued with her. He just up and left.

That's good, right?

Heaviness weighed her down as she switched off the table lamp. Her phone pinged.

Axe: *I still taste you. Nite.*

She reread the sentence several times.

Baylee: *Nite.*

Axe: *This Saturday?*

Baylee: *K.*

Axe: *Cool.*

That was it. Simple words which lifted the heaviness right up.

Lying back down, she burrowed her head in the pillow, a smile on her lips.

AT EIGHT-FIFTEEN IN the morning, Axe texted to tell her he was coming by to take her to her car. She hurriedly finished dressing then made her way downstairs.

The minute she entered the lobby, she saw the man—propped against the pillar, watching her like he had the night before. Something about his face seemed familiar to her. The man didn't try to hide from her like he had the last time; instead, he boldly watched her as she passed the pillar and stood by the large glass entrance door. He was lean and tall, and upon closer inspection, he appeared to be in his early fifties, with dark hair graying on his temples. He strolled down the lobby, coming closer to her.

She darted into the coffee shop and ordered a black coffee to go, and he followed her inside. She ignored him, moving over to the small gift store to flip through the local paper while she waited for Axe. Without turning around, she sensed his presence. Everywhere she went, he was there.

Why is he following me? Should I tell the front desk? The blood rushing to her head made her dizzy, and she dropped into a chair outside the gift shop. With her eyes closed, she rubbed her temples lightly as she tried to regain her composure. Her eyes fluttered open and locked with the piercing stare of her stalker. A strangled yelp escaped her as the space around her became smaller.

"Hey, babe." Axe's deep voice washed over her as relief replaced panic. "You not feeling so good?"

She brought her thin fingers to her trembling lips. "Not really. A glass of water should help." As she rose to her feet, Axe ran over to help. Behind him, she saw her stalker turn around abruptly.

"I'll get it for you." Axe pivoted. "What the hell?" Baylee watched Axe move toward the man. "Uncle Max?"

Baylee gasped as her tormentor stopped dead in his tracks.

Axe approached him. "What're you doing here?"

The man mumbled something Baylee couldn't understand. The last thing she wanted was for Axe to introduce her to his uncle—the man who'd been following her. She scampered out of the lobby, leaving the two men talking.

As she waited for Axe in front of the hotel, Baylee tried to digest what had just happened. The man who'd been creating such anxiety for her was Axe's uncle? What if his uncle was the one who killed her mother? He was around the same age as her dad, and she'd described the man as being tall and thin to her psychiatrist at some point during the years. Could Axe be the nephew of her mom's killer? It was too fantastic to imagine.

My mind is just conjuring up all sorts of unlikely scenarios. It's ludicrous. There has to be a rational explanation.

Axe came out of the hotel and motioned her to follow him, stopping at his Harley. "That was fuckin' weird, seeing my uncle Max at the hotel. Crazy."

"What was he doing here?" She hoped her voice didn't betray any nervousness.

"He said it was work-related."

"What does he do?"

"He's involved with a bunch of different things like construction, building management, and development." As he dusted off the bike's seat, he asked, "Why did you run out so fast? I was gonna introduce you, but you split."

"I didn't want to intrude. We better get going, I have to get to work."

He watched her closely for a few seconds. "Okay. Hop on."

"Oh, I forgot to ask you last night about the permit. What's going on?"

"The club thought it was all squared away. The person who was supposed to handle it flaked."

"I figured it was a problem. I have all the preliminary blueprints together, and I'm meeting the head of the zoning department for lunch. I'll schmooze him. No worries." She jumped on the back of the Harley.

"When you having lunch with the dude?"

"Next Monday. We're going to the French Bistro." She tugged at her hem, trying to pull down her dress. "Don't you have a car?"

"No. Don't like cages."

"My dress is all the way up. Maybe I should grab a cab."

"Not so easy to find a cab in Pinewood." He looked over his shoulder at her legs. "Besides, you have the sexiest legs I've ever seen, so why not show them off?" He winked. "Hold on."

The bike leapt forward, and she put her hands around his waist and enjoyed the ride.

They pulled into Le Crystal's parking lot next to her car.

"Thanks," Baylee said as she swung her leg over the motorcycle's seat. She grasped Axe's outstretched hand, falling in to him when her shaky legs hit the pavement. "I didn't expect—"

He captured her bottom lip with his teeth then kissed her, silencing her words. He ate her up with quick bites and kisses, and the taste and touch of him sent her reeling. Her eyes fluttered closed.

"Seeing you in your short dress makes my fingers itch to dig into your sweet, soft thighs, babe. Just like this," he breathed, burying his fingers into them.

"Oh, Axe," she moaned, pressing closer to him.

Her breasts were squashed to his chest, her legs surrounded by his powerful ones, and the long, thick bulge between them rubbed against her belly. Finding the hardness which stretched across his zipper, she palmed it firmly.

He leaned his mouth close to her ear. "Your touch, your body, your scent, it's all fuckin' messing with my mind."

A barely suppressed shiver ran through her body as his finger inched closer to her dampened panties, an unspoken need simmering just below the surface of her skin. She raised his head then flicked her tongue across his lips while she ran her hands over his broad shoulders.

"You're so sexy. You don't even know how much you turn me on," she murmured between feathery kisses along his jaw.

"Fuck, baby," he rasped.

Baylee threw her head back as he stroked her wet clit through her panties. Axe licked the tender flesh of her throat as he slipped his finger between her pulsing folds. She squeezed her eyes shut as his tongue and lips burned her skin, and his steady caress on her pussy made her explode into a million pieces in the middle of a parking lot in broad daylight. Waves of electrified shivers crisscrossed through her body, making her so weak in the knees she had to steady herself against Axe's bike.

"Wow," she panted.

A smile curled around his lips. "Love to watch you come. So fuckin' hot."

She caught his belt hoop with her finger and drew him to her. "What about you?" Her lips brushed against his.

"You can take care of me later. This was all for you." He kissed her, heavy and hard, before he pulled away. "Gotta get to church."

Baylee tugged her dress down, smoothed her hair, and supported herself against him as they walked to her car. She slid into the driver's seat and turned the ignition. Axe bent down and kissed her hard on the mouth.

"Drive carefully."

She nodded. She wanted to ask him if they were going to see each other that night, but what they had was casual sex—no emotions, no accountability, just sex. And was the sex ever awesome. A big grin stayed plastered on her face for the rest of the day.

As five o'clock neared, a twinge of disappointment pricked at her. She hadn't heard from Axe since morning—no phone call, no text, nothing. *Remember, Baylee, this is a casual fling. It's a sexual affair. Nothing is expected from you or him except pleasure, and he's definitely giving you that.* Keeping things casual meant no complications. As long as they were both giving and receiving pleasure, it was working; she could do as she wanted, and he could to. It was a mature, liberating "relationship," and it suited her just fine. She glanced at her Inbox for messages again. Nothing. She sighed.

As she approached her hotel, apprehension seized her as it had been doing ever since Axe's uncle followed her into the elevator. She still couldn't wrap her head around the fact that her creepy pervert happened to be Axe's uncle. Too strange. Did Axe know what was going on? He didn't act like it, but he was probably good at concealing things. It didn't make sense. Why would Axe be involved in this? Maybe he was just helping his uncle out, trying to keep an eye on her. Maybe the one-night stand in Denver wasn't as random as she thought. Chills danced up and down her spine at the idea.

Get a grip. I don't even know if his uncle scoping me out has anything to do with my mom. There may not be anything to be involved in. His uncle is probably just some perv who stalks young women. Axe was genuinely surprised to see him, after all.

She entered the lobby tentatively, surveying the area. Nothing out of the ordinary, and the sense that someone was watching her wasn't there.

"You just get back?" Logan's smiling eyes greeted her.

"Yeah. Where were you today? Played hooky?"

He jerked his head back. "No way. I'd never do that. I went out to the construction site with one of the engineers. All the trucks and machines are waiting to get started. I heard you were handling the permit issue."

"Yeah, I am."

"How's it going?"

"Okay." Baylee knew Logan was fishing for information to see who her contacts were and when they were meeting so he could pretend to bump into her. There wasn't a chance in Hell that she'd tell him anything until *after* she had the permit in hand.

"Any idea when it'll be done?"

"No, I'm working on it. I'm going to my room now. I'll see you around." She brushed past him and marched to the elevators.

The coolness of her room was a welcome after the stuffiness of the office. The building was having cooling problems, and most days Baylee came home feeling sticky and damp.

She peeled off her clothes then padded to the bathroom to take a shower.

The envelope icon on her phone blinked, indicating she had a message. A surge of joy ran from the pit of her stomach right to her head. She opened the text.

Logan: *Want to have some barbecue?*

A heavy sigh passed through her lips, and she sank onto the bed. The text wasn't from Axe. *Damn.* Her shoulders slumped. *It's casual. No expectations. Remember?*

Looking around the room, she realized that she didn't want to spend another night watching TV, ordering room service, and thinking about Axe.

Baylee: *Sounds good.*
Logan: *Great! I'll come by in about an hour…?*
Baylee: *I'll be ready.*

★　★　★

"THE SETTING IS beautiful," she gushed as she stepped from Logan's Mercedes convertible.

"And the barbecue is the best I've had. I discovered it when I was exploring around the backroads a few days ago."

Big Rocky's Barbecue was nestled among the evergreens on Aspen Lake, their reflection embedded on the diamond clear water. Bursts of pink, yellow, indigo, and red carpeted the lush valley. As summer dusk approached, the blue sky transformed into mulberry-purple, accented by the silhouette of ducks flying in "V" formation.

"It smells wonderful. I didn't realize I was so hungry," Baylee admitted as she glanced at the menu.

After ordering pork ribs, coleslaw, and buttered corn on the cob, she wiggled back in her chair and sipped her glass of Chardonnay as she enjoyed the view.

"Do you hike?" Logan's voice broke in on her moment of serenity.

"I used to when I was in college. I'd love to get back to it. Walking trails is a lot more scenic than watching other sweaty bodies on a treadmill."

He laughed. "I haven't done much of it, but I'd like to. Maybe this weekend we could go on a simple one. I'd be a beginner."

"Sounds like something that could work."

Their dinner arrived, and Baylee thought she died and went to Heaven when she took a bite of the juicy, succulent meat coated in a smoky barbecue sauce with a kick.

During the middle of dinner, Logan waved at someone behind her. "Hi."

She turned around in time to see Axe approaching their table, and he didn't look too happy.

Ignoring Logan, Axe fixed his flashing eyes on Baylee and growled, "What the hell are you doing here?"

She pointed at her plate. "Guess."

Crossing his arms, he said sharply, "You know what I mean."

"No, I don't." Dismissing him, she diverted her attention to the outside scenery.

"Hey. You. Is this business, or a date?"

Baylee heard Logan clear his throat then answer in a shaky voice. "No, not a date. Absolutely not. We're just having dinner as colleagues. Is there a problem with that?"

She glanced at Logan, and for a split second, she felt sorry for him. His neck and face were blotchy, and his hand trembled while he sipped his water.

"No problem… yet." Axe's piercing eyes bored into Logan.

He squirmed then leapt out of his chair when his phone rang, as though he were happy for an excuse to get away from Axe. "Will you excuse me? I gotta get this." He pointed to his phone while he sprinted away from the table.

Axe filled Logan's chair, staring at Baylee.

With narrowed eyes, she asked, "What?"

"I can't believe you'd go out with that ass-kisser."

"We're colleagues having dinner. What the hell is your problem?"

"I don't want you seeing other men."

"Whoa. Who do you think you are, telling me what to do? You're acting like some possessive jerk. You have nothing on me, like I don't on you. Remember, 'no strings attached.' God, you can be a real asshole."

"Watch the way you speak to me, woman. I don't let bitches talk like that to me."

"Did you just call me a bitch? Are you fucking joking? What cave did you crawl out of?"

Leaning forward, he grasped her upper arm, anger emanating from him. "You like bossing men around, don't you? Well, I don't go in for that shit. I'm not pussy-whipped."

"No, you're a bully who likes to beat on his chest and knock things around. 'Oh, look at me. I'm a man 'cause I have a Harley and a bad attitude.' Ha!" She yanked her arm away then shoved her face a few inches from his. "I say 'ha' to all of your posturing."

The vein in his neck twitched. "You finished?" His voice cut like a shard of ice.

A single shiver of apprehension coursed through her body—she knew she'd gone too far. Pursing her lips, she nodded.

With his index finger, he traced around her eyebrows, nose, jaw, and mouth. "Don't ever mock me again, *woman*." He grabbed a fist of hair at the nape of her neck then tugged her face closer, gently kissing her. "Not. Ever."

White teeth bit her lip and she tried to push back, but his hand held her like a vise. His tongue licked the pain away, then he sucked her bottom lip. She parted her mouth, allowing his tongue in.

"Now you're being a good girl," he muttered, driving his tongue in again, harder and more persistently.

His kisses were like molten fire, burning and scorching, and she welcomed them. She loved the dark danger that was Axe, and not knowing what he would do was a strong aphrodisiac for a woman who lived an organized, well-planned life. When he bit her lip, her whole body went on high alert, and she craved more of the pain and the pleasure. *Boy, am I fucked-up.*

Then she remembered Logan. Panic replaced pleasure, and she pushed Axe away.

"Why the fuck are you shoving me away?" His dark brown eyes flashed.

"Logan," she whispered.

"So?"

"I already told you about the situation with him."

"And I already told you I don't give a fuck. Now, give me your lips."

"This may not be a big deal to you, but it is to me, and *that* alone should make you give a fuck."

Taking her hand, Axe kissed it and held it in his. "You're right."

When she heard his words, she did a double-take.

"But I want you to know that if he pulls any shit that hurts you, or even stresses you out, I'll take care of him. It'll be my pleasure. I haven't liked the ass-wipe since I first laid eyes on him. A snitch always needs to be taught a lesson. Just sayin'…"

Axe had again mentioned "taking care of Logan." His veiled threats made her shiver as reality sank in. *Axe may be sexy, funny, and nice to me, but the truth is he's an outlaw.* She didn't doubt for a moment that he'd slit anyone's throat who threatened him or his club.

Logan's return to the table interrupted her thoughts. He glanced quickly at Axe sitting in his chair; Axe didn't move a muscle. Swallowing hard, Logan pulled a chair from the next table and sat down. He hesitantly slid his plate of food from Axe over to him, and finished eating his dinner.

The waitress came over to their table. "Hiya, Axe. You want your usual?"

"You know me, Maddie." Axe winked at the thirty-something woman, which made her smile.

"You finished?" she asked Baylee.

"Yes." She pushed her plate away.

When the waitress left, Baylee asked, "You come here a lot?"

"Yeah. Insurgents own the place."

Logan's eyes bulged, which made Baylee laugh.

"So this is the club's restaurant. When I did my research on the club, the name of the place wasn't mentioned."

"Your research?" Axe inquired.

"Baylee read everything she could get her hands on just to know who she was dealing with." Logan laughed, shaking his head as if it was the dumbest thing a person could do.

Axe raised his eyebrows. "Yeah?"

Heat rose up to her cheeks; she knew Logan was getting back at her for laughing at him a few minutes before.

"What did your research tell you about me?" His voice was thick.

"That you're persistent, loyal, and good at a lot of things other people aren't." Her cheeks had officially turned a new shade of red. How could she be flirting with him so blatantly in front of Logan? Axe made her lose all sense whenever he was near her.

Raw hunger brimmed in his gaze. In a low voice only she could hear, he said, "I wanna fuck you in the worst way."

The waitress placing Axe's beer in front of him diffused the sexual tension between them.

"You want anything more?" she asked Logan.

"No. I'll take the check."

From the strained look on his face, Baylee knew Logan couldn't wait to leave the restaurant and be far away from Axe.

After paying the bill, Logan stood up and looked at Baylee. "Are you coming?"

"Of course." Glancing at Axe, she smiled. "I'll see you at the office. Goodnight."

He just glared.

She and Logan walked out of the restaurant, but before Logan pulled out of the parking lot, her phone beeped.

Axe: *Don't fuck him.*

Baylee: *Logan? Would never do that. And don't tell me what to do.*

Axe: *The only one who gets near you in PWS is me.*

For unknown reasons, his one sentence made her stomach lurch, and a tingle of pleasure skated down her spine.

Baylor: *Yes, boss. *eyeroll**

Axe: *Cute. <wink>*

"Are you texting with that outlaw biker?" Logan asked. "What the fuck's his problem?"

"No. I'm texting with my friend. Axe is rough, and loves being a badass. He *is* a biker, after all. I wouldn't take it personally."

"I think for him, it *is* personal. He looks like he wants to beat the shit out of me." He sighed. "It'd be so much nicer if we had normal clients for this project."

"He's not that bad, really. I think he's just used to getting his way."

Logan looked hard at her. "You got the hots for this guy?"

She blushed. "No. He's hardly my type."

"I don't know, but you seem taken with him."

"I'm not *taken* with him. I do find him attractive, but I'd think most women would."

"Really? Interesting. I didn't peg you as the tattoo and leather type."

"I'm not. He's good-looking, that's all. Let's just drop it, okay?"

She stared out the window, wishing she were back in her room. The short car ride had never felt so long.

After thanking Logan for dinner, she sought refuge in her room. The whole day had been a roller coaster of emotions. Her casual fling with Axe was becoming more complicated as she felt herself being pulled into his world, and him into her heart.

CHAPTER TWELVE

H ARD ROCK BEATS filtered out from behind the clubhouse's closed windows as Axe approached. He needed a shot of Jack and a good game of pool in the worst way. Seeing Baylee with the ass-kisser enraged him, and he was ready to beat Logan to a bloody pulp. What the fuck was going on with him? Yeah, Baylee was a hot-as-hell woman, but he'd banged hot women before and moved on easily. He was the king of "no strings attached" liaisons, so why wasn't he screwing Rosie or Lola or any other chick? The simple answer was he didn't want to. He wanted to be with Baylee. It was like he couldn't get enough of her, and the more he tasted the more he wanted. He was like a goddamned junkie desperate for his next fix.

Fuck! The one thing that blew him away was he wanted to know everything about her—her backstory, her lovers, her fears. In all his twenty-eight years, he'd never felt like he did about Baylee. How was that for touchy-feely bullshit? *Fuck!*

It took a few seconds to become used to the low lighting in the great room. The Thursday night party was in full swing, and several brothers and a couple of club whores were already passed out, dead drunk. Axe wasn't in the mood to party. He only wanted some booze and a good game of pool, since the woman he wanted to fuck wasn't at the clubhouse—she was tucked away at the hotel. He had to fight his legs from jumping on his Harley and hauling ass over there. She wanted to keep it casual and so did he. It suited him just fine, but he wanted to beat the shit out of the ass-kisser for being with her.

That doesn't seem too casual. I can't get her outta my mind. Damn!

Before playing pool, he downed a few shots of Jack. The scorching smoothness hit the spot every time. Axe ambled to the pool table and saw Rock scratching his head.

"What's up, dude?" Axe asked.

"We're right in the middle of a goddamned game, and Throttle spots some prime ass and walks off. The horny bastard."

Axe chuckled.

"You wanna take his place? He was kicking my ass, pretty much."

"I'll play, but let's rack up a new game."

"You're not gonna quit on me, are you? I know you're a horny bastard, too."

"No chance of that tonight."

A busty hoodrat attached herself to Axe's side. "You want some company?"

He glanced at her. She was hot, with big tits, nice round hips, long legs—just his type. He should've been taking her back to his room, plowing into her pussy and ass for the next couple of hours. "Not tonight."

"You don't want nothing?"

"Yeah, I do. Be good and bring me a double shot of Jack. Tell the prospect it's for Axe."

Eager to please, she bounced away.

An hour later, Axe played the winning shot. Rock clasped his hand on Axe's shoulder. "Fuckin' good game. Can't say I'm happy, but it was a good one. You're a lucky sonofabitch." Rock placed his pool stick in the cue rack hanging on the wall. "Damn, I was psyched up to win and have some fun." He picked up his beer from one of the bar tables nearby, finishing it in one long pull.

Snapping his fingers, Axe said, "That's all good, but give me the cash, dude."

"The cash?"

"My winnings."

Rock grabbed two women from the spectators and shoved them toward Axe. "These are your winnings. A blonde who likes it in the ass and a brunette who loves a big cock in her mouth. We're low on redheads tonight, but you'll have fun with these two. I know you like more than one bitch in your bed. Enjoy."

The two women curled themselves around him.

Frowning, Axe rubbed his chin. "I thought we were playing for money."

"Fuck, this is better than money."

"I got something I gotta do." He pushed the women toward Rock. "You enjoy."

"What the fuck, brother? You won 'em fair and square."

The blonde whined. "You're the one who gets us, baby. You're the winner."

Two weeks before, he'd have been all over those two hot bitches, but all he could see was Baylee's face and ripe body as he checked them out. Shaking his head, he said, "Dude, I'm not feeling so good. You'll owe me two bitches next time we play."

Rock, Jerry, Chas, and Jax stared at him in shock. Fuck, he was shocked with himself. He'd never turned down prime pussy before, especially an eager double. The sexy minx at the hotel had made him all kinds of messed up.

"Later." He fought his way through the crowd and left the club-house. Raking his fingers through his hair, he swung his leg over his Harley. The engine revved and he peeled out of the parking lot, leaving the surprised looks and questioning eyes behind him.

The night air was warm, and the glittering stars dusted the dark sky. Summer nights were some of the best times he loved to ride his Harley. The wind whistled around him, and the nearly desolate back roads became his playground as he twisted the throttle, accelerating to high speeds. The open road, a purring bike, and good throttle control were some of the best feelings in life. When he made his bike soar, it was the ultimate act of freedom, one step above a prison break.

Riding hard and fast always cleared his head, and he needed to do it because he hated the feelings stirring deep down inside him. Feelings he hadn't entertained since he was a teenager and dated Amber back in high school.

Amber had been his first love, and after he'd found her fucking one of the jocks, she'd been his last. After a few days she'd come crawling back to him, begging for his forgiveness, and he'd left her sobbing without so much as a backward glance. But she'd broken his heart, even though he'd never showed it. From that day on, he'd never had any use for women except for pleasure.

How he'd hated high school; it'd been a pain in the ass. Axe had come from the trashy part of town. First from the trailer park, and then from a broken-down house that the city had condemned after he joined the Insurgents.

He'd always been able to hold his own, and he'd saved Derek from the bullies at their elementary school. From as early as he could remember, he'd always been an outsider, and it suited him just fine.

When he recalled his high school days, he couldn't remember a time when he hadn't been in trouble. Smoking, drinking, fighting, and skipping classes were how he'd passed his years in school. The truth was he'd been bored out of his mind, and by the middle of senior year, he'd just quit going to class altogether. His advisor had told him to stick it out a few months so he'd be able to graduate with his class, but he hadn't given a shit. He hadn't felt the closeness or unity the other classmates did. He'd been a loner.

Derek moved to Denver when they were sophomores in high school. He'd been Axe's only male friend. Axe hadn't had any problems with the girls, and most of them sneaked glances at him, loving his bad-boy attitude. He'd been exactly the type of boy a fine young girl's parents warned her about.

Axe had been a rebel, and the girls had loved it, but their boyfriends had hated him for it. When he'd walk down the hall, the girls would squeal and blow kisses at him, while the guys clenched their fists. They'd hated him for his confidence, his fuck-the-world attitude, for being what they lacked the courage to be. So they'd come after him in the gym locker rooms, the bathrooms, and after school. They'd always come in packs, too fucking scared to face him alone.

At first, he'd pretended to be tough, even though his insides quivered. But later, he'd welcomed them, wanted to fight them, to feel their bones crunch under his hard fist and see their blood spill. At that point, they'd realized he was the real deal, and they left him alone.

If Axe had to name the one person he'd hated more than anyone else during high school, Palmer Rodgers would be the one.

Palmer had come from the rich part of town, and he thought his shit didn't stink. When Axe had been fifteen, he'd been Palmer's and his pack of snobs' favorite punching bag. Palmer had despised Axe—saw him as nothing more than trailer trash.

When Axe had turned sixteen, they'd come for him, but he'd been prepared. He'd beat the shit out of Preston and Carter—two of Palmer's best buddies—and was coming for Palmer himself, but the wuss had run away. After the beating, they'd stayed away from him, but the looks, the whispers behind his back, and the cold shoulders had given Axe the message that he was trash and unworthy of their time.

But when he'd ride his loud, big-ass Harley to school, he'd see hunger in the girls' eyes, and respect in the guys'.

He'd bought the Harley after working two jobs non-stop over the summer for three years, and a full-time job during school. His uncle Max had told him if he earned half of the money for the Harley, he'd put up the other half. When Axe had brought the money to his uncle, he'd been surprised, but he'd honored his end of the bargain.

The Harley had been used, a bit beat-up, but in Axe's eyes, it'd been the coolest thing he'd ever seen. Right from the start, he'd started working on it, and he'd found out there was a kick-ass bike shop, Thunderbird Repair Shop. That was how he'd met Hawk, who introduced him to the Insurgents MC when he'd turned seventeen.

The year he'd fucked and dumped Palmer Rodgers's girlfriend to show the rich fucker he could make the girl scream louder than Palmer ever could, Axe had no more use for school.

His mom hadn't given a shit; she'd been too busy spreading her legs and popping pain pills. So he'd earned his GED and left all the bullshit of high school—especially Amber—in the past.

He hadn't thought of Amber in years, but Baylee stirred all this shit from his past. Having feelings other than lust for her pissed him the hell off. He didn't want to care about her. When Baylee had set up the "casual sex, no strings attached" liaison, Axe should've been elated. If any other woman told him that, he'd be thrilled. All the women who were on his fuck list knew his rules: no phone calls, no cuddling, and no repeats. Just fun and pleasure between the sheets. But when Baylee told him what he'd told countless women, disappointment and anger warred inside him.

The first time he'd touched her at the wedding reception, a current zapped him and surprised the hell out of him. He'd never felt such intensity from anyone.

The fact that she was in Pinewood Springs on the strip mall project was too freaky for it not to mean anything. Axe wasn't the metaphysical type, but even he had to admit it seemed like something was bringing them together. *What the fuck am I thinking? In two weeks, I've turned into a fuckin' pussy.*

On the way back, he turned off his brain and put himself in the ride and the wind. He swung a sharp left into the clubhouse grounds. The heavy bass could be heard out in the parking lot, the party in full-force.

After the fresh air, the scent of sweat, cigarettes, and weed was suffocating. He left the laughter, grunts, music, and conversation behind and entered his room, locking the door. He sat on the edge of the bed and took out his phone. Staring at the screen for a minute, he started to plug in Baylee's number, but stopped and placed the phone down on the nightstand. He lay down on the bed, covering his eyes with his arm as the moonlight spilled over him from the open window.

Saturday couldn't come fast enough.

CHAPTER THIRTEEN

THE MAN REACHED across his desk to grab a notepad, his cuff sliding up to reveal a white scar above his wrist. He blew out a breath and rubbed the back of his neck. "Are the shadows becoming any clearer?" he asked into his phone.

His contact on the other end tentatively replied, "In some aspects, yes."

"You're fucking the psychiatrist's nurse for *that*?" the scarred man asked, a sharp edge to his tone.

"She's only reading what the shrink puts in his notes in Baylee's file." There was a pause before the other man continued. "One thing's for certain: she is remembering more each session. Baylee called her shrink a few days ago and told him she recalls that her mother's killer had a thick scar on his right arm, starting above his wrist."

The scarred man took in a breath. "Fuck."

"I know. The images are becoming clearer."

"I have someone watching her. I can't take the chance of a full recall. I think it's time she joins her mother. I... *we* have too much to lose. Now that she's in Pinewood Springs, I'll take care of it. Something I wished you would've done years ago."

The baritone voice trembled. "Do you think that's necessary? Remembering a scar is not the same as a face."

"The face will come soon enough. I'm not willing to take the risk, are you?"

He let out a long breath. "No," he whispered.

"Didn't think so. Leave everything up to me. If you learn anything more from the nurse, let me know immediately. Understood?"

"Yeah, right."

"Baylee Peters would have been better off shrouded in darkness."

BAYLEE RUSHED AROUND, cursing herself for letting the time get away from her when she went antique shopping in west Pinewood Springs. As she finished putting on her mascara, her phone pinged.

Here.

She shook her head, smiling.

Baylee: *Running a tad behind. Will be down in ten.*

Axe: *Don't like to wait. Come down.*

Too bad, macho prick. For that comment, you get to wait ten minutes more. She slowed down, taking her time to apply her lipstick and gloss before she changed into her black jean skirt and lacy lavender crop top. It showed a bit of cleavage and the slight swell of her breasts, but the top didn't come off as slutty. The lace made the look sexy, but soft. The bottom came right above her belly button, and she dabbed bronzer on her flat stomach to cover up some of the whiteness of her skin. She never had time to sunbathe or enjoy the summer days, usually having her tans sprayed on her. She made a mental note to find out if the town had anyone who did that.

As she buckled her high-heeled sandals, her phone pinged again.

Axe: *What the fuck?*

Baylee: *Almost ready.*

Axe: *When I say 6:30, woman, I don't mean 7.*

She scrunched her face.

Baylee: *It's not 7. Be down in a minute. Chill, will you?*

Axe: *I never chill, babe.*

She rolled her eyes, combed out her hair, grabbed her purse, and headed out the door. While she walked down the long hallway, her insides were churning. She chided herself for being so nervous. Why did Axe make her insides twist? *Silly.*

She exited the elevator, and on her way to the lobby she spotted Axe, all six-foot-three of him in his tight jeans, black biker boots, and fitted t-shirt. His back was to her, and his firm ass, corded muscles, and drool-worthy tatted arms made her tingle. Each time he shifted from one foot to the other, the ink on his arms danced. She paused for a few minutes, watching him. He was gorgeous, and all hers, at least for the night. A flutter of arousal skated from the tips of her breasts, down her stomach, and straight to the dampness between her legs.

Baylee approached him as he turned around, his dark eyes slowly roaming over her body. His gaze began at her feet then moved up, lingering on her exposed belly button, then her cleavage. It finally rested on her mouth. He looked up at her, brown eyes smoldering, his full lips curved in a sensual invitation.

His shock of dark hair and perfectly formed eyebrows, along with an angular nose, chiseled cheeks, and five o'clock shadow always took her breath away. No doubt about it, he was all man—bulge and all.

He nodded to her, breaking the mesmerizing moment they shared.

"Sorry I'm late."

He drew her close to him, his rough chin scraping against her jaw-line. "It was worth it. You look beautiful."

Smiling, she pushed him back then looked around, making sure Logan was nowhere to be seen.

A crease crossed his forehead as his eyes turned stormy. "What the fuck? Don't pull away from me."

"Logan… Remember?"

"Give me your lips." He slammed her against his hard chest and captured her warm mouth with his.

She stiffened as his hand slid down her back, resting on her ass. As his tongue slipped into her mouth, she relaxed and kissed him back.

He broke away, a smile on his face. "That's the way I like it, babe."

Baylee's cheeks flamed and Axe laughed, squeezing her close.

Outside, the air was warm, even though the sun had started its western descent. As they rode, Axe looked over his shoulder, capturing her gaze. She pressed closer to him and kissed his neck, then trailed the nape of it with her tongue. He pushed her hand down onto his crotch, his hardness apparent. He looked over his shoulder again and winked at her. She buried her head in his back, not sure if he wanted her to jerk him off or not. Deciding it wasn't the safest thing to do while riding a Harley at a fast speed, she moved her hand up and kept it firmly around his waist.

The bike stopped in front of a fort—or at least, that was what it looked like to Baylee. Axe helped her off the bike then pulled her into an embrace, kissing her deeply.

"You naughty girl. You were teasing me on the ride out."

She giggled. "I didn't mean to. You're too tempting."

He growled and grabbed her ass cheek, squeezing it hard. "I've got plans for this ass later on."

A shiver whispered up her spine.

Taking her hand, he led her into the restaurant.

"Is this an actual fort?" Baylee asked.

"No. It's a replica of one. Most of the stuff inside is the real deal, though," he answered as they sat at their window table.

She looked around at the framed uniforms, the tin buckets, and other items lining the walls of this unique establishment. "It's rustic... and different."

"It's known for serving wild game."

"Not sure I want to be that adventurous. Well, at least not with my dinner." She squeezed his thigh lightly.

"Fuck, baby, you're giving me a slow burn."

They ordered their drinks and dinner—elk for Axe, trout for Baylee. Axe held her look then brought her hand up to his lips and traced her palm with his tongue, an intimate gesture which made her insides melt. *This is just casual, there shouldn't be any palm licking.* Baylee slid her hand away, pretending she wanted a sip of her wine. She had to steer the evening away from flirting and sensuality.

"Are you from Pinewood Springs?" she asked as she slathered butter on a piece of freshly baked corn bread.

"Yeah. You from Denver?"

"Yes. Did you ever live in Denver?"

"No. We got a charter club there, so I go hang with them sometimes."

"What about your uncle Max?" *Real subtle. Way to go.*

"My uncle? Uh, yeah, he did live in Denver for a bit."

Her pulse pounded.

"When did he live there?"

"I'm not sure. Why you asking so many questions about him?"

"It's just that I thought I'd seen him before. He looked familiar."

"It's probably because he's my uncle. Lot of people think we have the same features."

"Could be, but I could swear I saw him a few years back."

"Nah, couldn't be him. He was back in Pinewood. It's been a long time since he was in Denver. Let me see…" Axe took a long pull on his beer. "It was around 1998."

She gasped inwardly, her ears pounding from the rush of blood. *Oh, my God!* "Are you close to your uncle?"

"Sorta. I used to be closer when I was younger. Now that I think of it, he got kinda weird after he came back from Denver, but all in all, he's been okay—he helped me and my mom out a lot. I don't see him that often, though, not since I joined the Insurgents."

"So, it's just you and your mom?"

"Yeah. My old man split when I was nine. He never looked back." His jaw twitched.

"That must've been hard."

"It's whatever."

"At least you have your mom."

He snorted and slumped back in his chair. "Yeah, right. I'm not close to her. Fuck, I don't think anyone *can* get close to her. She only cares about one person—herself. Her whole goal in life is finding men, although she does a shitty job keeping them. She has a simple life when you think of it: men and pain pills. My mom's the biggest fuckin' junkie around."

"That must be so hard. Did you have a stepfather?"

"About five, I think. I lost count. She's getting married again. Fuckin' unbelievable. Her men mean everything to her. Her son… not so much." He motioned the waiter for another beer.

"It's hard when you're young to understand why a parent does certain things. I'm sure your mom was hurting after your father left, and being a single mom and having to raise a young boy must've been hard on her. She was probably just trying to do the best she could."

Axe mashed his lips together and stared at her. "You are so fuckin' wrong. You know, I remember when I was around ten or eleven years old, some of the guys my mom would bring home weren't so crazy 'bout having me around, so my mom would make me sit on the porch while she and her latest man fucked. Sometimes, the jerks would spend the night. When it was winter, I'd crawl under the trailer to stay warm until the guy left and I could go back inside. Sometimes, I'd stay at my buddy Derek's trailer, but his dad was a mean sonofabitch when he was drunk, so it was better to shiver under my own until I could get back inside."

Baylee felt tears behind her eyes as a lump formed in her throat. She caressed his cheek. "I'm sorry. I didn't know. I should've kept my mouth shut. We don't have to talk about this anymore."

Axe held her hand. "I want to tell you this. I've never told anyone about my past."

"How long did it go on?"

" 'Bout three years. It wasn't every night. Some of the guys acted like I was their kid, and they'd throw ball with me or other shit like that. Some ignored me—I liked them the best. When I hit fourteen, I told my mom to shove it, and at six feet and growing, the guys didn't want to mess with me. She always went for the puny fucks."

"I'm just so sorry."

He shrugged. "No big deal. My family is the Insurgents, and they're the best damn family. There isn't anything a brother wouldn't do for another. We always have each other's backs."

"You seem pretty astute with the engineering designs. Did you go to college?"

"Community. I got my Associate Degree. I was gonna transfer to a four-year college, but I began prospecting for the Insurgents, and I was so damn busy with my duties to the members that I never went."

"Have you ever regretted it?"

"Never. How the fuck did you get me to talk so much about myself? No more questions. What about you? Do you get along with your parents?"

"My mother was murdered when I was eight years old. It's just been me and my dad since then. My dad elected to withdraw from life after my mother was killed. I get along with him, it's just that he's a shell of the person he used to be." The lump in her throat grew larger.

Axe's eyes widened as his fingers touched his parted lips. A sigh escaped from them, his breath touching her face. He grasped her hands in his. "Fuck. That must be tough."

"It was and is."

Baylee felt calmer since she saw his reaction, noticing he was genuinely surprised. Her instinct told her he didn't know anything about her mother's death; however, Axe's uncle was far from exonerated in her mind.

"Who did it?"

"The killer was never caught. My mother's murder is a cold case."

"There weren't any clues?"

She pointed to herself. "I'm the clue. I saw the murder, but I can't remember it. I've repressed it, so all I see in my nightmares are shapes and shadows." She sipped her wine. "I wish I could remember. Sometimes, the gravity of it all drives me crazy. You know, you don't realize how important memories are until you don't have them. Our lives are a collection of memories, and such a large piece of my life is black." She purposely didn't mention her memory was coming back. That information was for her and Dr. Scott only.

"I don't know what to say except… fuck." He leaned over and kissed her gently.

"I'm used to it. It's been my way of life for seventeen years."

Silence surrounded them, each of them lost in their own thoughts.

The waiter placed their dinners in front of them.

"Smells good," Baylee said as she squeezed lemon over her trout.

"Take a bite," Axe ordered, holding a small piece of elk in his fingers.

"How does it taste?"

He laughed. "Don't ask me, try it."

She made a face and lowered her head to study the piece of meat.

"Fuck, it's not poison," he assured her. "Try it."

Baylee opened her mouth and he put his finger in, the meat falling on her tongue. He licked his fingers, his eyes dancing in amusement.

"Do you like it?"

A smile crossed her face. "I do. It's very tender and mild. I thought it was going to taste strong and gamey, but it's good."

"So, Baylee, how many boyfriends have you had?"

"Three. Since I graduated, I mostly date for a couple of months then move on. I'm too busy to have a boyfriend at this point in my life. Maybe later on. Who knows? Short-term flings seem to suit me better, but I hadn't been with a man for over a year before you."

"That's why you were so tight. It was an added bonus." He winked.

She ignored his remark. "I told myself I'd indulge in random wedding sex if I found someone I'd like to screw." She looked at him from under half-lidded eyes.

"I wanted to fuck you, too. How many one-nighters have you had?"

"One—you. I wasn't lying when I told you I'd never done it before."

"Would never have believed it. You rocked."

She shook her head. "Your turn. How many girlfriends in your past?"

"Just one—years ago, in high school."

"That's it? I'm surprised."

"Are you? I'm not good boyfriend material."

"Why's that?"

"I love pussy too much. The women I fuck know not to expect any-thing but great sex. I always leave them smiling." His gaze locked with hers. "But you already know that."

"I'm sure your Harley and leather attract quite a few women."

"You bet. When I first started with the Insurgents, it surprised the hell outta me how many women wanted biker cock. The free drugs and 'anything goes' lifestyle appeals to a lot of women. Some stay on and become club whores, others just come by to party with the brothers for a while then they move on."

"What kind of women do you like?"

"A beautiful woman with a great set of tits, and a rounded ass. Just like you."

She rolled her eyes. "Thanks for the compliment."

"What about you? What turns you on?"

"I like to be wined and dined—"

"Check."

"And I like getting flowers, candy—the whole cheesy, romantic nine yards." She paused. "You don't seem like the flowers and candy type, though."

"Damn straight. I don't do that shit for a woman. What I give her is sweeter than any candy. I give her a night she'll never forget. Fuck, flowers die, but a night with me will always be burned on her brain."

"A bit cocky, don't you think?"

He winked. "No, just truthful."

After Axe paid the bill, they stopped in the bar to listen to the live band play classic rock tunes. On the dance floor, they held each other so tightly Baylee was sure her ribs would be bruised. She loved feeling the music and swaying with Axe.

After a couple of hours of close dancing then groping each other in their corner booth, Baylee was burning with need. Axe couldn't ride fast enough back to her hotel.

They entered the lobby as two civilized people, but when the elevator door shut, they were clawing, biting and humping each other like two animals in heat.

By the time they arrived at her room, Axe had her ripped panties stuffed in his pocket, and she had his pants unzipped. Never releasing her, Axe kicked the door shut and slammed her against the wall.

"I've been wanting to fuck you since I first saw you in the lobby. You smell sexy," he snarled.

Her arousal mixed with his created a tangy, musky scent which drove her crazy.

He pressed into her, his hardness pushing against her. His teeth grabbed her bottom lip, sucking it before his mouth covered hers, his tongue darting in and out. In frantic moves, they tore off each other's clothes, touching, grabbing, kissing, and biting as if it were the last time they'd ever taste and feel each other again.

Axe hurriedly placed a condom on his dick then lifted her leg, and she wrapped it around him. She put her other leg around him, hugging him tightly as he held her up, his hands squeezing her ass checks. He thrust into her, her back against the wall, his mouth on hers and her heels digging into his back as he banged her hard and fast.

"So fuckin' good," he panted as he pushed hard and deeper.

"I'm close, Axe," she moaned.

The combination of his mouth, dick, and tongue crashing together brought Baylee to the edge of intense pleasure. Their grunts and moans filled the room, and she screamed out his name at the same time he grunted hers as they both came together in orgasm.

They slid to the floor, panting in each other's ears, their bodies sated.

After the wave of rapture faded, he helped her up and they lay on their backs on the bed, their bodies almost touching.

She looked at him sideways. "If we're going to keep having casual sex, I don't want you with other women."

He looked down at her, his eyebrows raised. "Sounds like you want a relationship."

"No, I don't. You told me you didn't want me to be with any other men, so what's the difference?"

"I'm a man."

"Totally lame reason. Care to try for a better one?"

He looked away.

She sat up. "I was an only child, so I was never very good at sharing."

Pulling her down, she fell against his legs. He propped himself up then bent over her, his eyes penetrating hers. "Neither was I." His mouth devoured hers before he abruptly pulled away. "Just remember, this monogamy thing goes both ways, babe. You don't fuck other men while we're doing this casual bullshit."

"Deal. Oh, and no sleepovers. Too intimate."

"What if I'm boozed?" She pointed to the couch in the sitting area of her suite. "Fuck no. I take the bed."

"Then no touching, okay? Just like we're related or something, okay?

He sucked air through his teeth. "Yeah, right, like that's gonna work."

"You're not boozed now, so… " Her voice trailed off as she pointed to the door. "Maybe I'll see you on Monday."

Axe yanked her close to him and kissed her hard, his hands roaming over her naked body. She moaned, rubbing her breasts against his chest while she cupped his firm ass cheeks.

He pulled away and jumped out of bed, dressing quickly before he gave her a crooked smile. "See you Monday. Make sure your pussy is wet for me."

The door slammed behind him right before she threw her shoe at it.

CHAPTER FOURTEEN

"WE'RE STILL WAITING on confirmation that the Skull Crushers are passing meth through our turf. They've started doing the same shit in Night Rebels' territory down south. This club is dangerous, they're nothing but a bunch of drugged-up punks who ride around on bikes thinking they're an MC." Hawk shook his head in disgust.

"I'm ready to beat the shit outta them just for the fact that they chose rice burners over Harleys. What a bunch of pussies." Axe tipped his chair back and looked around the meeting room. "Am I right?"

The brothers voiced their agreement. No outlaw MC would ever own anything but a Harley-Davidson. Many of the non-outlaw motorcycle clubs, and the new group of punks who thought an outlaw club consisted of having a motorcycle and committing crimes, owned Yamahas or Hondas—Japanese imports. Members of the Insurgents would rather be dead than own an import. In their mind, American-made Harleys were the only bikes to own, and anyone who rode a rice burner didn't have the soul of a biker.

"Once Steel gives us the word, we'll teach this club no one fucks with Insurgents," Hawk said.

"Fuck yeah!" many members chorused.

Banger stood up. "In other news, we got the fuckin' mess with the permit at the strip mall. What's going on with that, Axe?"

"One of the architects is having lunch with the zoning guy tomorrow. I'll let you know then."

"Good. Is there anything else we need to address?" No one said anything. "Our first priority is the meth shit we got going on. If we find out the Deadly Demons are involved with the Neo-Nazi gang, we'll have a war. If they're not, we'll have a battle. Church over. Go drink and fuck."

The sound of chairs scraping against concrete floors, biker boots clumping, and chains jangling bounced off the walls as the brothers left the cramped room to down a few beers and shots in the great room.

Axe and Jax went over to the dartboard to play a few rounds. Chas and Jerry joined them, and the group of friends drank beer and talked as the evening rolled on. Chas, Jax, and Axe were tight since they were prospects together then patched in just a year or so apart from each other. Jerry had become a close addition to their group since he'd patched in a year before.

As Axe waited his turn at the dartboard, he noticed Rosie kept staring at him from across the room, lust apparent in her eyes. He knew she wondered what was going on, but she was a club whore—she knew the score. He didn't owe her an explanation for shit. Anyway, she'd been busy with the brothers and a few of the members from their Utah chapter who were staying at the clubhouse for a couple of weeks. They'd all been running Rosie, Lola, Wendy, and the other whores ragged. The guys were insatiable. Axe laughed as he thought about it.

The way Rosie's ass peeked out from under her short skirt definitely made his dick twitch, but he wanted to see Baylee. The night before had been incredible. She was definitely his kind of woman, but he couldn't quite figure her out. Like, why the fuck had she asked so many questions about his uncle? Thinking back, she'd acted sort of freaked out when he'd bumped into his uncle at the hotel. Axe wasn't sure what was going on there.

Then she claimed she wanted casual sex, but came up with the "faithful casual sex" bullshit. What the fuck was that all about? He was okay with it because he didn't want anyone else but her, which irked him to no end. Axe didn't want to fall for Baylee. He didn't want any female complications or drama in his life, and with a woman that was always a given.

Rosie caught his eye and winked at him. He tipped his beer to her. A grin spread across her face, and she began shuffling over to him when one of the Utah brothers scooped her up and threw her over his shoulder. She laughed but Axe observed disappointment in her eyes as the brother carried her out of the great room.

Axe watched as the couple disappeared then whipped out his phone.

Axe: *Thinking 'bout you.*

He stared at his screen as he guzzled his beer. When it flashed, his groin pulled.

Baylee: *R u?*

Axe: *Ya. Thinking 'bout ur smile.*

Baylee: *What about it?*

Axe: *I like it.*

Baylee: *Do u?*

Axe: *Ya. It's the second best thing you do with your lips.*

No response. Axe motioned for the prospect, Blade, to give him another beer. Still the screen was blank. He'd wait—he had time.

The screen blinked.

Baylee: *And what's the best thing I do with my legs?*

Axe: *Spread them.*

Baylee: *Well, my legs are missing you between them.*

Axe took a long pull on his beer, his jeans suddenly tighter. *Damn, this is fun.* He'd never done this before. All the women he'd fucked just wanted his dick in them all the time. There was never anything more than two minutes of conversation, a major fuck-fest, then him or the woman leaving. Rinse and repeat.

Axe: *I can fix that. I can be over in twenty minutes.*

Baylee: *I'm working. Gotta get stuff finished by tomorrow's mtg.*

Axe: Ur a naughty girl. U get me all horny then leave me dry?

Baylee: I am naughty. What r u gonna do?

Axe inhaled sharply, his jeans growing increasingly uncomfortable while he pictured her soft, rounded ass cheeks reddened by his handprints, her big tits swaying. *Fuck.*

Axe: Ur gonna get a spanking 4 sure. The rest u'll see.

Baylee: Mmm…

Axe: Fuck, babe. I'm hard as a rock. Need u.

Baylee: Gotta work. Use ur hands.

He laughed aloud. Throttle came over. "What's so funny, dude?"

Axe: Later.

Baylee: Bye.

Axe turned his phone over. "Just watched something funny on one of the video sites I check out."

Throttle's eyes narrowed. "You know I'm not believing your bull-shit."

Axe shrugged and drained his beer.

"Who were you talking to?" Throttle asked.

"No one. Gotta go."

"Aren't you finishing the game?" Chas asked.

"Can't. I gotta talk to my uncle Max 'bout something. See ya." Axe pushed away from his chair and walked out of the clubhouse.

THE FOLLOWING MORNING, Axe went to the office to see Baylee.

"Sir, Ms. Peters is not in," said Tina.

"Where is she?"

"She's at a lunch meeting."

"Fuck, I forgot. She's with the zoning guy, right?"

"Yes."

"Where are they?"

"The French Bistro."

"Fuck, that's right. Shit, my head is fucked this morning, you know." Axe smiled at Tina's strained face. He scared the shit out of her, vulgar language and all, and he got the biggest kick out of it. Citizens were so damned uptight about things. "Thanks, darlin'." A loud laugh burst through his lips when fear crept into her eyes. *She probably thinks I've got the hots for her now. Too fuckin' funny.*

Axe walked into Carl's office to go over some of the structural details. Carl was one of the engineers who had joined the project. After an hour, Axe sauntered back to Baylee's office, surprised she hadn't returned. He left the building and headed for the French Bistro.

As he approached the eatery, he noticed Baylee sitting at a table talking animatedly, hands flying. The zoning man had his back to the window. The way she cocked her head and laughed, her legs elegantly crossed, made his crotch tighten. *She's beautiful.* A nice, warm buzz vibrated inside him—he could stand looking at her all day.

Warmth morphed to fire when he observed the zoning guy place his hand over Baylee's. Like a bull seeing red, he charged into the restaurant, kicking open the wooden door and bumping into patrons as he made his way to Baylee. He loomed in her field of vision. A smile curled her lips when recognition set in.

"Hey. I didn't expect to see you."

"I bet you didn't." His eyes flashed.

"What are you doing here?"

"Seeing what's taking you so long at your 'meeting.' You should already be back at the office."

Red blotches dotted her chin and cheeks. In a low voice, she said, "So now you're my boss?"

An awkward silence fell between them. The zoning man cleared his throat, and Baylee swiveled around. "I'm sorry, I should introduce you."

"No need." Axe's icy voice chilled her. Looking up at him, she gasped as a darkness she'd never seen accentuated his features.

"It's you," her dining companion said with contempt.

Axe's nostrils flared and his lips pulled back, baring his teeth. The fucking prick sitting next to his Baylee—she *was his*, at least for the summer—was his high school nemesis.

"If you don't mind, we're having a meeting between two *professionals*." Palmer pursed his lips.

With force, Axe jerked a chair from the table and sat down. The two men glowered at each other.

Baylee fidgeted and laughed too long. "Palmer, Axe is one of the professionals on the team."

"Is that what you call yourself now?" Palmer turned up his nose. "Figures."

"Why don't we go out back and I can show you how I earned my road name." The muscles in Axe's arms flexed, making his tattoos slither ominously.

"Guys, come on. We're all adults. This is silly." Baylee's shrill voice punctuated the tension between the two men.

Hatred emanated from them as each man glared at the other, neither backing down. Without breaking eye contact, Axe motioned the waitress over.

"Hand the check to him." He pointed at Palmer. "Lunch is over."

When the waitress handed the bill to him, Palmer turned away from Axe and gave the waitress his credit card.

Baylee lightly touched Palmer's hand. Axe growled, burning rage threatening to explode.

"If you could rush the zoning application for the permit, I'd be eternally grateful."

Palmer regarded her, his eyes softening. "I'll call you. I think I can make this happen." He squeezed her hand.

Every muscle in Axe's body went rigid as he began to push his chair back. Underneath the table, Baylee's hand curled around his inner thigh, her fingertips inching her way to his dick. He sat back.

"Until we meet again. I enjoyed our lunch." His brow creased when he darted his gaze at Axe. "That is, *most* of it. I only want to work with you. If that's not possible, then I cannot promise I'll be able to obtain the permit or speed up the process."

"I'm the only one involved in this." Her fingers had landed on Axe's hard dick.

"Excellent. Goodbye, Baylee. I will definitely be in touch."

Palmer marched out of the restaurant at the same time Baylee roughly poked Axe's firm bulge.

"What the hell is the matter with you? Do you want to fuck up the construction of your club's strip mall? You need a therapist or something to work with you on anger management. You're just lucky I can still salvage this."

"Like fucking him?"

Her face paled. "No! How dare you?"

"You two looked pretty cozy to me, holding hands and all."

"You are so out of control. Nothing was going on. I work with sleazy men like Palmer all the time. A little flirting always helps get things through faster. I'm not going to fuck a guy for a permit. Damn, give me a little credit."

Axe shook his head and stared out the window, watching the cars and people go by. He had to let the rage pass or he was going to break something. For a couple of minutes, he sat mutely, staring at small-town life bustling past.

"The fucker and I have some history."

"I picked up on that."

"I want to beat him to a bloody pulp."

"I figured as much, and I think he did, too." She held his hand. "Does this go back to high school?"

He nodded. "The asshole's probably a crook like his dad. That's how his dad got rich—extorting money outta small business owners, taking bribes to give permits to those who could pay, taking blood money, and all the time acting like he was fuckin' respectable. Palmer used to flaunt his Porsches and country club parties, and all the other bullshit trappings of wealth, but the family's money came from cheating."

"Don't outlaw clubs get the bulk of their money illegally?" When he threw her a dirty look, she shrugged. "I'm just saying…"

"Yeah, you're right. I don't give a shit where the money comes from, what I fucking hate is the hypocrisy. The truth is Palmer, his dad, his whole fucking family thought they were better than everyone else, and they were worse than trailer trash."

Baylee kissed his hand.

"I know the sonofabitch. He knows you want the permit, and he'll use it to his advantage. The fucker will tell you to fuck him or else he won't be able to get the permit for a long time. And if that happens, I'm gonna end up in the joint for life 'cause I'll kill him."

"That's not going to happen. I know how to handle myself, and believe me, I'm not going to sleep with him. If we have to wait, we do. Anyway, if we don't get it, I'm sure your club can be persuasive." She smiled.

Seeing the fucker touch Baylee ripped right through him. A lot of women considered Palmer a "good catch"—he was rich, had a position of power within the city, was good-looking, and he could be charming with the ladies. If Baylee fell for him, Axe would be crushed. Just thinking of her with Palmer, or any man, enraged him.

Baylee brushed the hair off his forehead, leaned in close, and whispered in his ear, "Why would I waste my time with him when you're here? I find you incredibly handsome and sexy. I only want to be with you." Her hot breath caressed him.

Axe captured her mouth, his tongue dipping in. Her soft moan went straight to his cock. Their tongues danced as they pressed closer together, heedless of the people around them.

"Let's get back to the office," he rasped.

A week before, she balked at any impropriety in her office with Axe, but since she'd tasted him again, all reason had left her. She couldn't get enough of him, and all she could think of was feeling him inside her.

He'd crept into her blood stream, and she needed and craved him just like a desperate addict.

She grabbed her purse and they left the restaurant, arriving at the office in less than ten minutes. When they entered her office, Axe closed and locked the door, watching Baylee as she set her purse down on the desk. In two long strides, he had her in his arms, twisting his hand in her hair, crushing his mouth on hers. He slid his hand under her skirt and growled when her bare ass greeted him. "You're wearing a thong. Fuckin hot, babe."

Digging into her flesh, he kneaded her cheeks while he trailed his tongue down over the base of her neck, nipping her soft skin along the way. His cock jerked as she shivered under his touch. The way she rubbed her tits against him, her soft groans, her quivering skin, all fucking drove him to the edge. He had to possess every inch of her.

Tugging at her lace shell, he grunted, "Take it off."

In one fluid movement, her camisole was on the ground along with her skirt, and she stood before him in a sheer bra and matching peach thong. *Fuck me.* He was close to shooting his wad. He buried his face between the swells of her breasts, licking their rounded magnificence.

She gasped when he covered her tit with his hand, her nipple hardening under his touch. He lifted her breast from her bra and pulled the red bud into his mouth, sucking, licking, and devouring it. Her back arched when he popped her other breast out and he stood back, admiring their beauty before he went in for a taste. Baylee's small cry of pain followed by a moan of pleasure when he bit her soft flesh, shot all the way down to his hard-as-shit cock. Later, when he'd see her naked breasts, he could appreciate the red love bites he'd made all over them. They turned him way the fuck on, and he desired to mark every inch of her exquisite body, but at that moment he had a pussy which needed his attention.

Dragging her over to the desk, he pushed her down, pinning her hands above her head.

She craned her neck, her lust-filled eyes locking onto his. "I want to feel you inside me now."

A feral growl rose from his throat as he spread her legs open with his. "You love my big cock in your tight cunt, don't you?"

"Uh-huh," she panted.

He splayed his hands over her ass, pinching and stroking her sweet cheeks. "Fuck. I love your ass. It's so juicy and tempting." He leaned over and bit her hard. She jerked, moaning.

"You like that?" He bit her again, harder.

Again she jerked, and the way her ass jiggled when she did drove Axe wild.

"I know you like that 'cause your pussy is dripping, babe."

He glided his finger over her wetness, his index finger flicking against her sweet spot. The more he flicked, his touch relentless, the more Baylee squirmed and moaned, her ass wriggling back into his hardness.

"Fuck, baby. You doing that is gonna make me come. You're being such a bad girl, teasing me like that." He pushed her ass forward then smacked it hard, red streaks just beginning to appear.

"Ouch!"

He chuckled and licked the red area, all the while playing with her clit. Another hard slap, followed by his soothing tongue.

"You ready for me to fuck you hard?"

"Yeah. Fuck me."

He reached in his back pocket and pulled out a condom, tearing it open with his teeth before quickly rolling it over his length. He'd have to ask Baylee if she were good so they could start fucking raw. The condom kept him from feeling her, and he craved to feel every inch of her.

Pulling her up by her hair, he shoved her on top of the desk, knocking everything on it, including the landline phone, to the floor. He hopped on then grabbed her legs and placed them on his shoulders. He kissed her hard then made a few more love bites on her reddened tits before he pummeled into her heated sex.

"Feel good?" he grunted between thrusts.

"Ohhh," was all she could muster as his cock hammered into her over and over. As he pounded in and out of her, her hips bucked up and down amid suppressed moans and gasps of pleasure, her ass jumping and flexing with each thrust.

"You're so hot and nasty, but you already know that, don't you?"

"I'm ready to come."

Axe rubbed the side of her nub as he pounded her, his self-control waning. Then her silky walls held him like a clamp, and he knew she was about to explode. The way her pussy gripped him and her face contorted in pleasure sent him over the edge, his balls tightening before releasing streams of hotness inside the sheath. Her tiny snorts and whines sent shocks through his body. Normally, she'd be busting his eardrums, but she couldn't do it at the office, so her subdued pleasure turned him the fuck on for some reason. He thought it was the sexiest thing he'd ever seen.

He buried his face in the crook of her neck as he lay on her, part of his legs and feet dangling off the desk. Her light kisses on his left temple touched him in a way that scared him.

"Totally awesome, stud," she said, her breath caressing his face.

Axe turned toward her, kissing her lightly on the lips. "Fuckin' awesome, babe."

A knock on her door made her shove Axe away as she leapt up, frantically grabbing her clothes.

"Yes?"

"Ms. Peters? Mr. Danesk asked me to give you the hard copies of the material he prepared for you to attach to your application to the City for the permit."

"Okay. Can I come to your desk and get them in a bit?" She hopped on alternating feet while she slid her shoes on.

"I'm leaving early today. I have to give them to you now."

"Shit."

Axe chuckled.

She glared at him. "Can you help instead of watching me?"

"I'd love to help you put your clothes on, but if I do, I think Tina will be waiting a long time for you to open the door."

"Help with all this." She waved her hands over the items he'd knocked off the desk.

"Sure." He tucked his dick into his jeans, zipped up, and bent over, picking everything up.

Another knock.

"Ms. Peters? I really have to go. I have a doctor's appointment, and I don't want to be late."

"Why can't she just leave the fucking documents with someone else?" Baylee whispered.

"She's probably a nosy bitch and wants to snoop."

He laughed when her face lost its color.

"Do you think she knows? Oh, God, I didn't think of that. Oh—"

He hugged her quickly. "I was only joking. Damn, you need to lighten up."

Baylee rushed to the door and opened it, blocking entrance to her office.

"Here you are," Tina said, her neck craning to see over Baylee's shoulder.

Axe caught her eye and smiled at her. He chortled when she turned away.

"Thanks. Axe and I were going over some things on the project. I was bringing him up to speed on my lunch meeting with the head of zoning."

Axe came up behind her, his hand resting on her ass. "We had a lot to talk about."

Tina scurried off while Axe busted out laughing.

"I'm glad you think this is so funny, and take your hand off my ass. We were reckless," Baylee admonished.

"That's what made it so great."

He pinched her behind, and she swatted his hand away.

"Too cute," he said, planting a kiss on top of her head. "I gotta shove off. Banger's expecting a full report. I'll make sure to leave out the juicy details. I'll come by later, we can get some dinner."

"Not tonight. My bosses—Bob and Gary—are coming in from Denver tonight, and we're all having dinner together. We're going to have to lay low for a few days. I can't risk them finding out anything about us."

"Okay, but remember, don't go out with fuckin' Palmer."

"I have to in order to get the permit. Don't worry, Logan, Bob, and Gary will be my chaperones."

Axe gave her a quick kiss, then left. When he pulled away from the curb, he looked up and saw Baylee waving goodbye. He lifted his chin, straddled his bike then rode away, wondering how he could go a few days without her.

Fuck, she's in my blood.

CHAPTER FIFTEEN

B EFORE BAYLEE ENTERED her hotel room, she knew someone had been there. Something didn't feel quite right, and she sensed her space had been invaded. Scanning the room, she didn't notice anything out of order, except the dresser drawer was not closed all the way.

She rushed over and opened it. Definitely her things had been moved. Did the housekeeper look through her drawers? Reaching under her folded cotton tops, she retrieved a jewelry box she'd hidden. Her face scrunched when she opened it and saw her jewelry was still there. *Funny. I* know *something's missing. I feel it. I know I'm not imagining this.* When she checked every nook and cranny in the room, however, nothing appeared missing. She brushed it off as being exhausted.

Baylee rubbed her eyes. The day had been an emotionally-wrought one. As she undressed, she thought about Palmer Rodgers. That man was a definite slimy creep. Axe had been livid when he saw Palmer's hand on hers. She didn't like that the creep did that, but he could either speed up the progress by a few weeks, or he could stall the whole thing for months. She'd flirted with him because she pegged him as being the kind of man who would think all women wanted him. She'd gotten her way by flirting before, but would she sleep with a man to get the permit or whatever job-related thing she needed? No damn way, but a little flirting never hurt anyone.

Butterflies fluttered in her stomach when she thought that Axe must see her as something more than a good fuck; otherwise, he wouldn't have been so angry when he saw her eating dinner with Logan a few nights back, and he wouldn't care that Palmer had his hand on hers. She hoped he cared, because she had stirrings inside of her, and they scared the crap out of her.

Her rational mind told her it would never work based on geography alone: she lived in Denver and he lived in Pinewood Springs. Also, he was in an MC, and she'd like a life free from rival gangs, turf wars, and all the other crap she read about when she did her research.

No, I can't let him get to me.

Forcing herself *not* to think of Axe, she concentrated on getting ready for dinner.

DINNER WAS A tennis match between her and Logan, trying to best each other in front of Gary and Bob. She let herself be sucked into it, and it made her feel uncomfortable, but her competitive nature had kicked in.

During dinner, a sweet, vinegary smell, like apple cider, wafted around her and a vivid memory of a tall, lean man with graying hair, piercing green eyes, and a long, sharp nose flashed before her. The man came toward her as she cowered on the steps, unable to move. Suddenly, a surge of overwhelming fear gripped her.

"No. No," she gasped aloud, her hand covering her pounding heart. *I can't fucking breathe!* She gulped air, but the more she did, the more her lungs refused to fill. All of her limbs were stiff, and her face turned red as she continued to gasp, both hands covering her heart. *I'm going to die. Oh, God! I'm going to die in front of everyone. I can't breathe. I can't think.* Black spots twirled in front of her eyes as the room spun, and Gary, Bob, and Logan stretched further away from her.

"Are you all right?" Bob asked as he leapt from the chair, rushing over to her.

Sweat poured down her face as she gripped the table, her knuckles white from the pressure.

"You're as white as a ghost," Gary said as he dunked a corner of his napkin in his water glass then dabbed it on her face.

The coolness soothed her, and Bob's hands massaging her shoulders began to calm her down.

"Sorry," Baylee panted. She willed herself to slow her breathing so she could calm down.

Shakily, she brought her water glass to her mouth and took two large gulps. After a few seconds, she fibbed, "The crab cake must have shrimp in it. I'm allergic to it. I guess I should've asked." "Now that I've drunk some water, I'm feeling much better. Sorry I scared you." She looked down at her plate to avoid their stares.

"Glad you're better," Bob said. "You gave us quite a start. Are you sure you're okay?"

Baylee nodded, her neck flushed from embarrassment. She'd made an idiot of herself, but seeing the killer stage-front in her mind had freaked her out.

Logan shifted the conversation back to him and all his wonderful accolades, but she just let it go, still reeling from her flashback. *Oh, my God! I remember the killer's face. For the first time since Mom died, I remember.* The face wasn't a crystal-clear picture quite yet, but it was definitely coming back. The minute she returned to her hotel, she'd call Dr. Scott. The enormity of the vision stunned her—this was a major breakthrough.

Back from dinner, she checked out her room before latching the deadbolt and security locks. She sat on her bed and, with trembling fingers, called Dr. Scott. He answered on the third ring.

"I saw the killer," she blurted out.

"You did? In your mind?"

"Yes, I had a flashback to the night my mom died. I *saw* him. I'm so shaky, but a part of me is jumping for joy."

"Can you identify him?" Dr. Scott asked.

"Not really, but the image was much clearer than any other I've had. I know he had green eyes. Intense, frightening, green eyes. This is huge, isn't it?"

Dr. Scott cleared his throat. "Yes, it is. You now know the killer has green eyes and a large scar on his lower arm. You are making progress. What were you doing when you had the memory?"

"I was out at a business dinner. Pretty routine. I don't know what triggered it."

"A certain scent, sound, or touch can trigger the mind to unlock the portion which holds the buried memory."

Baylee racked her brain, trying to remember what happened the seconds before the memory assaulted her. "Wait. I think it was the smell of fermented apples that did it." She scrubbed the side of her face. "Yes, that's what did it. When I smelled it, it seemed like a vaguely familiar scent."

"During our sessions, you spoke about the sweet and pungent scent surrounding the killer. You've mentioned that since you started therapy back when you were a child. Perhaps the killer smelled like fresh, harvested apples, or the air had the scent in it that night. Whatever it was, the smell triggered your memory."

"Wow. It was intense. I had a panic attack right at the table. I felt like such a fool."

"It's powerful when that happens. I'm not surprised."

"I was freaked out. It came out of nowhere, and there he was with his frightening green eyes coming for me. I was so scared." Baylee shuddered and ran her hand up and down her arm.

"Did you feel particularly stressed today?"

"A guy's been watching me. I don't know if it's related, but he's definitely targeted me. The weird thing is he's a friend of mine's uncle. Isn't that strange?"

"Does your friend know his uncle is following you?"

"I haven't told him. I don't know what to make of it. Sometimes, I just think he's a perv."

"It's possible."

"Also, I know someone was in my room. The drawer to my dresser was opened."

"Was anything missing?"

"Not that I can tell."

"Maybe the cleaning crew opened it and didn't close it all the way."

Baylee knew Dr. Scott didn't believe in her "hunches." He was a man of science and didn't consider intuitions or the sixth sense, but she believed in them, and she *knew* someone had come into her room.

"Are you all right now?"

"I am. I feel like I'm getting closer to having total recall, but I'm scared because the killer might be watching me to make sure I don't testify."

"I see. Baylee, we've gone over this many times. The chances of the killer hanging out for all these years on the off chance you'll get your memory back is extremely slim. Most of the time, murderers can't wait to leave town and relocate far away from the crime scene. You're safe. Recalling what happened on that tragic night is necessary to free you. If the killer is caught, that's great, but our therapy is all about setting you free from the past and the guilt. If you keep living in the past, you will never move forward. Understand?"

"Yes."

"All right. If you need to talk to me, I'll leave my cell phone on all night. Make sure you jot all this down in your journal."

"I will. Thanks for everything. Goodbye, Dr. Scott."

"Goodnight."

Baylee wished she'd been comforted by his words, but she couldn't shake the nagging feeling that someone had been watching her every move since her mom died.

She slipped into her nightshirt and turned on the TV, grateful for the distraction. After an hour, she went to the drawer to dig out her journal. She'd been keeping one ever since she'd started seeing Dr. Scott a few years back. It was a record of her nightmares, her fears, and her recalls—a very personal aspect of her life.

Wanting to write about her major breakthrough, she opened the dresser drawer and slipped her hand between her tops. Nothing. She felt around. Nothing but clothes. A slight tremor of panic weaved its way up her spine. She took out each item until her t-shirts, crop tops, and knit shells were piled on the bed. No sign of her journal. She emptied every drawer in the dresser, rummaged through her suitcases, overnight bag, tote, and purse. Nothing.

It was gone.

Clammy fingers squeezed her nerves as she realized what happened. Someone came into her room and took it—not the jewelry, cash, traveler's checks, or laptop, only her journal. She covered her mouth with her hand. The only one who would want to know her thoughts, her dreams, her memories was… She couldn't think it. It was too awful, too frightening, but her mind wouldn't let it go. The person who stole her journal was the killer.

Oh, my God! He knows I'm in Pinewood Springs. He was in my room. Oh, God! He knows everything about me.

She opened her mouth but nothing came out, and she stood frozen in the middle of the room, shaking like a leaf with her cold and sweaty hands clenched at her sides. Pounding against her temples made her lightheaded. The killer was after her, had been ever since he killed her mother. He'd tried to kill Baylee that night but was interrupted, and he was finally going to finish the job. She was trapped like a fucking hamster on a wheel, going around in circles and never getting anywhere. He had all the advantages; he orchestrated the game, and she was the pawn. All she could hear was the pounding of her heartbeats. Even though her drapes were all pulled, she felt like she was in a fishbowl and he watched her.

The phone rang. Baylee jumped, took a moment to compose herself, and then answered.

"Hi, Baylee. Do you want to join Gary, Bob, and me for a drink?" Logan asked.

"No."

"Sure?"

"Sure."

"Okay. You sound weird."

"I was sleeping when you called. Tell Gary and Bob I'll take a rain-check."

She placed the receiver on the handset and wiped her fingers over her face. She probably should've gone down and joined them; it would've been better than sitting alone and imagining horrible scenarios with the killer.

She had to stop; she couldn't let him have the upper hand. Being a victim again was *not* an option.

After crawling between the covers, Baylee opened her book, but it wasn't long before the hum of the air conditioner lulled her to sleep.

She woke up with a start, the room pitch-black. Did she turn the TV off? She didn't remember doing it. Something had woken her up. She held her breath, listening over the pulse booming in her ears. There, a rattling sound. *What is that?* Again, a little louder. It came from the door. Slipping out of bed, using the light from her phone, she tiptoed toward the front door then paused. The rattling sound grew louder. *Someone is trying to get in!* She covered her mouth with her hand, adrenaline rushing through her body. It sounded like someone was picking the lock and turning the knob, but she knew she'd locked the deadbolt and the security bar.

What should I do?

As she crept closer, the rattling stopped. She barely breathed, standing motionless as time passed. Nothing. Had she imagined the sound? After several minutes, she inched her way to the door and put her ear against it. Nothing. She exhaled forcefully.

Leaning forward, she grasped her neck and looked through the peephole. A piercing green eye stared back. She screamed and jumped away, the doorknob rattling and shaking as the person kicked the door.

Baylee ran to the phone and called the front desk, sputtering out her fear that someone was trying to break into her room. The clerk said security was on its way. She held onto the receiver like it was a lifeline, cold sweat trickling down her back. *He* was outside her door.

A loud knock broke her resolve, and the tears she'd been holding back flowed down her cheeks.

"Security," a loud, male voice boomed.

How could she be sure it wasn't a ruse? She walked back to the door, wiping her wet cheeks with the palm of her hand. She looked out the peephole again and saw two uniformed young men standing in the hall. Taking a deep breath, she opened the door.

"What's the problem, Miss?" one of the guards asked.

"Someone was trying to break into my room."

"Did you see him?"

"Yes. I looked through the peephole and he was staring back at me." Recalling the horror of it, the tears ran down her cheeks again.

"We'll take a look around. Lock your door."

About ten minutes later, they knocked again.

"We checked the hallways and down the stairwell. Everything is fine. If you have trouble again, call us." They gave her their direct phone number.

"Can someone pick the deadbolt?"

"Any lock can be picked, but it'd have to be done by an expert. The deadbolts are very secure, as well as the security bar."

"Thanks."

She closed the door then dragged the desk chair over, propping it under the doorknob as extra precaution.

Sitting on the bed, the lamp on, terror froze her. *What if he comes back?* Even with the three locks, the security guards, and the chair against the door, she didn't feel safe. Without hesitating, she opened her phone and sent Axe a text.

Baylee: *R u still up?*

Two seconds later, her phone pinged.

Axe: *Ya.*

Baylee: *Sorry to text so late.*

Axe: *Never be sorry, babe. Glad to hear from u.*

Baylee: *I need a friend right now.*

Axe: *What's wrong?*

Baylee: *Too long to explain. Can u come over?*

Axe: *Sure!*

Baylee: *As a friend. I'm scared.*

Axe: *I'll be there soon.*

Baylee: *Thanks.*

She set her phone down and rubbed her throbbing temples. Her phone pinged, and she smiled.

Unknown: *I'm watching you, Baylee.*

Her heart dropped to the pit of her stomach and she threw the phone on the bed, scooting away from it. Instinctively, she looked around the room then at the locked front door.

Another ping. She stared at the phone for a few seconds, willing it to be Axe who had texted. Slowly, she picked it up.

Axe: *No worries. I'm on my way.*

She exhaled then curled up in bed with the covers over her head, waiting for Axe to arrive.

A soft knock on her door sent her body in a downward spiral.

"Baylee? It's me, Axe."

His familiar voice brought tears of relief, and she rushed to the door, dragged the chair away, and looked through the peephole. His tall, strong body filled the view. When she opened the door, she flung herself into his arms.

"What's going on?" he asked softy as he held her and led her back into the room.

All the fear and tension for the past couple of hours drained from her, and she broke down crying, her body rising and falling as he held her close to him, stroking her back and her hair.

"Come on, it's going to be okay. I'm here now." His soft voice comforted her, and his powerful arms around her small frame lent her a sense of protection.

After a while, she pulled away. Axe reached out and wiped the wetness from her cheeks with his calloused fingertips.

"What's happened?" Concern creased his brow.

Baylee led him to the bed and they both sat down. She took a deep breath then told him everything, from when her mother was murdered to what happened before she texted him. The only part she left out was the bit about his uncle because she wasn't sure if it was related, and she didn't want to cause family problems.

When she finished, he nestled her in his arms, her head pillowed against his upper chest. "I'm glad you told me. I'm here now, so you don't have to be afraid. I've got your back on this. I'll take care of business. I won't let anything happen to you."

He stood up, taking her with him. Pulling down the covers, he said, "You need to sleep. I'll stay with you. No one's gonna hurt you. Don't worry about anything."

Baylee pulled the sheet over her, her arm wrapped around Axe's waist. His scent was intoxicating, and being in his arms made her pulse and heartbeat calm and steady. She glanced up and met his stare. Warmth flooded through her, and she grabbed his neck and pulled his head down, kissing him deep and urgent. Axe pulled her closer to him, his hands roaming down her sides. In one movement, he had her on her back and he hovered over her. She shook her head.

"I only want you to hold me."

Desire-filled eyes regarded her before he lay by her side, drawing her close to him. Safe in his capable arms, Baylee fell fast asleep.

CHAPTER SIXTEEN

THE FOLLOWING MORNING, Axe woke up and gazed at Baylee. She looked so peaceful sleeping, her head resting on his shoulder. It was a first for him—he'd never slept with a woman without screwing her. Pleasure from having her in his arms spread over him.

Baylee sighed in her sleep, and he simply watched her. His Baylee was in some deep shit, and he agreed with her that the killer was after her. After all these years, the sick fuck stood in the background, waiting for her to start remembering so he could off her. It had to be someone close to her or her family; an ordinary killer would've been long gone by now. It was someone she knew, he was positive. The only clue was the phone number from where the wacko texted her, but Axe bet he'd used a burner phone.

The minute she'd opened up to him the night before, he'd decided she needed protection. He could watch her, but he'd need help. Maybe the new prospect, Puck, could do it. He'd present the situation to Banger and hope he'd go along with it, but if not, Axe would have to watch her all the time. No way was he letting some sick fuck hurt his woman. After he dropped her off at work, he'd go and chat with his prez. If it was the last thing he did, he'd keep her safe.

After he had the protection issue covered, then he'd figure out what the hell was going on, and what to do to lure the killer. He looked down at Baylee again and pressed his lips together; he may have to use Baylee as bait.

Bending down, he kissed her. She yawned and opened her eyes, a big smile crossing her face.

"Morning," he said against her lips.

"What a wonderful way to wake up." She put her arms around his neck and pulled him down on top of her, kissing him wet and hard.

"I like you in the morning," he teased as his hand slid over her hips then rested on her ass.

"You're going to like me even more when I suck you."

"Yeah, something like that definitely earns you points. You gonna put my cock in your fuckable mouth?"

"Yes," she whispered as she pushed him on his back. "I can't wait to taste you." Her tongue trailed down his jaw before she peppered kisses on his neck, moving down toward his ready length.

She lowered her mouth to kiss the head of his dick, her sparkling eyes locked with his. When the tip of her tongue peeked out from her mouth, he sucked in his breath, watching as she made small circles around his crown while her slender fingers wrapped tightly around the base of his shaft.

"Do you like it when I do that, Axe?" she whispered before placing her lips over his crown and soaking up his pre-come. She smiled wickedly at him. "Do you like it when I swallow?"

"Fuck yeah. I love it. It's so hot watching you suck my cock."

The warmth and wetness of her mouth, the softness of her lips and tongue, and the awesome pressure of her hand on his balls fired every nerve in his body. Watching his dick in her mouth was the sexiest thing he'd ever seen. As she worked her magic on him, her tits swayed and glimpses of the curve of her ass drove his excitement higher. The deeper she took him in, the further he wanted to go until his head hit the back of her throat, and he couldn't hold back any longer. With his eyes rolled back and legs stiffened, streams of hotness released in her warm mouth.

"Fuck. Feels so good. Fuck," he grunted as his hands tangled in her hair.

"Mmm… love your taste," she murmured against him, the vibration against his dick causing him to moan deeply.

Breathing heavily, he gripped her shoulder. "Get up here."

Baylee shimmed up beside him, and he drew her close and hard against him. As they lay with legs and arms entangled, Axe tilted her chin, their gaze locking. Sweeping her hair from her face, he said, "I guess we've raised 'casual' up a few notches."

She chewed her lip, nodding.

He leaned down and kissed her. "That suits me just fine."

"Me too," she whispered.

"We gotta talk about what's going on with you." He placed his finger on her lips when she groaned. "We gotta. I have a plan, but it'll take some time to get together. For now, I have to keep you safe, so I'm gonna ask Banger if the club can spare a prospect to help me keep an eye on you."

"Like a bodyguard? I don't think I can live with someone always there in my space."

"Puck won't be in your space. He knows how to become part of the background. Anyway, you have no choice. I agree with you, the killer's come back for you. He has your journals, and he knows you're beginning to remember."

She shuddered against him, and he held her close until she calmed down.

"This isn't one of your nightmares, babe. That shit, you can wake up from. This is real, and I don't want anything happening to you."

"You're right. I'm just so angry my life isn't my own. He destroyed my life the night he killed my mother, and right when I'm healing, he's back for round two. Fuck!"

"I'm pissed, too, and we'll use our anger to track him. He made a mistake."

She looked up at him. "What's that?"

"He brought me into it. I'll fuckin' kill his ass."

Baylee's body felt soft and relaxed in his arms.

She chuckled. "I shouldn't be happy to hear those words, but I am."

"You should be. He took a life, your mom, and now he gives his. An eye for an eye, you know. That's the way my world rolls."

Winking at him, she teased, "I'll have to remember to stay on your good side."

Axe brought his face inches from hers. "Baby, you'll always be on my good side." Cupping her chin he kissed her, the lightest brush of his lips against hers.

Against his lips, she murmured, "I'd love to stay like this with you all day, but I have to go to work."

"I gotta get going, too. Want to talk to Banger."

They rolled out of bed.

"I'll take you to work," Axe said.

"On the back of your Harley? Use my car. You can have it for the day."

"No way am I driving in a cage in the summer. Fuck, you can't feel shit in a cage."

"Just to take me to work. You can come back and get your Harley. I can't have my bosses see me coming to work on the back of a motorcycle."

"Why the fuck not?"

"What will they think?"

"Who the fuck cares? Life's too short to worry about everything someone thinks about you. I don't give a shit if people like me, my attitude, or my lifestyle."

Watching him with earnestness, she said, "You're right. Fuck it. If they're going to fire me for riding on the back of a Harley with you, then I'll take them to the Labor Board."

Laughing, he tweaked the tip of her nose. "You're my kind of woman. Fuck the world."

"I've been meaning to ask you how you guys have these odd names, like Puck."

"They're road names. Your actions or something about you gives you your name. The names mean something to the person or the club. Puck got his after he smashed in the teeth of another biker who was bothering a group of young girls at a winter rally. He's a hockey fanatic and always carries a puck in his pocket. Anyway, he told this jerk to leave the girls alone, and the guy shoved him. A fight broke out and, at the end, the jerk was spitting his teeth out. Puck nailed him in his fuckin' trap with his puck."

Baylee grimaced. "I don't think I want to know how you got your name."

He hugged her. "No, babe, you don't. Trust me on this."

AFTER HE MADE sure she arrived safely at her desk, he rode to the clubhouse.

Knocking on Banger's door, Axe entered when he called out.

"Hey," Axe said.

"How's it going?" Banger replied.

"Not so good."

"What's up?"

"There's a problem with the lead architect who's almost got the permit situation solved." Axe continued to tell Banger about Baylee's dilemma, stressing that she was the one whose design would be used for the restaurant.

Banger listened, no expression crossing his face.

"So, you can see she needs some protection. I can handle most of it, but I'll need the loan of one of the prospects. Maybe Puck?" Axe slumped back in the chair.

"You done?" Banger asked.

Axe nodded.

Banger stared at Axe, wiped his hands on his faded blue jeans, and said, "You're fucking her, aren't you?"

Axe glared into Banger's clear blue eyes. "What the fuck does that have to do with it?"

"Everything. When a man's got his dick in a woman's pussy, he'll do anything for her."

Axe's face turned dark. "Whether I'm fuckin' her or not isn't the point. She's in danger, and if we're gonna get this goddamned strip mall finished, we gotta keep her safe."

Banger guffawed. "Bullshit. Don't try to pass some lame excuse over on me. Another architect could step in and finish the job. You got the hots for this one. Now I gotta check her out, 'cause I wanna see what the woman who made you fall looks like."

"What the fuck? No bitch made me fall. If you don't wanna help, then just say it. Don't tell me all this shit."

Banger stared at him. "Are you fuckin' her? Yes, or no?"

Axe rubbed his face. "So what if I am? I could walk away in a second. It's just good pussy with a great pair of tits. Shit, I could go out now and tell Rosie I wanna fuck, and we'd go at it."

"But you won't 'cause you haven't given Rosie or any of the other club whores the time of day for the past few weeks. This architect's got you by the balls." Banger smiled widely.

"You finished? You enjoying this?"

He nodded. "Yeah, I am. I just wanna see the woman who has you all fuckin' twisted."

Axe blew out a long breath. "You gonna help, or not?"

"I need to make sure the other members are on board with this. Using one of our prospects for guard duty for a week or two when shit may hit the fan with the fuckin' Skull Crushers may not be the wisest move."

Axe nodded. "That's fair. Let's call church and take a vote. I gotta know."

"Okay. I'll let the members know we got an emergency church this afternoon."

Axe walked to the door. Before opening it, he turned to Banger, arm straight up, fist in the air. "Thanks, brother." Then he left.

Later that afternoon, all thirty members voted to have Puck watch over the architect—who had Axe by the balls—for a week. It wasn't a smooth vote, but Axe put up with the ribbing because, at the end of church, an enormous sense of relief washed over him when his brothers voted to help him and his woman.

And she *was* his woman, even if she didn't know it yet. He'd never have guessed their one-night stand would turn into him loving her.

CHAPTER SEVENTEEN

FOR THE NEXT few days, everything was quiet, and Baylee and Axe fell into a routine: Puck watched her during the day, Axe was with her each night, and in the morning he'd take her to work on his cam-screaming Harley. They grew closer, but Baylee was still afraid to let Axe know how she felt, unsure of his feelings since he never told her if he cared about her more than a summer romance.

Securing protection for her had to mean he cared, but she'd heard some of his club buddies refer to her as "his woman," and Axe would bristle. At least she wasn't apprehensive all the time since Puck and Axe were around. The fear which strangled her a few days before dissipated whenever she saw Puck. Tall, muscled, and tatted over every inch of skin Baylee could see, Puck was an intimidating figure—she was glad he was on her side. He never smiled at her, rarely looked her in the eye, and seemed perpetually bored, but she knew he'd rip the head off anyone who came near her. For the time being, he was her protector. He'd stay outside her door at the office, sitting in a black leather chair, messing with his phone all the time, but whenever someone came into her office, his eyes were alert, his body tense.

Explaining him to Stan took a lot of creativity, but in the end, he was fine with Axe hanging around her. She knew the secretaries were petrified of him, but after a couple of days they were used to it and didn't pay him any attention.

Baylee glanced up from her computer screen when Gary came into her office. Bob had returned to Denver the day before, but Gary stayed on to make sure the permit was secure before returning to the city.

"Is that thug hanging around really necessary, Baylee?"

She motioned for him to close the door and sit down. When Gary was seated, Baylee said in a hushed voice, "Absolutely. Someone is trying to hurt me." Her voice dropped even lower. "I think it's the man who killed my mother."

"What? That's ridiculous. You're having paranoid delusions again. You've had them off and on for years. Your father was so worried, but you seem to have been improving with your new therapist. You're not going back to the way you were, are you?"

She shook her head. "No. And I never had delusions, and I'm not paranoid. No one will believe me. The killer has been studying me for years, watching me until my memory comes back. He's here in Pinewood Springs."

"Baylee. Stop. Will you listen to yourself? Why would the killer be in this town and not Denver? You've never been here, and I don't recall your mom or dad ever coming here. It doesn't make sense, does it?"

Running her hand through her hair, she gazed up at the ceiling.

"Does it?" he prodded.

"Um… Not really, but he *is* here. I know it." Gary's placating smile made her doubt her earlier convictions. "He is," she repeated weakly.

"Maybe you're working too hard. Why don't you take this weekend off and go back to Denver? See your friends and your dad. It'd do you good to be back in your house. It can't be too much fun living in a hotel."

He thinks I'm a paranoid nut. What if he's right? It really doesn't make sense that the killer would be in Pinewood Springs. She rubbed her forehead. *I don't know what's up or down anymore.*

"You know, the anniversary of my mom's death is in a couple of weeks," she said softly.

"I know. It'll be sixteen years?"

"Seventeen."

"Maybe that's what's made you so upset."

"My journal was stolen from my hotel room."

"And you think the killer came all the way up to Pinewood Springs to break into your hotel room to steal your journal? Really, Baylee?"

Tracing over pen marks on the desk with her finger, she avoided his eyes.

"Take some time off. I insist. It'll do you a lot of good. You'll see. You're so isolated up here. Logan tells me you rarely want to go out of your room. He told me he's always asking you to join him on outings, but you usually say no."

Yeah, Logan would say that. Stick the knife in deeper, asshole.

"I keep busy."

"You know, Logan would've been more than willing to take you to work and keep an eye on you. I could even have moved you two to connecting rooms to assuage your fears. You didn't have to call in a thug from an outlaw motorcycle club. It wasn't necessary. I wish you would've come to me first."

"I feel way more secure with Puck than I ever would with Logan."

For a few seconds, Gary stared hard at her then clasped his hands together, placing them on his knee. "Do you have something with Axe?"

Baylee stared back without answering.

He nodded. "I know you're aware of the firm's policy about getting involved with clients. Logan and a couple of the engineers on the team have noticed that he is quite taken with you… and you with him. You've come to work many times on the back of his *Harley*." He wrinkled his nose. "Baylee…"

"Axe is a representative, but the club, especially the board, is the client. Axe has to pass everything through the president and vice president."

"Even if that were true, you know he is not the man for you. If your mother were alive, she would never approve of an outlaw biker covered in tattoos, and your father will be very disappointed."

"You're mistaken. The only thing on my mind is proving I can do a stellar job on the strip mall project. I'm vying for the partner position."

"Now, that's what I like to hear." Gary smiled. "Brief me on the zoning requirements and your second designs you submitted the other day."

Gary stayed in her office talking business for a couple of hours. After he butted his nose in her affairs, he calmed down, and they had a good working session and made some progress.

Baylee was hard at work when a delivery man rapped on her doorframe, holding a huge bouquet of pink roses. Her insides fluttered, and excitement coursed through her body. After signing the delivery slip, she opened the card and read it.

To a beautiful woman who is most persuasive. I'll call you. With much respect, Palmer.

Her shoulders slumped. The flowers were from Palmer, but she'd wished they were from Axe, even though he'd told her he wasn't the flower-giving type. The phone rang and she answered it.

"Hello?" she said.

"Hi, Baylee. This is Palmer. Did you get my flowers?

"Yes, they just arrived. They are lovely. Thank you."

"Why don't we have dinner tomorrow night? I have the zoning permit, and I threw in the building one, as well."

"Wonderful. Thank you so much, Palmer. It makes my job much easier."

"Anything for a beautiful lady. Tomorrow night at seven?"

"That would be fine."

"Excellent. I'll pick you up at the hotel."

"Sounds good. Thank you again."

She placed her phone down. *Yes! I got the permits.* They could finally break ground and lay the foundation. As an architect, it was always thrilling when the actual building started and all the ideas, diagrams, and designs became reality.

Her mouth went dry when she realized she'd made a date with Axe for the following night. They were supposed to go out to dinner that evening, but he'd called earlier in the day and told her he couldn't come over because he had club business. He wouldn't tell her what it was, but he'd told her he'd see her the following night. Axe was not going to be happy when she told him she couldn't go out with him because she was having dinner with Palmer. Even though he would be pissed, he had to realize it was very important for her to have the permits in hand, and she wasn't going to jeopardize the project because Axe and Palmer couldn't play nice in the sandbox. Axe would have to deal with it. This was business, and it benefitted the Insurgents.

She sighed, knowing she was in for a battle with him.

Exhaustion weaved through her muscles and Baylee packed up her laptop, deciding to skip out an hour early and have a glass of white wine at the hotel bar.

With her trusty bodyguard beside her, she stepped into the hotel bar, the familiar wood paneling and red-leather chairs a welcomed sight. Grabbing a table away from the lobby—she didn't want to risk Logan joining her—she settled in the comfortable swivel chair and kicked off her shoes. Four-inch heels had to have been invented by a man—they were pure torture, but damn pretty and sexy. Digging her toes in the plush maroon carpet was nirvana. Turning her head, she spotted Puck at a table behind her. She smiled.

"Would you like something to drink?"

He shook his head.

"You don't mind if I do?"

"You can do whatever you want. Axe just told me to keep you safe." He crossed his massive, inked arms.

She nodded. *So, he* is *capable of forming sentences.* Her phone rang, and Axe's name flashed. Her heart soared.

"Axe."

"Who the fuck sent you the flowers?"

"Hello to you too."

"Who sent them to you?"

Baylee glanced at Puck, who watched with an impassioned face. "News travels fast, huh?"

"Who?"

"Palmer Rodgers sent them." She heard his low growl. "I impressed him, which is good news, because he's signing off on the zoning permit. He's throwing in the building permit, as well."

"What color are the roses?"

"Pink. Did you hear what I said?"

"I heard you. You're done with him?"

Baylee paused, breathed deeply, then said, "Not quite. I have to get the permits."

"He can drop them off at your office."

"He could, but he's in all-day meetings tomorrow, so we're meeting for dinner." She licked her lips. "It's just a quickie dinner. I'll have both permits in hand tomorrow night."

"You don't really believe his bullshit line, do you?"

She whispered, "It's just business, Axe. You know that."

"I thought we had a date."

"We can get together later, or the next day. I can't blow all this because you're feeling insecure or threatened."

A very long pause ensued. When he spoke, Axe's voice dripped ice. "I'm not fuckin' insecure. Threatened? That's a load of shit. I don't like being number two. Tell the motherfucker you can meet him the day after tomorrow. We have plans."

"Axe, you're being unreasonable. I have to get the permits, you know that. I said we can meet later, at around ten o'clock. You can come to the hotel, and we can have some fun."

"I don't have to wait in line to have fun, baby. Plenty of willing chicks who're dying to show me a helluva good time. So are we on for dinner tomorrow, or not?"

Baylee's skin pricked. Why the hell was he being so unreasonable about this? He was acting like a macho asshole who wanted his way. Well, too bad; she needed the permits. She compromised by asking him to come by later, and then he threw the threat of fucking other women in her face? No way was she putting up with *that* nonsense.

"I can't make it. Sorry. I explained all this to you. If you want to be unreasonable, then that's your choice. If you don't want to come by later and be with me, that's your choice, as well. As far as I'm concerned, this discussion is over."

Axe laughed dryly. "Suit yourself. Have a good time with asshole."

The phone went dead. *Did he just hang up on me? This is ridiculous!* Baylee stared at the blank screen. She wanted to call or text him back, but her anger got in the way. How dare he hang up on her! She was having dinner with a pompous ass in order to get the stupid permits so the project for *his* club could begin, and he was giving her a hard time. *What an arrogant, pig-headed asshole.* She refused to call him back. He was in the wrong, and he owed her an apology. *Men!* She should've stayed on her celibate-until-made-partner plan. This whole whatever-you-call-it thing she had with Axe was getting too complicated. Why did she let him get to her so much? Why the fuck had she fallen for such a prick?

Baylee gulped her wine then turned to Puck. "Thanks for telling Axe about the flowers. I thought your job was to protect me. How did you figure me receiving flowers into that equation?"

Puck lifted his eyebrows and shrugged.

Shaking her head, Baylee stomped out of the bar, Puck at her heels. Without even a glance at him, they rode the elevator in silence, then she went in her room and slammed the door. Heat flushed through her body as she pounded her fist on the mattress several times. The fact that Axe didn't understand pissed her off. He acted like she *wanted* to go out with Palmer instead of understanding she *had* to for business reasons. Axe was out on club business that evening, and he expected her to understand why he couldn't be with her, and she did. So why couldn't he extend the same courtesy to her? How could he even think she was interested in Palmer? She couldn't believe Axe couldn't tell she was crazy for him.

Men! They're a pain in the ass.

A soft knock on the door shifted her attention. Looking through the peephole, she saw Puck standing outside with his arms crossed over his enormous chest.

"What is it, Puck?" she said after opening the door.

"Blade, another prospect, is coming to relieve me since Axe won't be here tonight."

"Oh… okay. I guess you do have to sleep." She smiled.

Puck just stared at her.

"Thanks for letting me know."

"He'll be here in about twenty minutes. I'll let you know when he comes." Puck turned around.

"Thanks," she said to his broad back, closing the door.

As promised, twenty minutes later, another soft knock rapped on the door.

When she opened it, a tall, tattooed and pierced man with blond hair stood before her.

She looked around for Puck.

"Puck left. I'm here for the night. He'll be back in the morning."

"Okay. You're Blade, right?"

"Yep."

"Can I get you anything, like a drink or a sandwich?"

"I'm good. Brought stuff with me." He patted the backpack he had slung over his left shoulder.

"If you need anything, please let me know. Don't worry about waking me up, either."

Blade lifted his chin then turned around and moved the padded office chair closer to the door.

"Goodnight," Baylee said.

Ignoring her, Blade plopped down on the chair and took out his phone. She shut the door, exhausted. After changing into her pajamas, she pulled down the covers and slipped between the sheets. With her sentry standing guard, she drifted off into a deep sleep.

CHAPTER EIGHTEEN

PUCK WAS BACK at his post the following morning. Baylee was dying to ask him how Axe was, but she knew he wouldn't tell her anything. He was definitely a man of few words. Half-expecting Axe to call her, she pretended it didn't bother her, but her clenching stomach told her otherwise. Each time her phone rang, a light-hearted feeling would seize her only to be replaced by heaviness when the calls weren't from him.

No calls. No texts. Nothing.

When the lunch hour drew near, Baylee couldn't stand staying in her office, wondering if she'd hear from Axe. She had to have some fresh air. She'd heard the sandwich shop around the corner was simple and very good, so she walked over, enjoying the sun's rays.

In the restaurant, she scooted into a single booth, and noticed Puck stood in the small vestibule. He practically took up the whole space, and it made her laugh. She wished he'd sit with her and have a sandwich, but she knew he never would. His job was to protect her, not keep her company.

Coming into the eatery was Axe's uncle, his eyes fixed on hers. Puck was gone, and panic set in. When she needed Puck the most, he'd abandoned his duty. The uncle waited for an available table; the shop was so tiny it only fit twenty people at a time. She scanned the room then breathed a sigh of relief when she spotted Puck stuffed into a booth, watching her.

She ate quickly and scampered out of the shop just as Axe's uncle was shown to a table. Was it a coincidence he was at the restaurant? She hardly thought so. She was grateful Puck was there. It was amazing how much more confident she was with her massive bodyguard watching her back.

A SKY-BLUE LINEN sheath was the only dress she had which showed no cleavage. With simple, low-heeled pumps, she hoped her outfit would keep Palmer's mind on business.

At seven o'clock sharp, Palmer arrived in a gleaming, silver Porsche. Dressed in an expensive camel-colored sports jacket, white pants, and a blue pin-striped shirt, he looked like he'd just stepped out of *GQ*.

Baylee wondered how he afforded his expensive tastes. After all, he was only a government employee.

"You look beautiful," he said as he approached.

She gave him a half-smile in return.

Driving in his Porsche wasn't near as much fun as riding on Axe's Harley, and it wasn't all because of Axe. The space inside the sports car was small, and Baylee missed the rush of wind around her. Thinking about Axe made her chest tighten—he hadn't called her all day.

"Here we are," Palmer said as they pulled up to the restaurant.

Greyston Restaurant overlooked the picturesque Aspen Grove Valley, offering refined seating filled with upscale class and elegance. It was a popular eatery among Pinewood Springs's rich and sophisticated elite.

Seated at a small table for two, Baylee admired the valley covered in wildflowers which glowed with bright-colored butterflies searching for nectar. On the horizon, the mountains rose, jagged rocks dotted with clusters of evergreens; on the base, white-trunked aspen trees softened the sharpness of its angles. Sherbet-pink and orange hues from the descending sun reflected off the crystalline lake.

"What a beautiful setting," Baylee said.

"Not as beautiful as you," Palmer countered.

Ignoring his comment, she looked at the menu, her stomach twisting. She wasn't very hungry, and she wanted a quick dinner so she could go back to the hotel, curl up under the covers, and watch a sappy love story. Out of the corner of her eye, she spotted Puck's colorful tattoos and smiled inwardly, guessing the tough biker hated this part of his assignment.

"Are you from Denver?" he asked.

"Yes, born and raised."

"Which part of town did you grow up in?"

"Southeast Denver. Greenwood Village area."

"Nice."

"Why?"

"I was born and lived in Denver until my parents divorced and my dad moved me up here."

"I didn't know you lived in the city."

"My dad used to be head of the zoning department. He transferred up here, and when he retired, I took over his job. I'm young to be running the department."

"How old were you when you moved?"

"Eleven."

"Well, you've done well for yourself."

"I have. Having a rich dad didn't hurt." He laughed.

I wonder if Axe is with another woman. He wouldn't do that to me, would he? We agreed to be monogamous, but he was so mad at me...

"Baylee? Am I boring you?"

Her cheeks flushed. "No, of course not. I'm just so busy at work with the strip mall, and a few new projects I picked up today. I can't seem to turn my work brain off. Sorry."

He reached over and held her hand, squeezing it. "I get it. You need to slow down. Life isn't all about working. You have to have some fun. I'd like to show you around the area, and we can throw a little fun into the mix. What do you say?"

"I can't commit to anything right now. My whole focus is on the strip mall, and the sooner it gets finished, the easier it will be for me to explore the area with you." She pulled her hand gently away from him. "And have some fun." She gave him her best doe-eyed look.

He swallowed hard then put his hand inside his jacket, taking out a legal-sized envelope. "Here's my contribution to speeding the process along." He handed it to her.

"Thank you," she said as she opened it and inspected the permits. *Perfect. I wish I could leave now.*

"You know, I did this for you, not that loser, Axe."

Her muscles tightened. "He's not a loser."

Palmer shook his head. "You don't know him. I went to high school with him, and he was nothing but trailer trash, a real bum. He thinks he's something just because he belongs to that motorcycle gang." He leaned closer to her. "If it were up to me, I never would've given a zoning permit to an outlaw club."

"I thought it *was* up to you," she said sweetly, biting back her bitterness.

"Normally, it is, but the go-ahead came from higher up. I think the club is keeping hard drugs out of the county, so the officials rewarded them with the permit. I'm not a hundred percent sure, but someone did them a big favor."

"So, I'm thanking the wrong person?"

"No, I made sure you got them fast. Anyway, I'm giving you some friendly advice. Stay away from Axe. He's a jerk who isn't worth spitting on."

"I disagree. I think he's a great guy. It's probably time you left high school behind."

"He charms the ladies then, when they fall for him, he treats them awful. I can see he's charmed you."

"We're friends and colleagues."

"If you're smart, you'll keep it that way."

If I were smart, I'd be having dinner with Axe instead of you.

For the rest of the meal, Palmer told her what a great catch he was, and Baylee feigned interest.

After Palmer signed the credit card receipt, Baylee pushed back her chair, gearing up to leave.

"I thought I'd show you a bit of the landscape," he said.

"In the dark? I'll take a raincheck." She drummed her fingers on the table. "I have a few more hours of work ahead of me, and I'm exhausted." She pretended to yawn.

"That's too bad." He grabbed her hand, brought it to his mouth, and kissed it. "You're a beautiful woman, and I'd like to get to know you better."

She slid her hand out of his and smiled. "Let me make some headway with the strip mall, then we can have some time." *That oughta keep him satisfied for a bit.* Of course, she had no intention of starting anything with him. Axe was the one she wanted. It was her bad luck that she had to go and fall for a bad boy who didn't know what the word *commitment* meant. The man in leather was definitely going to break her heart, she just knew it.

They arrived back at the hotel, and when Palmer leaned over to kiss her, she jerked back, his lips grazing her cheek. *Shit. Puck is watching.* Rolling out of the car, she said, "Thanks, I had a nice time."

"Let me walk you up to your room."

Fat chance.

"I'm good. Thanks again, Palmer."

"I'll call you," he said at her retreating figure.

She acted like she hadn't heard him. Passing through the thick glass doors, she entered the hotel.

Back in her room, she spied through the peephole until she saw Blade take Puck's place. Her heart sank, knowing Blade's presence meant Axe wasn't coming. She bit her lower lip. Axe must've really been mad at her and, in her opinion, for a silly reason. Men were such babies at times. Maybe she should have postponed Palmer for the next night. He still would've given her the permits, but she hadn't wanted to take the chance. She needed to one-up Logan; she let ambition make the decision. *A lesson learned.* She'd hurt Axe's feelings, and he was too proud to ever admit it. What was a business decision for her was a betrayal for Axe. She should've been more sensitive.

Of course, none of this would've happened if she'd stuck with her plan of a casual, summer fling. She'd let one night of random sex turn into casual sex then into an emotionally charged relationship. And then she went and fell for him.

If he doesn't call tomorrow, I'll text him. The mature thing to do would be to call him and tell him goodnight, but she was afraid if she did, he'd be with another woman. Her mind couldn't go there. She wouldn't let it.

After changing into her nightshirt, she turned off the light then cried herself to sleep.

THE MOMENT PUCK entered the great room, Axe motioned him over.

"Anything?" Axe asked.

"Nah. Same as always. Oh, I saw your uncle Max at the restaurant she had lunch at."

Uncle Max? Wasn't he at the hotel last week? His uncle rarely came to town, yet within the past week he'd been at two of the same locations as Baylee. Something was off. What, if any, connection did his uncle have with Baylee? *What the fuck has Uncle Max gotten himself into?* Axe didn't know, but he was sure as hell going to find out.

"What happened with the motherfucker she had dinner with?"

"Nothing. They had dinner."

Axe hated transforming into a pussy in front of any brother, let alone a prospect. He despised that the spell Baylee cast over him made him ask pathetic, stupid questions, but he couldn't fucking help himself. "Did anything happen between them? You know what I mean."

"Not that I could see. He kept coming close to her, but she always pulled back. And he tried to kiss her when he dropped her off, but she pushed him away. Your woman was good." Puck smiled.

"She's not my woman," Axe grumbled.

"Really? Would've guessed she was."

Axe glowered at the prospect; he was out of line with that comment.

"Go." He waved his hand, dismissing Puck, and the prospect ambled away.

In his mind and heart, Baylee was his woman, but he wasn't ready to admit it to the brotherhood, not until he knew how she felt about him. He doubted she wanted anything past the summer. The way he saw it, she wouldn't have gone out with Palmer for dinner if she cared anything for Axe. It was a slap in his face, and it pissed him the hell off. Since she'd broken their date to go out with Palmer for the fucking permits, he'd felt funny, like a small piece of him shattered. He'd never felt like that before. She did wrong, and she should have called or texted him, telling him so.

Axe scanned the great room, checking to see if Rock had come back yet from some club business—the dude owed him a pool game. A busty blonde caught his eye, and she headed his way, her hips swaying, licking her lips. He grabbed his beer and slipped away, snaking through throes of people until he reached his room.

After he finished his beer, he took out a bottle of Jack and poured it into a water glass. His aim was to get good and drunk so he could forget about long, dark hair falling down an elegantly curved back, soft, full lips, and big, hazel eyes that pulled him in every time. He wanted to hear her voice, should call her, but he didn't. This was all new to him. For so long, he'd numbed himself on mindless sex, never giving himself enough time between fucking to think. Up until Baylee, the only one he had to care about was himself. Love and tenderness had been dead inside him for such a long time, he'd forgotten how they felt. He hated change, and this was change in a big way. The wall he'd built around his heart a long time back was crumbling, and he couldn't fucking stop it even if he wanted to.

Chapter Nineteen

BAYLEE TURNED LEFT into the clubhouse parking lot, relieved to have found it after thirty minutes of driving up and down the same stretch of highway. It was only after Banger had guided her on the phone as she drove that she'd discovered it down a narrow road off the highway. It was set so far back that no one could see if from the road.

She'd filed the permits with the court earlier in the morning, but Banger needed to sign a few documents before the construction crew could start breaking ground. Since she'd agreed to go to the clubhouse to see him, her stomach had been rolling and gurgling. She hadn't heard from Axe, and she wondered if he'd be at the club. She hated she'd taken extra time fixing up before leaving the hotel; she'd even curled her hair, and she hated doing that. In her pretty coral dress and strappy wedge-heel sandals, Baylee looked amazing. The high-low hem showed enough leg, and her sleeveless arms were toned and golden from the spray tan she'd had the day before. Finding a salon that offered spray tanning had made her day—a bit of cheer in an otherwise "Axe-less" day.

Her gold bangles jangled as she opened the heavy front door. For a few seconds, she couldn't see anything. Then, as her eyes adjusted to the low lights, she saw men in jeans and leather on bar stools, at a couple of pool tables, and at a few regular tables. The minute she locked eyes with a couple of them, the hoots and wolf-whistles began.

"Fuck, what a hottie," a tall, bearded man said as she passed.

With head down and cheeks flaming, she made her way to the bar, praying Banger wasn't one of the men in the room leering at her. As she waited for the bartender to finish serving some of the men, she surveyed the room and noticed a few women kneeling in front of a few guys, their dicks in the women's mouths. Baylee turned away in embarrassment and focused on a pretty dark-haired, busty woman who wore a scrap of material which barely covered her rounded butt. The woman, hunched over a seated man, was saying something in his ear, her breasts practically in his face. He turned his face away then his dark eyes locked with Baylee's. Covering her mouth with her hand, she watched as Axe leapt out of the chair, knocking the brunette against a tall man who caught her, his arms wrapped around her waist.

Baylee spun around, her back to Axe, a lump forming in her throat. "You." She pointed to the bartender. "Where is Banger's office?" Her breath hitched, her voice cracking on the last word.

He tilted his head toward a hallway. "Last room on the left."

"Hey, aren't you gonna say hi?" Axe asked from behind her.

"You seem busy." Her eyes darted to the brunette straddling the tall man while he sucked her breasts.

Axe looked over. "You mean Rosie? Nah, nothing was going on."

Baylee tossed her hair. "You know, Axe, you *are* a free agent. I mean, what *we're* doing is just for fun. So do whatever the fuck you want, I don't care." She swallowed the lump in her throat, yanked out of his grasp, and headed down the hall. Behind her, Axe's boots stomped on the linoleum as he followed, the jingling of his chains grating on her nerves.

A second after she knocked on the president's door, a voice boomed, "Come in."

Grasping the doorknob, she started to turn it when Axe's arms circled her waist, drawing her in to his chest. He nuzzled her neck and whispered in her ear, "Don't be like this. You know you're the only one for me. I haven't looked at another woman since we met at the wedding."

His breath scorched her neck, and goosebumps pricked her skin. She fell back in to him, enjoying being in his arms again.

"You comin' in?" Banger asked.

Baylee wriggled out of Axe's embrace and opened the door. The president reclined on a brown leather desk chair, his legs on his desk, crossed at the ankles. His blue eyes were filled with surprise when she walked in.

She started to close the door when Banger looked over her shoulder and said, "That you, Axe?"

"Yeah," Axe replied from behind Baylee, entering the room. "Banger, this is our architect, Baylee."

Banger smiled widely, the lines around his eyes crinkling. Nodding, he ran his gaze up and down her body. "Now it all makes sense." He winked at Axe, who grinned like a Cheshire cat.

Baylee resisted rolling her eyes, but if she had a bat she'd knock them both over the head.

The meeting with Banger went better than Baylee had expected. She hadn't anticipated liking the president, but he was an easy-going man, although she was sure he could be hard and ruthless if the situation demanded it. After all, he couldn't be a softie and be the national president of a one-percenter club. He was around forty-five and a nice-looking man. What amazed her most was how solid he was—he was all muscle.

After the meeting, Baylee marched back to the great room, ignoring Axe as he tried to convince her to go to lunch with him. Storming out of the club, she slammed into Puck.

"Sorry," she said as she rubbed her head. The man was powerfully built.

"Didn't see you," Puck muttered, his eyes focused on Axe.

"It's okay." She headed to her car, smiling as she overheard Axe's and Puck's conversation.

"Why the fuck didn't you warn me she was coming to the club?" he asked in a low voice.

"Tried. You didn't pick up."

She glanced at Axe as he scrolled through his phone, then shook his head and cursed. She slid into the driver's seat then zoomed out of the parking lot, giving Axe nothing but a cloud of dust. A few minutes later, she caught sight of Puck in her rear mirror, the chrome on his Harley blinding under the hot, summer rays.

IN THE MIDDLE of the afternoon, as she replayed Axe and Rosie's scene in her mind for the umpteenth time, Baylee decided that she may have jumped to the wrong conclusion. Axe had turned his head when the brunette leaned over him, and he definitely wasn't touching her. Maybe he was telling the truth about her coming on to him, and he was just getting ready to push her off when he saw Baylee. He kept repeating the same story in the deluge of texts he'd been sending her all afternoon— the ones she hadn't answered.

Maybe she'd hear him out and give him the benefit of the doubt. The previous night, Palmer caressed her hand many times, and, to the onlooker, it would seem as though they were an item. Looks could be deceiving, however.

She missed Axe.

"Puck?" she called from her office doorway.

The gruff man looked up from his phone.

"Do you know if Axe is at the clubhouse?"

"He's at the shop. He's closing up for Hawk 'cause him and his ol' lady got shit to do."

"I need the name and address of the shop, please."

A few minutes before six o'clock, Baylee switched off the motor and tried to relax her frazzled nerves. Breathing in deeply, she touched up her lipstick then locked her car door, noticing Puck against his Harley as she walked into the repair shop.

Axe glanced up from the cash register, his head jerking back as he gave her a double-take.

"Hey," he said.

"Hey."

"Did you need something?"

She nodded. "You."

Tingles skated across her skin when he sucked his breath in. His eyes captured hers in a piercing gaze.

Axe came out from behind the counter and yelled to Puck, "Take off."

When he shut the door and locked it, Baylee's heartbeat skipped.

"Want a beer?"

"Sure."

He handed her the cold bottle then bent down and kissed her softly on the lips. "I'm happy you came by." Pleasure lanced through her every pore. "I'm gonna wash up. You can wait in the showroom. It's cooler."

"You sell motorcycles here?"

"It's Hawk's shop, and he has a few restored vintage bikes he sells."

Axe showed her a small room that housed about five motorcycles. She spotted Axe's bike. "You selling yours?"

"Fuck no. I like to keep it in when it's hot out. I'll be back after I wash up." He padded away.

"Is anyone else here?"

"No. I closed up. It's just you and me. Why? You wanna get kinky?" He chuckled.

"Just wondering."

"I won't be long."

Baylee settled down on the small leather couch and picked up a biker magazine, flipping through the pages absentmindedly. She wanted to do something unexpected when Axe came in. She always wanted to be adventurous with the men in her life, but whenever she'd tried, it wasn't their thing. They'd look at her as if she were a deviant, but with Axe, there were no bounds. He brought out her nasty, sexy side, and she loved him for it.

Without thinking, she hurriedly stripped down to her ivory lace bra and panties, then went over to Axe's bike and swung her leg over, straddling it. Her body tingled like a thousand live wires, and her heart thumped against her chest as she waited for him to come in. She'd never been this bold in taking the initiative before. Sucking in her breath, she hoped she didn't chicken out before he came in.

"Fuckin' hot," Axe said thickly.

Since his bike faced out, she hadn't seen him come in. All of a sudden, she felt shy and foolish. Baylee swung her leg over the seat, but before she could get off the bike, Axe was all over her, his hands wandering over her body as he seized her mouth with his, his tongue devouring hers. It was as though he was starving and she was his sustenance.

"Get back on the bike," he said harshly.

Baylee swung her leg back over and Axe came to her side, massaging her tits while he licked her neck. She threw her head back as he kissed and sucked before his mouth trailed up to her ears. She moaned and tilted her head sideways as Axe ran his lips down her neck to her shoulder, lightly biting and sucking her delicate skin while he continued to massage her breasts. Each nip, lick, and kiss scorched her skin, and her body hummed with desire.

"I love your skin, so soft in my hands," he whispered between kisses.

With her eyes closed, Baylee let herself feel the way her skin pebbled while he gave her soft bites. The hairs on the nape of her neck stood up when he blew against the wet trail his tongue left on her shoulder.

Axe's mouth came up to her face, his tongue tracing her jaw line as he cupped her breasts and squeezed them. She leaned back on her arms, making her chest stand out. He groaned and his mouth seized hers hungrily as his tongue charged in, sending shivers of desire racing through her. Leaving her lips, his mouth seared a path down her neck to the swell of her breasts. With a ferocity that took her breath away, he shoved down her lace bra, revealing her fleshy tits. He sucked in his breath as his gaze lingered on them, the skin around her nipples puckering from the anticipation of what was to come.

"Your tits are perfect. I fuckin' love touching them, and I can't wait to fuck them with my hard cock."

Baylee buried her hand in his thick hair, her mound damp from his filthy mouth. She loved a dirty talker, and Axe had a knack for it. Each time he'd say something dirty, her pussy tightened and an aching, sweet sensation sent quivers up her body. This biker knew how to make her burn.

Pushing his head between her tits, Axe chuckled against her skin as he kneaded them, pinching and flicking her nipples.

"Harder," she said hoarsely.

"That's what I love, babe."

His sucking turned into biting as his teeth clamped down on her stiffened red buds, pain mixed with pleasure shooting through her. She leaned back further, the thin layer of skin stretching tautly. As he pinched her nipples hard, he sucked and bit the delicate flesh around them. Each bite electrified her body, and she feared she'd orgasm while he played with her.

Gliding one hand down past her belly, he rubbed her pussy through her panties while he continued kissing, biting, and sucking her tits. Moving her panties to one side, he caressed her glistening sex then put his fingers between her swollen lips and stroked up and down. Bending at the waist, he opened her lips wide and licked her. With her head back, lips parted, a guttural moan escaped Baylee's throat. She then held her breath and listened over the pulse booming in her ears, savoring his rasping sounds as he licked, sucked, and kissed her.

"Fuck, babe. Your pussy is so hot and wet. And its taste is intoxicating. You're so sweet."

As he tasted her, his tongue swirling around her clit, he continued playing with her tits. She swayed her hips, trying to rub against the Harley's black leather seat. Axe raised his hand and put his finger, drenched with her juices, in her mouth.

"Taste your sweetness."

She drew his finger deeper in her mouth, sucking it wildly, then looked down and met his lustful gaze as he watched her lick herself off his finger.

"That's fuckin' hot, babe."

He withdrew his digit then shoved back inside her with such force her ass jumped up from the seat. She whimpered, watching his glimmering finger shove in and out of her. When his tongue flicked over her clit, a thousand jolts of pleasure erupted in her, and her body stiffened then quivered as waves of ecstasy washed over her. Not able to talk or move, she rested on the seat, her head back, legs splayed open, panting harshly. Axe stood up and plunged his hot tongue through her parted lips.

"You're so fuckin' sexy. I love watching you come."

Regaining some sense of normalcy, Baylee pushed up and drew Axe to her, hugging him tightly, her red nipples rubbing against his chest.

"You are awesome. I've never felt like this with a man before. I love the way you touch me. Now, I want you to fuck me."

"I can't wait to fuck your wet pussy. I know your tight cunt loves my big cock filling it up."

The things he said would make any decent woman blush, but Baylee was thrilled to hear them. They made her hot and horny, and her body tingled as she thought of him pounding into her.

He helped her off the bike, then pushed her drenched panties down. She stood naked before him and he stared, devouring her with his gaze. She pushed his t-shirt over his head then unzipped his pants, his hardness jumping out. He discarded his jeans and boxers and they stood together, grinding against each other, feeling naked skin against naked skin.

"Let me help you on my bike," he rasped.

Axe seated Baylee on his Harley as though she were going to ride it, then placed her hands on the handlebars. "Just relax," he whispered as he gently kissed the side of her face.

She turned sideways and saw him take out a condom from his wallet, rolling the sheath over his long, thick dick. Her sex clenched when she felt his hands on her back. His touch was electrifying, and the jolts it sent through her body were intense.

"I'm gonna pick up your legs and pull them back. Don't be afraid. You're not gonna fall. I got you."

Baylee nodded as she held her breath and looked over her shoulder.

Axe stood behind the bike, then reached on either side of her. He picked up her legs, extending them backward over the end of the motorcycle. Supporting her back end by holding her legs up, he moved his dick over her slick pussy before he entered her.

The feel of having almost full body contact with the bike turned Baylee on, as did his big dick.

"I love having you in me, filling me up. It feels so good."

"I love being in your tight pussy. I'm gonna fuck you good and hard."

He pulled out then slammed back in. Each time he thrust, her clit rubbed against the leather seat, sending currents of pleasure through her. Soon, her body vibrated with liquid fire as she shattered into thousands of glowing stars, soaring to a shuddering ecstasy while she screamed in pleasure. Axe began to pant, and she felt him go rigid as her pussy walls clamped around his dick.

"Fuck," he groaned, thrusting a few more times inside her.

Baylee clenched, milking his cock for every last drop. He leaned over and kissed her ass cheeks then let her legs down slowly, guiding her into a sitting position on his bike. When he helped her off, her legs felt like rubber, and she fell into him. Catching her, he leaned against his bike and gathered her in his arms, holding her close while he stroked her hair.

"Fuckin' awesome," he murmured into her tresses. "Damn, I won't be able to ride again without thinking how hot you looked while I fucked you on this seat." He patted the seat he leaned against.

"It was amazing. For me, it was the first time on a motorcycle."

"Me, too."

"Are you joking?"

He shook his head. "There's no way in hell I was gonna fuck a chick on my bike. No woman gets on my bike unless I ask them to."

"I didn't know. I'm sorry."

He laughed from his belly. "Sorry? I'm sure the fuck not. I've been fantasizing fucking you on my bike since I met you. I wanted it." He kissed her tenderly on the lips.

Surges of joy filled her, and her stomach fluttered in a good way. "I'm glad we shared this together."

"Me, too. You're special to me." He embraced her tighter. "Are you cold? You're shivering."

"A little. The air conditioning is really cold."

"Let's get dressed and get some dinner."

"Sounds good. I haven't eaten all day. I'm starving."

She picked up her clothes and went to the bathroom to freshen up.

EARL'S RESTAURANT WAS known for its juicy prime rib dinners, so when Axe suggested it, Baylee readily agreed. She was ravenous, and a juicy prime rib, a salad and baked potato sounded divine.

They elected to dine on the patio, the heat of the day dissipating with the advance of the setting sun. The restaurant sat atop a hill, and the view was spectacular—the Rocky Mountains towering high in the sky, the verdant valley below teeming with wildlife, and the majestic fir forests.

As she and Axe enjoyed their dinner, her phone pinged.

Unknown: *All the bodyguards in the world won't keep you safe.*

Baylee blanched, her mouth quivering as she stared at the message. "Who is it?" Axe asked.

Opening her mouth, no sound came forth. Shaking her head, she handed her phone to him.

"What's up?" he said as he read the message, his face reddening. "What the fuck?" he hissed.

Axe: *Listen fucker, you're a dead man.*

Unknown: *You think you scare me? Your little cunt is first, then you're next. Enjoy your prime rib dinners.*

Axe leapt up, knocking over the glasses on the table. Stalking around the patio, he surveyed the valley, then went inside to search, leaving

Baylee alone with her thoughts.

A few minutes later, he returned and handed her the phone.

"Fucker could be anywhere, peering at us through high-powered binoculars," Axe seethed. He slammed his fist on the table, causing Baylee to jump. "I've gotta find this bastard. The asshole has just declared war."

The tremors started from her arms and ran all the way down to her toes—she couldn't stop them. She hugged her arms, but they racked her body until she was one vibrating mess.

Axe pulled her into his embrace, tucking her hair behind her ears as he whispered, "It's gonna be okay. I won't let anyone hurt you," over and over in her ear.

She clung to him, his soothing voice calming her. He held her for a long time, and the fear seeped out of her. Cupping his chin, she stretched up and kissed him. "Thanks."

"Never need to thank me for helping you." He kissed her back, harder and deeper.

"You know what?" she muttered against his soft skin.

"Hmm?"

"I've decided I can't play the victim anymore. This psycho gets off on my fear, and I can't live like this. I have to put the fear aside so I can concentrate and let my mind bring the memory of him forward. I can't end up like my mother." She rubbed her neck, pushing the fear down which threatened to rise again.

"That's my woman. In this world, you gotta fight. You can't wait to be trampled, you gotta do the trampling first. Besides your bosses, who knows you're in Pinewood Springs?"

She looked up, racking her brain to remember who else she told about her summer gig. "Claudia. She's a very good friend of mine, and she has the hots for Logan, but that's not important. I know, TMI."

"Who else?"

"My dad, my therapist, and that's about it. I didn't tell too many people. I don't have a lot of friends since I work so much. That's all I can think of. Maybe my dad or Claudia told some people?"

"It's someone you know. Just have to figure out who. No way this shit is random."

"The anniversary of my mother's death is soon," she said softly. "I have a sick feeling the killer is waiting until then to strike. I'm scared, but I don't want to be a victim."

Axe held her close. "I promise you I'm gonna find the sonofabitch and make sure he pays for every tear he's made you shed, and for every dark shadow he's planted in your brain."

An hour later, they were back at the hotel. Baylee searched the lobby for Puck, but he was nowhere to be seen. Joy filled her.

"You coming up?" she asked as she waited for the elevator.

He nuzzled her hair. "Yeah. I'm spending the night. You good with that?" She nodded. "And not on some fucking couch."

She giggled. "I gave up on that plan a while back."

When she opened her door, she scanned the room. She'd fallen into the habit of searching it ever since someone had broken in. Sure no one unwanted had come in, she pivoted and snaked her arms around Axe's neck.

"I'm glad you're here."

"Me, too, babe. I belong here with you in my arms."

"You're sweet." She kissed his chin. "I'm beat. Long day with a lot of emotions. I'm gonna change."

When she came out of the bathroom, Axe was already under the covers, the TV barely audible.

"Come here, sweetheart."

She molded herself against him, his arms holding her tightly. He ran his fingers through her hair as he watched the TV screen, the lights flickering in the dark room. Each time he stroked her hair, her limbs loosened, and her mind recalled a comforting, loving memory from her past—her mother brushing her hair before bedtime.

Baylee snuggled deeper in to Axe, content to be back in his arms.

THE MORNING SUN spilled into the rooms, forcing Baylee's eyelids open. She squinted against the intruder, too lazy to leave the warmth of Axe's body to close the curtains.

He yawned. "Fuck, it's bright in here."

"I forgot to pull the curtains last night. Sorry." She buried her head against him.

"What's the time?"

"Too early," she said into his side.

Chuckling, he rose from the bed and grabbed his phone. "Damn. I gotta go. We got church."

Peeking out from between the fingers over her eyes, she asked, "You want me to relieve that?"

He squinted, looking down. "Would love it, but I gotta go. I'm already gonna be late, and I'm not even dressed."

"Not into quickies?"

"With you, babe? Never." He hovered over her, bending down to kiss her.

"What do you want for breakfast? I'm going to order room service. I can't figure out the coffee machine."

He laughed. "The coffee machine has you stumped? Nothing for me. I don't have time. I gotta haul ass."

As he showered, she ordered a pot of black coffee. Axe came out with a white towel tucked around his waist, small drops from his wet hair trickling down his bronzed chest. Baylee rubbed against him and licked the drops off him. A growl passed through his lips.

"You keep teasing me and I'm gonna have to spank you, babe."

"That's what I'm planning on."

"Fuck, you make me want to skip church and spend the day fucking you."

"Sounds good."

He yanked her head back and slammed his mouth to hers, their tongues twisting and lashing together. With a frustrated sigh, he pulled back. "Later on, okay? Fuck. You don't know how this is killin' me."

She feigned a pout, then sat on the chair, tucking her legs under her. "When you were in the shower, I was thinking about all the crap that's happening to me, and I decided to call the police. I have the text messages, so I have the proof now."

Putting his jeans on, Axe stopped midway. "Are you crazy? No fuckin' badges."

"Why not? Isn't that what people do? They call the police when someone threatens their life."

"We don't. We take care of our own." He zipped up his jeans.

"I'm not a part of your world. I'll feel better if I call the police."

Axe gave her a hard look. "You are so damned stubborn, woman. The badges aren't gonna do shit. You have to either be attacked or killed before they do anything. In my world, we don't sit around and wait, we act."

Baylee averted her gaze, shrugging. She wanted to believe he could make everything all right with her, but she'd still feel better if the cops were involved. After she arrived at the office, she'd call the police—it couldn't hurt.

"After church, I got some work to do. I'll send Puck over." Axe scrubbed the side of his face. "Fuck. I forgot about you gettin' to work."

"I'm sure I'll be okay driving alone. It's only ten minutes away."

"A lot of shit can happen in ten minutes." He tapped his fingers against his lips. "I'll have to be late for church. I'll send a text."

Baylee watched him, her eyes lit with an inner glow.

"Don't just sit there smiling, woman. Go get ready. I'm gonna catch enough shit for not being on time."

Twenty-five minutes later, the Harley jerked to a stop.

"Thanks for taking me." Baylee gave him a quick kiss on the cheek.

"I'm making sure you get to your office okay." He held her elbow and tugged her into the building.

When they walked into her office, an arrangement of wildflowers and baby's breath in a country basket greeted her.

"Where the fuck did those come from?" Axe asked as he surveyed the room.

She saw his eyes land on the bouquet of roses she'd placed on the table a few days before.

She shrugged, set her briefcase on the desk, and pulled out her laptop from its case. As she plugged it in, she watched Axe open the card out of the corner of her eye.

"He wants in your pussy so bad, the piece of shit," he gritted.

"Who?"

"Mr. Fuckface Palmer Rodgers, the motherfucker."

She blushed.

"Why're you turning red? You want something with this asshole?" Axe's expression tightened.

Shaking her head, she said, "No. I already told you I didn't, like, a dozen times. I'm not interested in him. It's just that a girl likes to receive pretty flowers. At least, I do. It makes me smile. Nothing more than that."

"Is that all it takes to get into your panties?"

"No one's getting into my panties unless I let him and, for now, I'm letting you." She smiled sweetly and looked at her computer screen.

Axe clenched his jaw. "You got the permits, so no reason to see the asshole again."

Looking up from her keyboard, she leaned forward, her elbows on the desk. "Is that a request or an order?"

"Take it whatever way you want, but your contact with the motherfucker ended today. I told you before, I don't like sharing, especially when it comes to things that belong to me."

Before she could answer, he was at her side, pulling her to her feet. He took hungry possession of her mouth, his tongue slipping in through her parted lips. She moaned and leaned in to him, her arms circling his neck.

He pulled back, looked intently into her eyes, and whispered, "And you, sweetheart, *definitely* belong to me. Don't ever doubt it."

Then he was gone. Baylee stood in the doorway, staring at him as he swaggered along the corridor. Before he exited the lobby, he looked over his shoulder and winked at her, put on his sunglasses, and left the building.

Baylee touched her lips, the intense current that was always between them hot under her fingertips. Her insides were still tingling from his kiss and declaration that she was his. That was what he said, wasn't it? He said she belonged to him. *Do I* want *to belong to him? Hell yeah, I do.*

She smiled then looked at the flowers, wishing they were from Axe. She picked up the phone and buzzed Tina.

"Would you like to have the flowers in my office? I'm allergic to them."

"The beautiful ones that came this morning?"

"Yes."

"I'd love to. I'll be right down."

"You can also have the roses."

"Thank you."

Focusing her attention back on her computer, Baylee smiled when her phone pinged, anxious to see what Axe had written.

Unknown: *You cannot escape me.*

Baylee's stomach shot to the floor. She glanced around the room, went over to the window, and looked out. Everything seemed normal, like any other day.

Baylee: *Stop it!*

Unknown: *Why? Aren't you enjoying our little game?*

Baylee: *I don't remember anything. My mind is still foggy. Leave me alone!*

Unknown: *It's not that simple.*

She sat at her desk, stunned. The psycho enjoyed taunting her, and he was trying to drive her over the edge.

Unknown: *You look pretty in your white dress.*

Baylee threw the phone across her desk, glancing down at her white linen dress. He wanted her to know he was aware of her every move, and it didn't matter if Puck or Axe were with her—he was in control.

Baylee picked up the phone and called the police, who basically told her what Axe had—there was nothing they could do at that point. No crime had been committed and, as far as she knew, it could be a crackpot with nothing better to do than taunt her.

Axe had been right—the police weren't going to help her. She'd rely on Axe and his club, and on herself, to beat the killer. With tightened fists and a set jaw, Baylee agreed with Axe.

The asshole just declared war.

CHAPTER TWENTY

A XE SAT ON the ripped vinyl chair and listened to the squeaky click of the oscillating fan on top of a scratched filed cabinet. The portly gentleman behind the paper-strewn desk spit as he spoke on the phone, his fingers drumming on the desk every few seconds.

The man looked at Axe and rolled his eyes while he pointed at the phone, shaking his head. Axe tilted his chin. He'd hoped this guy could help him. Cara said she used him for most of her cases, that he was a top-notch private investigator. Coming to the PI's office was huge for Axe since he didn't like asking for help outside the club, but he figured he needed someone experienced in investigations. The moment the killer revealed he knew Axe was involved, that was when Axe decided to bring in someone who wasn't in the Insurgents.

The slam of the receiver startled Axe, and he looked up into the man's crinkled face. The PI extended his stubby-fingered hand. "Dean Wesley." His voice sounded like he'd been smoking for a long time.

"Axe." He shook back, then wiped his hands on his jeans.

"Sorry for the sweat. Fuckin' air conditioning never works. All that damn fan is doing is circulating hot air." Dean wiped his face with a tissue. Reclining in his chair, he smiled. "What can I do for ya?"

"I need some information about someone who's stalking my woman."

"Okay. Do you know who it is?"

"I'm sure it's the fucker who killed her mother years ago."

Dean whistled. "Was he caught and released?"

"Never caught. It's a cold case, but he's in Pinewood scaring the shit outta her. He's aiming to kill her."

Axe explained the whole situation to Dean, who took notes on a legal pad. After he was finished, he looked at the PI and asked, "Can you help with this? Cara said you're gold."

Dean laughed as he wiped the sweat from his face again. "She's a nice lady. Pretty, too. I can try to find out who he is, ask some questions. He must've had someone do his dirty work at the hotel. I want to find out who let someone in your girlfriend's room, so I'll need to get in there. Chances are high the room's been bugged."

"I've thought the same thing. I'm one step ahead, though. I changed Baylee's room."

"Good move. I still want in there. I can stop by today. Is there any chance your girl can stay at your place?"

"She won't go for it, but if things get too intense, I'll insist she stay at the clubhouse."

"No doubt the stalker is using burner phones to contact her. They're hard to trace 'cause a person doesn't need to sign anything to get the phone. A true cash-and-carry transaction. Everyone thinks calls from pre-paid can't be traced, but they can. Calls made on burners are generally transmitted over existing networks. I can check the records of the towers around the areas when the correspondences were received." Dean finished his bottled water in one long drink.

"Cara's on board with getting whatever you need."

"She's a great gal. Pretty, too, but I already said that, didn't I?"

Axe nodded.

"Cara can get the subpoenas I'll need. I'll keep you updated, but since this guy probably has someone tailing you—"

"No one's following me. Believe me, I'd know it."

"Yeah, you coming from the biker world gives you a real edge here. The guy's probably got some high-powered binoculars. It's best we meet away from Pinewood."

"You can come to the clubhouse. It's secluded, and we know exactly what's down."

"Sounds like a plan. Is your girlfriend gonna pay for the services? I ask for fifty percent down, and the balance after the job's done."

"I'm picking it up," Axe said.

They finalized the price for the investigation, and Axe left the office. Having Dean Wesley on the job eased some of the pressure he'd been feeling the past few days. When he sat in the PI's stuffy, suffocating office, he realized he couldn't lose Baylee. He wanted to keep her close to him, but he didn't know how she felt about him. In less than five weeks, she'd no longer need to be in Pinewood Springs; she'd be able to work virtually from Denver. But Axe didn't want to think about Baylee leaving.

As he straddled his Harley, ready to switch on the ignition, his phone rang. Unable to see the screen because of the sun's glare, he answered.

"Yep."

"Hi, Michael. This is your mother."

He cursed under his breath. "What do you want?"

"I want to know how you are and—"

"I'm good. I'm in a hurry. I have something I gotta do."

"We never talk. You can give me a few minutes."

"Go ahead."

"I'd love to see you. You rarely come around anymore. I'm getting married—"

"What'll he be? Number six?"

"I just had bad luck. You'll like him. He's so good to me, and he's rich. His name is—"

"Save it, I don't wanna know. I gotta go."

"Wait! You're coming to the wedding, aren't you?"

"No."

"You *have* to come. You're my only child, and I want you there."

"It's bullshit, and I'm not wasting my time. Gotta go."

"You have to come. I could die, and then you'd be sorry you didn't come."

"Don't lay that guilt trip on me. I'm not a kid anymore, it doesn't work."

"Okay, but remember that you and me are all we have. You have my blood in you. We're all we got." She sniffled. "Please? I want my son with me at my wedding. Can you just think about it?"

Axe clenched his jaw. Whenever his mom wanted him to do something, she'd start the 'family blood' shit, and if that didn't work, she'd throw in some sniffles and tears. *That* got to him every time. He should've just told her to fuck off, that she'd been a selfish, shitty mom and he was done, but he never did. He'd freeze her out for a time, but he'd never cut ties with her completely. He couldn't do it.

"Okay, I'll *think* about it," he gritted. "Will you let me get off the fuckin' phone now?"

She chortled and blew her nose. "Thank you, honey. You've made me so happy. I thought it'd be nice if you, me, and Stephen go out to dinner before the wedding. I want you to meet him."

"No way. You got me thinking about coming to your hook-up. Don't push it. You know it isn't gonna last, anyway."

"This time, it's different."

"I've heard that five times before. Whatever. Do you know where Uncle Max has been? I've been trying to get a hold of him for a couple of weeks."

"I saw him the other day. He told me he has to go out of town on some business, but he'd be back in time for my wedding."

"What business?"

"He didn't say. Why?"

"I need to talk to him. Gotta go."

"I know. I'll see you at the wedding in two weeks. Bye, dear."

He grunted then hung up. *Fuck! If I go to the sham wedding, at least I can talk to Uncle Max.* The more Axe thought about his uncle being where Baylee was, the more convinced he was that the man was involved. Axe had done the math, and his uncle was in Denver around the same time Baylee's mother was killed.

HAWK RECEIVED THE confirmation from their brothers down south: the Skull Crushers were dealing meth in Insurgents' territory. Steel had told Hawk they were starting shit on his turf in Puebla, and he and his brothers were preparing for a war.

"We think there's only three of them. It's like they're scouting the area to see how far they can go," Banger said.

"They didn't get far last night. I threw them outta Dream House then me, Rags, and Jax beat the shit out of 'em." Rock put his fist in the air as his brothers congratulated him and the other two for keeping scum out of the gentleman's club the Insurgents owned.

"They need to be taught respect," Banger said, his blue eyes blocks of ice.

The other members nodded and sounded their agreement.

"We need to show them to stay the fuck outta Insurgents' territory. These fuckers are the tip of the iceberg. We gotta stop it now. I'm sending Jerry, Axe, Puck, PJ, Rags, and Chas to confront them tonight. Make sure they can never do this shit again."

After church, the brothers shuffled out to the great room to eat the barbecue buffet Banger had brought in from the club's restaurant.

"How's it goin' with the sexy architect?" Chas asked.

"Fine, but some fucker is doing some bad shit to her. I'm trying to find out who the fuck he is. No way I'm letting him hurt my woman," Axe explained.

The minute he said "my woman," he regretted it; Chas, Jerry, and Jax stared at him, then laughed.

"Fuck, never thought I'd see the day when the mighty pussy-chaser would fall. Welcome to the club, brother," Jax said.

Axe brooded as they teased him.

"What happened to you tellin' Chas and Jax they were fucking stupid to take old ladies? You've worn the stud title too long. Now us single brothers can take over." Jerry poked Axe in the ribs.

Axe glared at him. "At least I'm hot after a woman I can have. You're so fucked up over Kylie that you can't even talk right when she's in the room."

"You're fucked. No way," Jerry protested.

Axe tilted his head back and glanced at the others. "Am I crazy, or does he get a boner every time Kylie's around?"

They all laughed. Jerry slammed his shot glass on the bar, shattering it.

Jax patted his back. "Lighten up, dude. We're having fun fuckin' with you, but you must know you're asking for a whole lot of trouble if you get your dick anywhere near Kylie."

"Banger will kill your ass," Chas said.

Jerry wiped the blood oozing from his cut finger. "Kylie's hot, but she's too innocent. I like women who know what the fuck they're doin'."

"Who says she doesn't? She's on her own at college, and I hear the parties can be pretty wild," Axe teased.

Jerry stiffened. "Shut the fuck up. No one's messin' with Kylie at college."

Jax cuffed Jerry's shoulder. "Maybe *she's* messin' with someone." He wiggled his eyebrows.

Jerry shoved Jax who, smile gone, puffed up his chest and moved into Jerry's space. "What the fuck?"

Jerry, tense and rigid, said, "Just shut the fuck up 'bout Kylie. She's not a whore. She's not doin' shit at college."

Axe smiled. "Sounds like you got some personal information. You wouldn't be checking on her, would you?"

Jerry pushed away from the bar. "I'll see you all tonight." He stormed off.

"Fuck, he *has* been stalking her. Well, I'll be damned." Axe took a long pull of his beer while the other guys snickered.

"He has it bad." Chas shook his head. "He's also got a death wish."

"Last thing I'd wanna do is fuck with Banger." Axe popped the top off his beer.

"Now, tell us what's goin' on with *your* woman, and how we can help," Jax said.

Axe clapped Chas and Jax on the back. "This shit started when Baylee was eight years old…"

CHAPTER TWENTY-ONE

STANDING IN THE alleyway, smoking joints, the Insurgents brothers cussed up a storm as they waited for the three Skull Crushers to show up.

"They're late. When they get here, I get the first punch." PJ inhaled deeply. "Fuck, this is good stuff."

"You know we only cultivate the best," Chas said as he lit up another roach.

Everyone stiffened and grew silent as a slight clack on the concrete reverberated against the brick walls. Rock stealthily crept toward the alley's entrance then hid behind a commercial dumpster as a lone figure entered the alley. When he passed Rock, he stopped and surveyed the area then moved on. Before he passed the second dumpster, Rock was on him, pounding him to the ground, his knee pushing into the man's back.

"Where are the other fuckers?" Rock slammed the guy's face into the pavement.

"No. Stop. It's me, Rodney. Stop."

Axe came over and, with his boot's toe, he turned the man's face sideways. Even though it was a dark, moonless night, Axe could see the blood flowing from Rodney's face. In the darkness of night, it appeared as misshapen birth marks.

"That you, Rodney?" Axe asked.

"Yeah. Get him off me. I can't fuckin' breathe."

Rock jumped up, his thick fists gripping Rodney's shirt, taking him up with him as he rose. "Didn't know it was you," he said when he set Rodney on his feet.

"What the hell you doing here?" Rags asked as he and the others approached the wiry man.

"Came to update you on the Skull Crushers." He darted his eyes from one member to the other.

Rodney had been an informant for several years for the Insurgents. He was a pothead, and he ran in junkie circles. If someone new was dealing in Pinewood Springs, he'd know it. In exchange for information, the brothers papered his wallet and gave him prime weed. They had a working relationship, but Rodney was never a part of the club. If he betrayed them, they'd slit his throat in a second.

"So, what's the word?" Axe asked.

"They split. They got word you were aiming for them, so they got out. Went back south, as I heard it. They had a few meth deals, but they skipped."

"Who told them?" Rock leaned down and put his face an inch away from Rodney's. "It wouldn't have been you, would it?"

"No. No way. Absolutely no way." Rodney stepped back from Rock, bumping into Chas's strong chest.

"You wouldn't be fuckin' us around, would you?" Chas stared at him. "You didn't tip them off for a few baggies of crystal, did you?"

"Fuck no. Shit, guys, we go back some years. I never did you no wrong. No way. No fuckin' way. I heard they split from some junkies who wanted more crystal. They said they weren't around, but would let them know when they'd be back. I'm cool, guys. I didn't do you no wrong. I swear."

"He's cool," Jax said as Rodney's shoulders slumped.

"If we find out you're shittin' us, you're a dead man." Rock punched Rodney in the kidneys.

The man howled and doubled over. Axe threw five crisp one hundred dollar bills along with a paper bag filled with quality marijuana. "You did good, man. Later."

The members shuffled out of the alley, their boots clicking on the pavement. As they rounded the corner, Axe saw Rodney, bowled over, collecting his pay and weed.

BAYLEE WAS A welcome sight to Axe as she stepped aside and let him pass into her new room. It resembled her old one except it was reversed, the bed on the left. He drew her flush to him, loving the way her tits crushed against him. He kissed her, savoring the minty taste in her mouth.

"You look beat," she said while she stroked his back.

"I am, babe."

He led her to the bed, pulling her down with him as he sat. Axe kicked off his boots then stretched out on the bed, tugging her close to him. Twisting a few strands of silky hair around his finger, he kissed the top of her head.

"I see you're settled into your new room. How was your day?" he asked.

"Okay."

"No more flowers?"

"No. I gave the flowers to Tina, and when Palmer called to see if I received them, I asked him not to send any more."

He squeezed her hard, trying to bring her as close as he could to him without suffocating her. "I'm glad."

She traced the outlines of the tattoos on his arm. "I fell asleep a couple of hours ago. I had another nightmare."

He brought his lips to the top of her head and asked, "Same as the others?"

"Yes and no. No in that I could see the killer's face clearly, but it looked like a mixture of Palmer, Bob, Gary, and you."

"Me?"

"Yeah. Crazy, huh?"

"Maybe there are features in each of us that the killer had. Like my hair color, you know?"

"Maybe. Bob has green eyes, so maybe that's why. Maybe I am crazy. Maybe whoever is tormenting me found out about my mom from archived newspaper clippings and gets his jollies doing this. I don't know."

"Believe me, babe, you're not crazy. I'll get to the bottom of it."

"Or maybe it *is* the killer, and he's trying to drive me insane. Give me another nervous breakdown like I had years ago. When I had my breakdown, all the progress I'd made to that point disappeared—all clarity was gone. The killer has my journal, and he knows I'm remembering, clearer than I ever had. Maybe that's the point, to make me have a meltdown so my mind returns to darkness."

Axe squeezed her. "Don't worry, I've got your back. You're my woman. I'm not gonna let anything happen to you."

"Why would you do that for me?"

"Because that's the way the Insurgents do it. They take care of their own."

"Don't you think we're rushing into all this too fast? We're having fun together, but I don't expect you to risk your life helping me. I do appreciate all you've done for me, and just being here for me, helps a lot. You know, we don't *really* know each other."

"I know enough. Some people spend years with each other, and they don't really know each other. There's no fuckin' way I'm letting some asshole hurt you." He chuckled. "And don't worry about me, I can take good care of myself. No fucker's gonna take me out." He pulled her in closer to him, her stiff body resisting. "Baylee, what the hell's going on in your head?"

She cast her eyes downward, then shook her head. "Nothing."

Lifting her head up with his thumb under her chin, Axe stared intently at her. "You're not alone. I'm here, and the brothers are willing to help, if it comes to that. And this shit about not knowing each other means nothing." A long breath blew through his parted lips. "From the first time I touched you, I felt a connection to you. I'd never fuckin' felt something like that with a woman. It was like a spark, like static electricity. It fuckin' freaked me out. I know you felt it too."

Baylee nodded.

"That means something. I don't know what, but I feel it when I'm with you. So don't be tellin' me not to take care of you. I'll always have your back."

"I know. I'm just freaking out about stuff. This whole situation with the killer has put me on edge with everything. It's like I no longer have any control, he knows everything about me, and I know nothing about him. I'm not even sure if he has green eyes or a scar, they could just be figments of my dreams. Since all this crap started, I think about my mom all the time. I miss her like crazy." Her voice cracked.

Axe didn't know what to say. He wished he could eliminate the sonofabitch who was causing her so much pain. She was also freaking out about them, and he couldn't blame her because it scared the crap out of him. He didn't plan on this, and he'd never have guessed that he'd have opened his heart to another woman again. Once he took care of the killer, she'd be less nervous. He didn't want her to walk out of his life, but he was also unsure on how they could make what they had work. *It's so complicated. I shoulda left it at casual, but how could I? She's fuckin' amazing.*

Axe held her in his arms, stroking her upper back, and with each stroke his desire for her grew. Each time he came near her, he wanted her more than he'd ever wanted another woman in his life, and if it was the last thing he did, he'd keep her safe. In a short time, she'd become very important to him, and he wasn't about to lose her to anyone or anything.

Baylee's heavy breathing filled the room.

"Baylee?" he whispered, nudging her a little.

"Uh?" she said groggily.

"You sleeping, babe?"

"Took a sleeping pill a half hour before you came. I need to sleep without the nightmares."

Soon, she was fast asleep, and Axe's hard-on would have to wait.

Shit.

He turned off the lights and watched the boxing match on television.

THE FOLLOWING MORNING, Axe woke up with a raging case of morning wood, hornier than hell. Reaching over, he patted the mattress. He rolled on his side and stared at the empty space. Thinking Baylee was in the bathroom, he shimmied out of his boxers and waited for her to come back to bed.

The minutes ticked away, and Axe padded over to the bathroom door to see if she was feeling all right. A sudden coldness hit to the core as he shuffled back a couple of steps. Dashing over to the nightstand, he took out his phone and called Baylee.

"Don't be mad at me," she said.

"Where the fuck are you?"

"I'm fine. I went for a drive. I had to have some time to myself."

"What the fuck does that mean?" Axe ground his teeth.

"Everything is a jumble of emotions for me right now. I feel like I'm on a roller coaster speeding down hills and curves, never able to just stop and think."

"I thought we resolved this last night. Come back home. Do you realize the danger you're putting yourself in? Fuck, Baylee, you're alone. Damnit!"

"And that's the point—I'm alone. I don't have anyone around. I need this for a while."

"You may not be as alone as you think. Hell, if you wanted to be alone today, you should've told me. I was gonna tell you last night, but you fell asleep. I've gotta help a buddy of mine who's doing a charity poker run. I'll be gone for about four days. I got you covered with Puck and Blade. You'll have four days of alone time."

"I'll have my bodyguards. I just wanted to feel free, that's all. I needed to think about us, too. I'm not sure how the 'casual sex' plan went so off-kilter."

" 'Cause we found out we really like each other. That we're connected. Were you listening to anything I said last night? Fuck."

"I feel like I have to regroup, that's all. At work, I've done a half-assed job on the project because I'm distracted by you."

"And that's a bad thing?" He laughed.

"It can be. I want to make partner. I just have to regroup."

"Regroup, my ass. What we have blows my mind, too, but I'm not running away from it. I thought I'd be the last person who'd be tied to one woman, and I'm getting plenty of shit about it from the brothers. As far as your career, I'm not stopping you from your goal of partnership."

"I think about you all the time," she said softly.

He chuckled. "I like hearing that. I think about you, too."

She groaned. "My job is important to me. How can we have anything living so far apart?"

"I don't know, but we got something now. We'll have to see how it plays out. You're in danger, babe. Come back to the hotel."

"Okay, but we need to slow down a bit. If what we have is real, then bringing it down a notch won't hurt."

"When it comes to women, I don't know how to slow down." He exhaled. "You're afraid to give your heart to me 'cause you think I'll be taken away like your mom was. That's not gonna happen."

"How do you know? When my mom kissed me goodnight, she definitely didn't think that was going to be the last time. She didn't know she'd be dead an hour later." Her voice hitched.

"Life is fucked sometimes, I know, but you can't hide from it because of something that might happen. If we did that, none of us would be living—we'd only be existing. Come on back. Come on, babe."

"I'm on my way back. I have a question."

"What?" His stomach tensed.

"What's a charity poker run?"

As he roared with laughter, all tension seeped from him. "This one's for charity. Some of 'em are to raise money for the club. Bikers must visit five to seven checkpoints, drawing a playing card at each one. The point is to have the best poker hand at the end of the run. You gotta pay fees to be part of the event, and sometimes people sponsor you. It's fun, and money is raised. I wasn't sure I was going to go with all the shit goin' on, but my real good buddy organized it, and it's for his son who has cancer. Fuckin' sucks."

"How sad. You need to go. Are there women at the run?"

"Only men can play and make the run."

"Are there women there to service the men?"

"Yeah. It happens."

There was silence on the other end. Ready to hang up and redial, Axe heard Baylee breathing. He smiled.

"You don't have to worry about that. I'm going to help out my buddy, not to fuck other women. You almost here?"

"Yes. I'll be up soon." She hung up.

Axe lay back on the bed. He understood where Baylee was coming from. This thing between them blindsided him, too. For the first time since he walked through the Insurgents' doors, he wanted to be with someone other than his brothers. The women he fucked for years were for draining his cock only, but the brothers were his family, his core. With Baylee, everything had changed. Most of the time, he'd rather be with her than the brothers.

He would have to force himself to go on the poker run, because he didn't want to be away from her. He'd never imagined he'd ever be indecisive with the brotherhood.

The click of the key card was music to his heart.

Baylee entered, a small smile whispering on her lips.

In a husky voice, Axe said, "Get over here. Your ass needs some spanking for that stunt you pulled."

Giggling, she ran and jumped on the bed. Axe caught her, pinned her underneath him, and covered her face with kisses.

CHAPTER TWENTY-TWO

THE GREEN-EYED MAN observed the other as he came into his office—his shoulders slumped, his gait slow.

"Did anyone see you come in?" the man inquired when his visitor crumpled in the black leather chair by his desk.

"No," he replied, wiping the sweat off his forehead with a crisp, linen handkerchief.

"What brings you here?" the green-eyed man asked, drumming his fingers on his wooden desk. He didn't like the measly guy in his space. He hated weakness and insecurity, and his collaborator was guilty of both. The slouched man was quickly becoming a liability.

"I think we need to back off. Baylee is scared enough. She doubts her sanity, and that's making her question everything she thinks she remembers. From her journals, she still only recalls shadows and shapes. I think we're safe. We can leave her alone."

He looked at the whiny piece of shit in front of him. He questioned his judgment in becoming involved with the weak guy years before. Even back then, his gut had warned him about partnering with the spineless man. Greed pushed back his instincts, however, and he entered into a business arrangement with the man who sat before him, weak as ever. After all these years, and all they had been through, the fucker still hadn't developed a backbone.

"I told you I'd take care of her. All you have to do is stay the fuck out of it. You brought me the journal. Your part is finished."

The man slumped further into his chair. "I don't want to know the particulars."

His green eyes hardened. "You won't know anything. I'll take care of it. Having the goons from the Insurgents MC hanging around has caused a kink in my plan, but I'll work around it. The good thing is that the members are high in brawn but very short in brains." His thin lips curled up.

Wiping his forehead again, the man in the chair nodded before his mouth turned downward. "I hate to see this happen to her." A sheen of sympathy covered his brown eyes as he looked into the clear, glinting ones on the other side of the desk.

"It's simple. She's a liability."

"I don't really think she is."

"Do you want to upset your safe, well-orchestrated life?"

Head hung, he whispered, "No."

"I didn't think so." Contempt laced his voice. "You're out of it. I'll take care of the rest. You can go now." He dismissed the gutless man with a wave of his hand.

Sighing deeply, the brown-eyed collaborator rose to his feet, turned around and walked slowly out of the room, his shoulders hunched and his head down.

When he left, the stalker tapped his pen against his desk. He hated not being alone in all this. The more people involved in a killing, the more risk there was in getting caught. Baylee would be the first one to deal with, the lowlife biker next, then he'd eliminate the loose end—his cowardly partner in crime. After doing that, he could finally put the murder of Cassandra Peters behind him.

CHAPTER TWENTY-THREE

F OUR DAYS WITHOUT Axe seemed like a lifetime. Baylee had become accustomed to seeing Puck during the day and Blade at night. Each morning, when she peeked out the door, Puck's broad shoulders and colorfully tatted arms greeted her. He never said a word to her, only grunted or shook his head when she'd ask him if he wanted anything. At night, Blade took over, and his muscular build and stern face gave her comfort when she slept. Like Puck, Blade never spoke to her of his own volition, but he'd at least give her an audible answer if she asked him a question.

She'd been excited to share with Banger the news of breaking ground on the strip mall. The following Monday, the foundation would be poured. All the months of hard work had paid off, and her designs would soon be brick and mortar. Logan's input had been minimal, since most of the ideas and designs he delivered had been slightly altered copies of hers. Gary and Bob had seen right through that, and Baylee was pretty confident she'd be offered the partnership. Besides, she could handle Banger and had no problems meeting him on his turf. When she'd suggested Logan go to the Insurgents' clubhouse for a meeting, he freaked out.

Thinking of the partnership, nausea overcame her. Before the summer, adrenaline pumped and surged through her core when she visualized securing the brass ring, but since her liaison with Axe, the partnership weighed on her like lead. The day before Axe left on the poker run, Baylee had freaked out about their relationship. Since he'd been gone, however, she realized how much he'd slipped into her life.

Not having him around didn't seem like an option. She loved Axe.

Plain and simple. She'd take a chance on them, but she wondered if they could sustain a relationship from three hours away.

Her phone pinged, and she bit at her lips as her breathing accelerated. Was it the killer? Since her last text from him several days before, he hadn't contacted her; nevertheless, her stomach churned as she stared at her phone. She picked it up then looked at the Inbox—Axe's name. Lightheadedness overcame her, making her giddy as she opened the message.

Axe: *How r u?*

Baylee: *Okay. I miss u. Wish we were together right now.*

Axe: *Doing what?*

Baylee: *Kissing and...*

Axe: *U want my big cock fucking u?*

Baylee: *Yeah!*

Axe: *Me too. I'm home tomorrow, and ur all mine.*

Baylee: *Can't wait. The way u hold and kiss me is hot.*

Axe: *Fuck. U've worked me up now.*

Baylee: *I'll take care of u later.*

Axe: *I know u will. Gotta go, babe.*

Baylee: *Think of me.*

Axe: *Always do.*

Baylee's face flushed, and a sweet pull clenched her pussy. Her nipples had hardened while she was texting; she was so damn horny. Axe did something to her. She couldn't wait to ride him hard. Just thinking about it made her thighs quiver and her core pulse.

Another ping.

Axe: *Forgot to tell u. Family picnic tomorrow.*

Baylee: *With ur mom?*

Axe: *No. Insurgents. Meet u at Clermont Park at 2. Puck knows to take u there.*

Baylee: *On his Harley?!*

Axe: *No. U follow him. U only ride on the back of my bike. Ur mine. Gotta go.*

Baylee: *:)*

She reread the text many times. *I'm his.* The words bubbled inside her, spreading warmth throughout. Her hazel eyes danced, and she hummed as she sat behind her desk and returned to her work. The next day couldn't come fast enough.

THE AIR WAS warm, the sunbeams glowing on Baylee's skin as she entered Clermont Park. The green grass tickled her sandaled feet as she approached a large group of men, women, and children. She figured it must've been the Insurgents because the men sported leather vests and blue jeans—apparently the uniform for the outlaw group.

Wisps of smoke curled above large grills, and wooden picnic tables with brightly checkered oilcloths shone in the afternoon sun. The painted wings of butterflies shone under the sun's rays as they flitted, like fairies, from flower to flower in the rectangular flower beds spaced evenly over the expanse of grass. Oak trees provide ample shade throughout the park, and a large, clear lake sparkled under the brightness of day. A playground near the area where the Insurgents converged brimmed with children. Elderly couples sat on concrete benches that dotted the park.

Baylee turned to thank Puck, but he had already joined the group, waiting for orders from the members. As a prospect, he and the others were there to do the bidding of the patched brothers.

When Baylee joined the group, a woman with long, chestnut-colored hair and twinkling green eyes came up to her.

"Hi, you must be Baylee. I'm Cara. Come on over and I'll introduce you to the other women."

As Baylee followed, she spotted Axe standing among a group of nice-looking men. Arousal flared within her like a torch when she saw how fine he looked in his tight, sleeveless t-shirt, each muscle outlined underneath. The dark five-o'clock shadow over his chiseled jaw took her breath away, and his snug blue jeans showcased his bulge, making her mouth water.

Their eyes locked, and he flashed her a wicked grin that caused her heart to skip a beat. She fought the urge to run and jump into his arms, wrapping her long legs around him as she peppered kisses on his face and neck. He raised his arm and waved, and Baylee so wanted to lick and squeeze his iron biceps while running her hands over his sexy shoulders.

"Uh, Cara? I see Axe. I'll be right back, okay?"

"Sure."

Baylee ambled over to Axe and he stopped mid-sentence, scooped her into an embrace, and kissed her deep and hard. Her cheeks turned crimson as the men in the group stared, smiles and snickers on their lips.

Nuzzling her neck, he whispered, "I've missed you, babe." His breath tickled her skin.

"Me, too," she said, kneading his solid biceps.

"Missed your smell and your taste." His deep chuckle reverberated through her, coming to rest between her legs.

"You done with the kissy-face shit? We got some stuff to discuss," Throttle said.

Baylee's face burned and she pulled away. "Cara wants me to meet the other women. I should go."

Axe said in a low voice, "I'll come get you when we're done." He patted her ass, and his touch scorched her. At that moment, she needed him bad.

As she passed three large grills, she waved at Banger who stoked the glowing charcoals. He tilted his chin to her, his blue eyes sparkling.

When she found Cara again, Baylee smiled sheepishly. "I'm sorry about that."

"No reason to apologize. Let me introduce you to everyone." Cara pointed to two older women who were setting up the picnic table with condiments, plates, and utensils. "This is Doris and Marlene. Ruben is Doris's husband, and Billy belongs to Marlene. The women opening the chips are Sofia—she belongs to Tigger—Emma, who is with Danny, and Lacey, whose husband is Bruiser. Finally, you have Addie and Cherri." Cara walked over to the two women who were seated on the picnic bench. "Chas is Addie's husband, and Jax is Cherri's man."

"I'm sure I'll have to ask everyone's name again," Baylee said, her brow creasing.

"No worries. Ladies, this is Baylee, Axe's woman."

The women welcomed Baylee then handed her a beer.

"Can I help with anything?" she asked.

"Not right now. When we're ready to eat, you can help put the food out on the table," Cara said.

"Did you make all the food?" Baylee inquired as she popped a tortilla chip in her mouth.

"We all brought something," Cara answered.

"Cara always brings a taste of Italy," Addie joked. "Banger is crazy for her sausage and peppers, so we always have that at family gatherings."

"Banger loves to eat good food, and I keep telling Hawk that the woman who catches him will do it through her cooking," Cara said.

The women laughed.

"I don't know if he wants to be caught," Doris retorted. "He and Grace were tight. I think he still misses her a lot."

"He's lonely since Kylie went away to college. Having a nice woman around will do him good." Cara walked over to where Baylee, Cherri, and Addie sat.

"And what does Hawk have to say about your matchmaking mind?" Addie asked.

"To keep out of it." Cara looked at the women. "So that makes me want to do it for sure."

They all busted out laughing.

Comfort enveloped Baylee as she sat among the group of women who made her feel as though she were one of them. She could get used to spending time with them. She could even see herself becoming friends with Cara and Addie.

A cute blonde girl toddled over to Baylee and set a bright purple pony with electric green hair in her lap.

"Oh, how pretty your pony is," Baylee said as she picked up the toy. "You're pretty, too. What's your name?"

"Paisie," the toddler said then ran back to the white-blonde seated next to Addie. The little girl put her head in the woman's lap, peeking out to watch Baylee.

"Is she your girl?" Baylee asked.

"Yeah. Her name's Paisley, but we call her Paisie." She stroked her daughter's hair.

"Is this your baby, too?" Baylee pointed to a baby's carrying case.

"No, she belongs to Addie."

Addie smiled and pulled the mosquito netting away. The pink-cheeked infant with a patch of red hair looked like an angel.

"She's beautiful," Baylee murmured.

"Thanks. This is our special little girl. My miracle. I didn't think I could have kids, but here she is." Addie leaned over and grasped her daughter's tiny hand, kissing her fingers. "Her name is Hope. Even though she has my red hair, she has her daddy's dark eyes."

"How'd you ever get Axe to calm the fuck down?" Cherri asked as she watched Paisley play with two other small children.

The question took Baylee back. "I don't know. Has he slowed down?"

"Yeah," they all said.

"I love it! Axe was always giving Chas crap about us going out, and now he's joining the ranks. Too much." Addie covered her mouth as she laughed heartily.

"I love watching this," Cherri agreed. " 'Bout time he settled down.

Jax's been having so much fun with all this."

"Chas, too." Addie and Cherri both chuckled.

Afraid to ask, Baylee said, "How was he before?"

Before anyone could answer, Cara said, "Lost. Now he's found you. It's good."

As Baylee spoke with the women, she was very aware of Axe nearby. Even though he talked with his buddies, drank beer, and played horseshoes, his eyes were on her, building her arousal.

Banger, Ruben, and Bruiser signaled the grills were hot, and they began lining them with burger patties, brats, and steaks.

"Time to set the food on the tables," Cara said.

Baylee jumped to help. Bending over an ice cooler, she jerked when a hand curled around her bare waist. As she was lifted, the scent of Axe filled her nostrils. He smelled purely male, leather and motor oil and fresh air. A single shiver rode her spine.

He held her back against his chest, his hard length poking at her butt. Feathery kisses around her shoulders brought goosebumps to her skin.

"Come on," he commanded, taking her wrist and dragging her behind him.

"I have to help the women. Cara asked me to," she balked.

"Fuck that. Cara knows the score. They all do."

He took her to the other side of the park in the middle of a cluster of pine trees, their boughs laden with long, thick needles. Pushing the branches aside, they entered a hidden space surrounded by the trees. Inside, it was cool as the branches overlapped, forming a roof, while the sun filtered thinly in.

Before Baylee could take it all in, Axe had her back against a tree trunk, his mouth on hers, his tongue charging in. She welcomed the swirls of his tongue as he consumed her mouth, the flaming touch of his fingers as they slid under her short jean skirt setting her on fire. Her large breasts brushed against him with each breath she took, her nipples hardening at the contact. She'd missed him so much.

She gasped when his hardness jutted against her. He pulled back, their eyes reflecting one another's desire. Placing her fingers on his crotch, he winked and said huskily, "See what you do to me?"

She held her breath and listened over the pulse booming in her ears. His voice, his touch, his scent—the very feel of him—sent her reeling, and she pressed closer to him, trying to fuse their heat together.

"How do you make me think of you all the time?" he rasped as soft nibbles glided across her shoulder.

She moaned, squirming under his mesmerizing touch, her panties dampening.

His mouth moved from her shoulders upward, capturing her bottom lip with his teeth before kissing her hungrily. Axe slid under her panties, parted her swollen lips, and pushed his finger deep inside her wet slit. Baylee instinctively ground against his hand, gasping from sweet agony.

"Is it good?" His voice was hoarse with unfiltered lust.

"So good," she panted.

"I love it when you're wet. It tells me how badly you want me."

She clenched her fingers in his hair. "I want you bad."

With his other hand, Axe shoved her tank top up and unclasped the front of her bra, her heavy breasts popping out.

"Beautiful," he said as he played with her nipple, tweaking then tugging it.

When he took the stiffened bead into his mouth and sucked it, electric shocks coursed from Baylee's tightened buds straight down to her pulsing sex. Strangled yelps of pleasure passed through her lips, and she dug her fingernails in his back. Urgently, she grabbed at the hem of his t-shirt, pushing it up so she could feel his skin on hers. Pulling back, he whipped off his shirt and she leaned forward, licking his tattoos before flicking his nipples with the tip of her tongue. A feral growl broke from him and he spun her around, placing her hands on the tree trunk.

"Bend over," he ordered.

He pushed her skirt over her hips and moved her red lace panties to the side as he spread her legs wide, exposing her ass and pussy to him.

"Fuck," he muttered under his breath.

"I want it raw," she said as she wriggled her ass against his erection. "Are you clean?"

"Yeah," he panted, and she heard the *whir* of his zipper as he opened it. "You protected?"

Swallowing, she tried to speak, but her nerves were a thousand circuits of desire zig-zagging through her. She nodded instead.

"I've been wanting this for four fuckin' days, babe. I don't know what you've done to me, but I'm addicted to you—your taste, your scent, your pussy. I need you like an addict needs a fix." As he spoke, he rubbed her clit, her sweet spot growing rigid with each stroke, slick with need.

The tip of his dick against her heated slit threw her body in a tizzy; her legs stiffened, she held her breath, her nipples ached. Then he pushed inside, and her greedy pussy grabbed hold of him, encasing him inside her heated core.

He spoke low in her ear, cupping her tit and twisting her beaded nipple. "I want you begging for me to slam my hard cock into you."

Desire seared her every pore; his dirty-talking set her on fire.

"Tell me to fuck you hard. Harder than you've ever had it."

Baylee craned her neck and he looked down at her, black eyes smoldering, his full lips curved in a sensual invitation.

"I want your big dick fucking me. Do it now, please."

His low growl floated up to her ears.

Axe pulled out of her, and she watched as he looked at his cock glistening with her juices. Then his hungry eyes locked with hers as he slammed into her. His fingers dug into her hips, shoving in and out of her as she braced herself against the tree trunk, her tits bouncing and swaying.

"You are mine. Don't ever forget it." He slammed back into her. "You belong to me, and I'm never letting you go."

Breathlessly, she said, "And you are mine."

As he pummeled into her, the burning pleasure from earlier consumed her like a bonfire. Baylee's body screamed in savage ecstasy, her orgasm washing over her in searing waves of intense pleasure. With ragged cries, she tried to hold her quivering legs up while the burn of his seed filled her, his grunting pants echoing in her ears.

Axe pulled her torso tight against his, squeezing her as he breathed heatedly in her ear. "I fuckin' love everything about you, baby."

She placed her hands behind her, around his waist. Tilting her head back, she caught his gaze. "I've never met a man like you," she said softly.

He brushed a gentle kiss across her lips. "I love you. I'm your man, and I'll take care of you."

A warm glow flowed through her as her heart sang in delight. Swinging around, she placed her arms around his neck, her eyes shining. "I love you."

Then a kiss as tender and light as a summer breeze sent her soaring, and she relished the sweetness of it.

When they returned to the picnic, hand-in-hand and her hair mussed with bits of bark stuck in it, some of the brothers hooted and whistled. Axe laughed and Baylee turned several shades of red, but inwardly, she hooted and whistled louder than any of them. Axe loved her, and all was well.

CHAPTER TWENTY-FOUR

T HE NEXT MORNING, Axe's angry voice woke Baylee up. He sat on the edge of the bed, speaking with someone on the phone. Short seconds of silence, then his responses held a note of frustration. From where she lay, she noticed his clenched fist on the mattress, his knuckles white from the pressure.

"I'm done with this. Hangin' up now." He ripped out the words in a hoarse voice.

The discarded phone by his side, he sighed loudly then rubbed his eyes with his fingers.

"You okay?" Baylee asked softly.

Turning his head sideways, his gazed lingered on her mouth. "Yeah. Get over here, sexy." Clutching her wrist, he dragged her to the middle of the bed where he twisted and hovered over her, kissing her deep and wet. "Morning, beautiful." One lock of hair fell forward onto his forehead.

A bemused smile whispered across her lips, prompting him to hug her close to him.

"Who were you talking to? You seemed annoyed." She swept the lock from his forehead.

"My mom. She can be a pain in the ass."

Giving a small laugh, she asked, "What's she done this time?"

"I told you she's getting married. She's been bugging me 'bout going, for some fuckin' reason. This is hubby number six, so why the hell she cares if I go or not is beyond me."

"Who's she marrying?"

"Fuck if I know."

Baylee's eyes widened. "You don't know who your mom's marrying?"

Axe shrugged. "I think she told me, but I tune her out most of the time, so there you go. It pisses me off that she wants to play 'mom' in front of a bunch of people when she has no clue what it means to be a mom. Fuckin' irks me." He punched the mattress to drive the point home.

Bringing his fist to her mouth, Baylee kissed it. "You should probably go." She put her finger on his lips. "I know you're going to argue with me, but hear me out. Even though the two of you don't get along, she's still your mom, and you still talk to her, so that means you want some kind of connection with her. Sometimes we do things for people because it makes them happy and, in turn, it makes us feel better. Who knows, maybe this will bring you closer to your mom." Baylee looked away from Axe and studied the patterned curtains covering the large window.

Axe tucked a few tendrils of hair behind her ears. "You finished?" he asked softly.

She dipped her head.

His dark eyebrows slanted in a frown. "First off, babe, my mom wasn't a good mom like yours. She was shitty, at best. Secondly, I need a fuckin' scorecard to keep track of the men she's had in and out of her life since my dad split. And third, I'll feel pissed as shit going to her stupid-ass wedding, and her pretending we're so close and shit like that when it'll all be lies. I mean, who the fuck even has a wedding the sixth time? What a pathetic, delusional joke."

Baylee drew Axe against her and ran her fingers down his back. "I get that. If you don't want to go, then don't. It's hard for me to relate because there have been more times than I can count when I wished I had my mom around for special moments. But I adored my mom, and she was the best. You shouldn't do what makes you uncomfortable."

Axe drew his lips in thoughtfully, then let out a long breath. "I kind of need to talk with my uncle Max. He hasn't returned my phone calls, and he's never around when I go to his office. I know he doesn't expect me to be at the wedding since I've only gone to the first one." He leaned in and kissed her on the cheek. "I want you to go with me."

Baylee's face turned white and her insides quivered. How could she go to the wedding and come face-to-face with the man who'd been following her, making her petrified? "Me? I don't feel comfortable going to your mom's wedding. I don't even know her."

"You're going for me, not her. If you're with me, it'll make it tolerable. You're a part of my life. I want you to go." A big grin spread across his face. "We can find somewhere to fuck and pretend it's random." Light twinkled in the depths of his brown eyes.

She punched him lightly as her cheeks heated. "You're so bad. It'd be like an anniversary, right?" she joked.

He winked at her. "Fuck yeah. So, what do you say?"

She bit her bottom lip. Part of her recoiled at the thought of seeing his uncle, but she *would be* with Axe and all the other people. Maybe she'd learn why he'd been following her. Another part of her swelled with happiness that Axe wanted to take her to a family function. He wanted to tell his family that she was his, that they were together. The thought of being his made her toes curl.

"Okay. I'll go."

He squeezed her so hard, she could barely breathe. "Thanks, sweetheart," he whispered huskily.

Her insides tightened and a gush of pure joy washed over her. *Damn, he's adorable. I'm so crazy about him.* She had to be honest—he'd had her body from the first time they fucked. As hard as she tried to keep it only about pleasure and a summer fling, he'd begun to infiltrate her heart, and they'd officially professed their love for one another. With him in her life, nothing could harm her. Axe would take care of everything, and it would all be good.

The room phone rang on the nightstand, and she reached over then picked it up.

Logan's cheery voice greeted her, telling her that Gary wanted them to meet over at the site. "We can go together," he added.

"Since Axe has to report the progress to the club, he should be there, as well."

Logan groaned. "I don't think it's necessary. I'll take pictures of the progress, and you can drop them off at the clubhouse. You seem fond of the club." His tone was cold. "Anyway, I don't like him, and I know the feeling is mutual. I'm not comfortable around him."

"I think Gary would agree that Axe needs to be there."

A long pause ensued. Over the phone, she heard Logan clear his throat.

"Then I'll meet you there."

Click.

Baylee looked at her phone, shook her head, and muttered, "Men."

"Who were you talkin' to?" Axe asked as he sat up.

"Logan. We're meeting at the site."

"On a Sunday?"

"Yep, and you're coming, too."

"Wouldn't miss it. The club's been waiting a long time for this. They'll be stoked when I update them at our next church."

"Good. I'll be done in about fifteen minutes, then it's all yours. We'll take my car." When he opened his mouth, she said sweetly, "No arguments."

Then she closed the bathroom door, holding her hand over her mouth to quell the laughter bursting from her lips. Axe's look of disbelief was priceless.

She was downright giddy, and it wasn't all at his expense. She was blissfully happy, fully alive. Axe did something to her no man had ever been able to do—he erased the shadows across her heart.

CHAPTER TWENTY-FIVE

THE WEDDING WAS at the Primrose Hotel in one of the small banquet rooms. The windows faced a medium-sized pond stocked with golden carp, surrounding a fountain, its water spraying up in the dry summer air from the parted lips of two bronzed cherubs.

Ten round tables covered in alternating tablecloths in orange, green, and pink looked like bowls of sherbet. The head table held a spray of baby's breath and white and pink roses. Wait staff bustled around, putting the last touches to the place settings. Off to the left, in front of a picture window, the bridal arch bloomed with pink roses, purple hydrangea, passion vines, and olive branches, which lent a sweet aroma to the room.

Axe and Baylee made a striking couple. He sported black pants, a light gray pinstriped shirt, and his leather cut, while she wore a sleeveless chiffon dress in rose and forget-me-not print with silver, barely there platform sandals.

When they entered the banquet hall, Axe wrapped his arm around her waist, tugging her close to him as he scanned the room for his mother. Spotting her speaking with the minister, he led Baylee over to the bridal arch.

Axe's mother was an attractive woman in her late forties. Her toned body was testament to her diligence in keeping her figure. For her wedding, she wore her shoulder-length dark hair loose, the long layers softly framing her face while her wispy bangs danced over her forehead. Her nutmeg-brown eyes—lighter than Axe's—were heavily made up with black eyeliner, mascara, and dark purple eyeshadow. Her wedding attire was a simple ivory suit with a lacy, lavender camisole underneath.

She smiled broadly at her son. Placing her hand on his shoulder, she kissed him firmly on his cheek. "It's been a while. Let me look at you." She stood back and ran her eyes over him then leaned in and gave him a quick hug. "You look so handsome, Michael."

Axe groaned inwardly as he saw Baylee's amused eyes sparkle, her sensuous lips curling into a smile. He took a step backward, breaking away from her grip. "The name's Axe, Mom. It's been that for eleven years."

His mom shook her head. "Not for me. You're my Michael, my sweet baby boy." She laughed too loud, and her glassy eyes tried to focus on him.

He detected gin on her breath, and wished he hadn't come. *She's probably high on pain meds.* He could never trust his mom to act the way a mother should. *Fuck.*

She turned her attention on Baylee. "Are you Michael's girlfriend?"

Shyly, Baylee nodded.

"This is Baylee, Mom."

His mother opened her mouth just as Axe's eyes grew dark and threatening. She closed it and extended her hand. "I'm Lorinda."

Baylee shook her hand. "Nice meeting you."

Lorinda squeezed Axe's arm. "She's beautiful."

Baylee blushed, and Axe's eyes locked with hers. "I know," he said, his voice thick, hunger creeping into his gaze.

Lorinda grabbed her son's hand and pulled him behind her as she walked toward the makeshift bar across the room. "I want you to meet Stephen."

Axe snatched Baylee's wrist and tugged her with him as his mother snaked her way around tables, wait staff, and padded chairs.

A tall, lean man spoke with the bartender. From the back of him, Axe could see his hair was salt and pepper and he wore a very expensive suit. His shoulders were straight, and his voice commanded respect.

"Stephen." Lorinda released Axe's hand as she came behind her soon-to-be husband. She moved her hand up and down his suit jacket.

"I want you to meet my son, Michael."

Stephen turned slightly. "Please don't interrupt me when I'm talking with someone. I've told you that many times." He clamped his hand around her upper arm. "Pace your drinking, okay? I told you I didn't want you getting sloppy drunk at our wedding. Understand?" His voice was hard as steel.

Axe didn't like the way he spoke to his mom, and if he cared more for her, he would've had this jerk against the wall, knee positioned to slam him in his aged balls. Instead, he just stood there, eyes narrowed, jaw tight.

Lorinda laughed, but her cheeks turned crimson, and Axe knew she was embarrassed he and Baylee witnessed the exchange between the couple. *So much for a long-lasting marriage.* Axe gave the whole farce about six months. He knew his mom would tire of the guy's sharp tongue, and it'd just be a matter of time until she started looking around, getting antsy, wanting male attention from someone other than him. He'd be surprised if it went longer than that.

His mother looked at Axe, smiling weakly. "He'll be done in a minute. Then you can meet him."

The sonofabitch purposely continued talking, way after he should've stopped. Axe read him like a book; the fucker was punishing his mother. He stared at the asshole's back and did all he could to hold himself back from punching the guy. He was stuck there like a pansy-ass, waiting for his mom to introduce him to a man he didn't give a shit about. All he wanted was a beer, and Baylee snugly tucked into the crook of his arm.

Finally, her fiancé turned around, and Lorinda practically squealed. She grabbed Axe's hand again and said, "Michael, this is Stephen." She clasped her hand around Stephen's. "Stephen, this is Michael."

Her smiling face slackened as she looked at both men. Axe's face was dark and brooding, and Stephen's was tight and stern.

"This motherfucker is the one you're marrying?" Axe growled, his eyes never leaving Stephen's face.

"Michael, watch your language!" His mother dropped his hand and raised her fingers to her gaping mouth.

"You outdid yourself this time. This fucker is the worst you could've chosen."

"Stop it. Right now." His mother's eyes flashed and she stood by Stephen, her arm looped around his.

"Lorinda, *this*—" Stephen pointed his long finger at Axe "—is your son? How didn't I know that?"

" 'Cause you're a dumb fuck," Axe snarled.

On the verge of tears, his mother covered her ears with her hands. "No. This can't be. You're supposed to like each other. Why're you saying these things? What is wrong with both of you?"

Axe snorted. "Fucking reality, that's what, but you always liked delusions. I'm outta here. You deserve one another."

Axe spun around and strode away, dragging a startled Baylee behind him.

"Wait. Michael, wait!" his mother's high-pitched voice pierced his ears. "Michael!"

Baylee, struggling to keep up with Axe in her four-inch heels, stopped in her tracks, making Axe slow down. "Axe, what is going on? You need to talk to your mom."

Axe whipped around, a storm brewing in his eyes. "I don't *need* to do shit. And where the fuck do you get off telling *me* what to do? *Nobody* tells me what to do."

When he saw her crestfallen face and glistening eyes, he knew he'd crossed the line, but he didn't care. He was pissed, and he didn't need Baylee interfering. She didn't know shit about what was going on, about his life and how it'd been. She needed to fuckin' back off. Axe didn't need her telling him shit. Period.

Lorinda caught up to the couple, who stood still staring at each other. Fury emanated from Axe, and hurt and disappointment were etched across Baylee's face.

"Michael, please don't ruin my day."

His anger moved from Baylee to his mom. "It's always about *you*, isn't it? You don't give a shit about anything but yourself."

"That's not true. I love you, you just never let me in."

Axe threw his head back and gave a dry, bitter laugh. "Do you *really* believe the shit you say? The only one you ever loved was Lorinda Tomlinson, or whatever the fuck last name you have now. I'm sure you didn't give Tomlinson as your name to your fiancé. If you had, he never would've considered dating trailer trash."

Lorinda wiped a tear rolling down her cheek. "Do you know Stephen from somewhere?"

Axe shook his head then looked at Baylee. "You see what a great mother I have?" He turned back to his mom. "You were so strung-out on prescription meds and busy screwing any guy who would have you, you didn't even know how much shit the Rodgers gave me when I was in high school. His piece-of-shit son, Palmer, made it a point to belittle me every chance he got. And his dad? He made sure I didn't get the scholarship I was vying for. That asshole also made sure that I had constant contact with the fuckin' badges. And you didn't do shit. I dealt with that, but you *marrying* him? No fuckin' way am I gonna watch that."

His mom reached out and ran her hand down Axe's shirt. He jerked away, like his mother's touch burned his skin. "Oh, sweetie, I never knew."

Axe gave her a hard look. "No, you *knew*, you just didn't give a shit." Turning his back on his mother, he took Baylee by the hand. "Let's go." He walked toward the doors.

"Michael. Wait," a deep voice said.

Axe continued walking, but a firm hand grabbed his arm and spun him around. Axe took a swing, but Stephen managed to duck in time.

"Get your goddamned hands off me," Axe growled.

Stephen let go. "Look, I'm just as surprised that you're Lorinda's son as you are that I'm going to be her husband, but the shock has passed, and it doesn't really matter, does it?"

Axe didn't answer. He didn't trust himself right then. He was seething, and he wanted to punch this smug, arrogant sonofabitch right in the mouth. Then he wanted to smash and destroy all the cutesy fucking wedding decorations, starting with that damned bridal arch. The whole thing disgusted him. His mother had gone too far. The fact she looked clueless when he was so pissed told him everything. His family was the Insurgents, always had been from the moment he began prospecting. And he had Baylee. He didn't need this shit.

"Make your mother happy today. You and I don't have to be friends, but today is special for her." He tilted his head in Lorinda's direction. She stood there, dabbing the corners of her eyes, a small smile on her mouth.

"Special," Axe gritted. "Aren't you, like, number six?"

Stephen shrugged then trailed his gaze over to Baylee, staring intently at her. "Who is this lovely lady?"

Baylee leaned in to Axe, her body tense. He placed his arm around her. "You're checking out my woman? You keep it up and you'll be visiting the morgue instead of dancing the night away. I'm on to you, asshole. You can pretend you're this rich, respected man in the community, but I know better. You made your money by crooking people."

"And you and your hoodlum club are so innocent?"

"I've never pretended not to be a ruthless, cocky sonofabitch. You're the hypocrite. You don't matter at all to me or the Insurgents, 'cause we don't give a shit about the citizens' world. So, fuck you." He tugged Baylee toward him and nuzzled her ear. "Let's get outta here, babe."

As they opened the glass doors, his mother sobbed. "Please, Michael. Come back. Do it for me. Please, don't ruin my day. Can't you forgive and forget?"

Axe whirled around. "God forgives. I don't."

The doors shut behind him as he left the hotel without a backward glance. Red blotches floated in front of his eyes; his anger was palpable. The only thing he regretted was that he wasn't able to speak with his uncle. *I'll find him tomorrow and make him tell him why he was everywhere Baylee was.* Axe had grown weary of all the shit associated with his blood family.

When he started the car, Baylee leaned over and kissed the side of his face. "Are you okay?"

"Yeah, I'm fine. Since we're dressed, let's go to Aspen, have a steak, dance, and fuck like hell in a suite I'm gonna get. Sound good?"

She grinned, nodding in agreement. "The one thing I'm bummed about is I was craving wedding cake," she joked.

He brought her hand to his lips. "You want cake? I'll get you some. We can share it." He winked at her and veered his car on the two-lane, paved Highway 82.

CHAPTER TWENTY-SIX

BAYLEE, CALMED DOWN from the earlier scene at the wedding, looked out the window. She watched as they passed clear rushing rivers, steep-sided valleys, and extensive aspen groves whose rounded leaves looked like green disks shaking in the breeze, shimmering under the August sun.

"Aren't you gonna ask me what the fuck happened back there?" Axe's deep voice broke the pool of silence around them.

"I figured you'd tell me when you were ready. I gathered you weren't too crazy about your mom's choice." She cocked her head and smiled.

"That fuckwad is Stephen Rodgers, Palmer-asshole-Rodgers' dad. Fuck it!"

Baylee gasped. "Wow. That was Palmer's father?" She put her hand over Axe's and patted it. "I'm sorry. Your mother should have known that would've upset you. I wonder why she insisted you come to the wedding."

" 'Cause she's a selfish, self-absorbed bitch. She probably didn't put it together when she heard the name. Even if she did, the asshole's money would definitely come before me. I'm so done with all her shit."

"Maybe she really doesn't remember. You said she's hooked on pain meds. That crap can mess you up. Maybe she didn't intend to hurt you." She saw Axe's jaw moving back and forth. "It's just a thought," she added softly.

"Yeah, well, she's been doing shit like this for years. I'm done with it."

Baylee leaned over and kissed him on the cheek, then ran her fingers through his hair.

Axe exhaled. "I didn't mean to yell at you back there. It's just that I was super pissed, and it seemed like you were taking her side."

She continued to rake her fingers through his hair. "I know you were upset. I really didn't know the whole situation, I was just trying to defuse the tension that was escalating. I'm on your side. You can count on me."

Axe reached up and caught her hand, bringing it to his lips and kissing it softly. He turned on the radio, and the two of them listened to classic rock while they made their way out of Pinewood Springs.

AFTER A SHORT forty-five-minute drive, they arrived in Aspen, a charming mountain town at the base of the majestic Maroon Bells peaks. Forests of evergreen carpeted the verdant valleys. The climate was cooler than Pinewood Springs since Aspen's elevation was higher, and it was a welcome change for the couple.

Axe checked into a small hotel right in the heart of downtown, making restaurants and shops easily accessible. When they entered their suite, the large sliding glass door opened out to an awe-inspiring view of the mountain range.

"How beautiful," Baylee gushed as she stepped out onto the balcony, the cool air lightly caressing her skin.

Axe joined her, looping his arm around her middle, drawing her to his chest. He rested his chin tenderly on the top of her head while he squeezed her to him.

"You're beautiful," he said.

She smiled. "I've never been here."

"Really? I'm glad we came. I'm happy to share this with you."

The sun began its evening descent, and the lights in the town twinkled like fireflies in the night. Baylee's stomach growled loudly, and she giggled.

"Are you going to feed me?" she teased.

He spun her around and kissed her, a devilish look in his eyes. "I'll feed you now, and you can feed me later."

SEBASTIAN'S STEAKHOUSE WAS located in the heart of downtown Aspen. Warm, soft lights from individually crafted lanterns created the perfect atmosphere for romantic dinners, while the lit onyx bar added to the ambiance. A fire crackled in the large bluestone fireplace to ward off the summer night chill. Cedar beams and rustic wood tables completed the natural feel of the restaurant.

Axe scooted closer to Baylee before pouring the red wine in her glass. He loved being next to her, watching her full lips press against the wine glass as she sipped, breathing in her faint scent of white musk, and brushing against her soft skin. He couldn't get enough of her, and the electrical jolts he experienced when they touched blew his mind. Baylee made him feel complete and settled—something he'd never had before.

"You zoning out on me?" Her lilting laugh wrapped around him.

Shoving against her playfully, he answered, "No. I'm just taking you all in."

Leaning in to him, she brushed her lips on the side of his mouth. With his arm around her shoulders, he pulled her flush to him, crushing his mouth on hers until the waiter placed their steak dinners before them. They reluctantly pulled apart to eat their meals.

As Axe cut his New York strip, Baylee said, "I want to talk about Stephen Rodgers."

Darting his eyes up, he bristled. She reached over and squeezed his arm. "It's not about the wedding or the crap from the past." She took a sip of wine. "It's about the way I got the creeps when he looked at me, and it was more than him just checking me out."

"I noticed you tensed up."

"I did, and I'm not sure why. I got a strong, negative vibe when I saw him. I couldn't look at him. Honestly, I don't even remember what he looks like, I turned away so quickly."

"Maybe it's because you got the vibe he's an asshole, and you'd be right. Let's not ruin our night talking about that fucker. I'm already getting pissed."

"You're right. Let's have some fun."

After they finished their dinner and enjoyed a couple of drinks, the couple strolled down West Main Boulevard. Baylee shivered against Axe, and he guided her into one of the many boutiques lining the street.

"Pick out a sweater or something."

Shaking her head, Baylee protested, "I'm okay. It's just for tonight, and we'll be back at the hotel soon."

"Pick something out." He walked over to a rack of cotton sweaters in bright colors and patterned designs. "Like any of these?" He waved his hand over the clothing rack.

"I don't have my wallet. I left it back at the hotel."

"You don't need a wallet when you're with me. Pick something out, or I will."

It irked Axe that she was uncomfortable with him buying her something. That was bullshit. He didn't know her history with men, but he'd never expect a woman to pay for something while he was around. It wasn't his style. Since she was his woman, he'd provide for her; whatever she earned was for her alone.

After an hour of trying on jackets, sweaters, and shawls, Baylee finally decided on a lemon-yellow cardigan with ribbed cuff and hem.

"You like it?" she asked as she spun around, modeling it.

Axe, hunkered down on a cushioned ottoman, nodded. "I like you in anything. I'm just trying to figure out why it took you an hour to decide on it."

Laughing, she went over to him and mussed up his hair with her hand. Bending low to his ear, she whispered, "I love you." She ambled away, sweater in hand.

Axe watched as she waited in line to pay for the purchase. If he lived several lifetimes, he'd never understand women. He rose in one fluid motion and joined her at the cash register, the sales woman staring at Axe with interest. When he handed her the money, she brushed his palm with her fingers. Glancing at her, she smiled broadly, her eyes shining. While he was waiting for the receipt, he helped Baylee on with her sweater. Baylee kissed his jaw, muttering, "Thank you" against it.

The saleswoman handed Axe his receipt and mouthed the words, "Call me." Axe looked at the receipt and saw a number scribbled on it. Snorting, he wadded up the paper and pitched it in the trash bin then, with his arm around his woman, he walked out.

As they trekked the three blocks back to the hotel, Axe realized a few short months before, he would've taken the sales clerk up on her offer and banged her. With Baylee in his life, he couldn't think of being with any woman but her. The idea of being with one woman after years of fucking so many comforted him. Baylee was all he wanted and needed, and *that* stunned the hell out of him.

The striking rhythm of a BB King song drifted in the soft breeze as the couple passed a jazz bar. During tourist season, the bars were packed, and the shops on West Main stayed open until late in the night. A block before the hotel, Axe noticed a bakery and coffee shop.

"Let's stop in here for a minute." He opened the door for Baylee.

A few minutes later they exited, Axe carrying a small bakery box containing a three-layered white cake with white frosting. Winking at Baylee, he said, "When my woman wants something, I get it for her."

"You're crazy sometimes." She looped her arm in his.

"I'm always crazy for you." He tugged her next to him.

Back at their suite, Axe order two bottles of champagne with room service, and two toiletries bags with housekeeping. Sitting on the edge of the bed, Baylee kicked off her high heels, rubbing her feet and groaning in pleasure. Axe chuckled as she massaged them.

"Men should be made to wear these for one day. I bet you guys couldn't last a half hour in them." Baylee flexed her foot.

Axe's chuckles deepened into full-on laughter as he padded to the door. Room service set the two champagne glasses and bottles on the table. When they left, he gazed at Baylee.

"Come over by me." His voice was deep and sensual.

As she came over, he took off his shirt and boots then opened one of the champagne bottles, pouring it into the glasses. Baylee took hers, and her eyes, brimming with tenderness and passion, met his.

"To us," she said softly as she clinked her glass against his.

"Fuck yeah."

He drained his glass then looked her over seductively before tugging her to him. Setting her glass on the table, he gathered her into his arms, holding her snugly. Baylee buried her face against the corded muscles of his chest. Grabbing a handful of her hair, he tipped her head back and took her mouth savagely. Their tongues stroked each other's, their passion building. Baylee threw her arms around his neck, pushing his head closer to hers, their bodies melding together.

Axe pulled the zipper down on the back of her dress while the pads of his fingers smoothly glided down her spine until they landed right above the curve of her ass. Breathing heavily, he ground his hardness against Baylee, her small moans setting him on fire. Afraid he was going to shoot his load in his pants, he pulled away, then guided Baylee to the couch. She slipped out of her dress and stood before him in a rose lace bra, matching panties, and thigh-highs. He groaned and nestled his face in her cleavage.

She fell onto the couch, and he dropped down beside her.

"What about the cake?" she asked, grazing his jawline with her finger.

Eyes smoldering, Axe took the cake out of the box, broke off a piece, and placed it in her mouth. Her lips closed around his fingers and she sucked on them, her eyes locking with his. He slid his wet fingers from her soft mouth then trailed them down to her tits and tweaked her beaded nipple. Her gasp went straight to his cock.

"That's good cake," she said against his cheek. She scooped some frosting on her finger, placing a dollop on his lips, then licked it up. "So good."

Growling, he slammed her against him, his lips crushing hers, his tongue dipping into her mouth which tasted of sugar and vanilla. Their hands moved over one another's body frantically—they were all tongue, lips, breaths, and movement.

Breaking away, Axe tore off her bra, hungrily sucking her beaded buds while his fingers slipped under her panties, burying themselves in her wet folds. The more he tasted her, the more he craved her—he'd never have his fill of her.

"Lie down," he commanded.

Reclining against the floral cushions, she let him pull down her lace panties then spread her legs apart. But for the thigh-highs, she was naked; he watched as her skin broke out in goosebumps, and she shivered in anticipation.

"Fuck, you look hot."

Leaning over, he scraped the top of the cake and coated her nipples in frosting. "Don't you look tasty?" he said thickly.

Hovering over her, he gently kissed her eyelids then moved his lips down to her cheeks then jawline, lightly trailing his tongue down to her earlobe. He pulled it into his mouth and sucked it slowly. "You drive me fuckin' wild, babe," he said against her ear.

Trailing his tongue from her ear to her neck, he kissed the pulsing hollow at the base of her throat. Baylee raked her fingers through his hair as she squirmed underneath him.

"I like that," she murmured.

"I love how soft your skin is. You don't know what you do to me."

Dipping his head lower, he nipped and bit her soft flesh as his fingers skated across her sides, causing shivers to race across her body. He licked the top swells of her tits then made red love bites on the sides of them as she bucked under him. Circling her breasts with his tongue, he saw the stiff, white-covered tips of her nipples. Covering his mouth over them, he sucked and lapped up the frosting while softly biting the hard buds.

"Fuck. That feels amazing," she panted.

Grabbing each side of her tits, he pressed them together then dipped his tongue down the crevice, licking and nipping. He reached over and scooped up some more frosting, which he painted on her ribs, her belly button, and her inner thighs. Baylee squeezed her eyes shut, her head tilted back.

"Open your eyes, sweetheart. I want to see the desire in them," he said as his tongue skimmed over her body, licking and sucking up the icing.

Locking his gaze on hers, Axe slid one hand under her soft ass, kneading it as his tongue trailed down to her sweet inner thighs, where he teased her with his tongue, tracing figure eight patterns on them. Each time he looked up from beneath his hooded lids, Baylee's lustful eyes met his.

"You taste so sweet, but I can't wait to taste your pussy. It's the sweetest of all."

He heard her suck in her breath as the tip of his tongue flicked against her clit.

"You like that, baby? I bet you do. Feels real good, doesn't it?"

She moaned her response and he locked onto her clit, sucking it while his finger slid into her pussy. Baylee arched her back which pulled his mouth closer, trailing kisses on her inner thighs. Trailing back to her pulsing heat, he blew on it and she cried out in pleasure.

"Do you know how fuckin' beautiful you are?"

He pulled out his finger only to insert two more into her slick slit. As he shoved them in and out hard and deep, his wicked tongue swept long, full licks from the back of her pussy to the top of her clit, purposely avoiding her throbbing sweet spot.

"You're driving me crazy," Baylee moaned.

She dropped her hand to her mound, two fingers touching her quivering clit before he grabbed it and pushed it away.

"Not yet, baby. You're so close."

She groaned in frustration, and he chuckled against her swollen lips as he continued pistoning his fingers in and out of her.

"Believe me, it's gonna be stronger and better if you wait."

"Just let me come."

He felt her pulsing pussy against his tongue as he played with her, licking everywhere but where she wanted it the most. Her thighs clamped together, trapping his head between them, but he still laved her steadily, missing her aching spot each time. Each stroke of his tongue over her beautiful, pink pussy had his cock bursting to sink into her. The musky, tangy scent of their arousal blended with the sweet grape smell of the champagne and the sugary frosting. He didn't think he was going to be able to hold out, so he sucked her clit gently in his mouth, the tip of his tongue flicking the side of the hardened nub, over and over again.

Her pussy squeezed around his fingers, telling him she was ready to explode.

"Oh, God!" Baylee pulled Axe's hair hard as her body bucked and quivered below him.

As he watched her face contort, he leaned down and swallowed her cries of ecstasy with his mouth. The way she thrashed, moaned, and pulled his hair was turning him way the fuck on. He unzipped his pants, pulling them down hurriedly, then gripped her ankles, pushing her bent knees further toward her.

"I'm gonna fuck your sweet pussy. I can't get enough of it," he said, running his length over her slick sex then thrusting into her. "Fuck, you feel good, baby."

Panting and grunting, he pummeled her hard and fast, his hands slipping under her ass and lifting her further so he could push in deeper. As he dove in, she tilted her hips up, meeting him, taking every inch of him, until they moved together as one, their bodies fused by heat and lust.

His gaze dropped and he watched himself enter her over and over, stretching her wider, his dick glistening with her juices.

"Fuck, you're irresistible," he panted.

As they moved together, her soft hand lightly touching his balls sent jolts of intense pleasure up his spine. He couldn't remember ever wanting a woman as badly as he wanted her. Bending down, he captured her mouth, kissing her hard before he pulled back, his eyes fixed on hers.

With his finger, he caressed the side of her clit, watching her face crumple as she cried out in pleasure, her warm walls tightening around him as he pushed into her. Her arms circled him, her nails digging into the skin on his back. Then his body went stiff and a feral growl sprang from his throat as his seed rushed out in streams, filling her up.

"Baylee. Fuck. Fuck!"

He collapsed on top of her, loving the feel of her quivering body as it slowly relaxed from her orgasm. Flipping over, he held her close to him, their legs entwined. They lay together, sated, Axe playing with her hair as he kissed the side of her forehead. He never wanted to move.

Baylee, naked and warm, and in his arms, was perfect.

CHAPTER TWENTY-SEVEN

Two weeks later

THE ANNIVERSARY OF her mother's death came and went without incident. Baylee hadn't heard anything from the killer for the past three weeks. Perhaps someone was playing a sick joke on her, after all, and all her worry was for naught. Banger nixed the guard duty since everything was quiet and he needed the prospects at the club.

Baylee had felt vulnerable at first, but Axe made sure he was around most of the time when she wasn't at work, so the fear was held at bay.

The end of the summer, and her services in Pinewood Springs, were coming to an end. The foundation had been poured and the strip mall construction had begun. Banger was pleased, and he rewarded Baylee with a very large bonus. Logan accused her of sleeping her way into the good graces of the club, and Baylee knew when she was chosen for the partnership, he'd cry foul.

She sighed. She had mixed feelings about going back to Denver. On one hand, she missed her condo, friends, and the feel of a big city, but on the other, she was hopelessly in love with Axe. How could she leave him? In ten days, she'd be back home. For sure, she'd have to come back to Pinewood Springs to make sure everything was going okay, but the majority of the process on her end was finished; the rest could be completed by Skype.

Her heart lurched when she thought of Axe. They loved each other, something she never would have predicted. A one-night stand had turned into mutual love and respect. She smiled weakly when she remembered her plan to engage in a summer fling with him.

She packed up her laptop just as her phone pinged. Her heart leapt when she saw it was Axe. *He must've finished with his uncle.* Axe had finally tracked his uncle down and went to talk with him. Baylee was dying to know what transpired.

> **Axe:** *Hey, babe. Want Mexican for dinner?*
> **Baylee:** *Sounds perfect. Did u see ur uncle?*
> **Axe:** *Yeah. He's sorry he scared u. Just thought u were pretty.*

Bullshit.

> **Baylee:** *U believe him?*
> **Axe:** *Yeah. Know him. Dead end.*

Is he telling me the truth? Why would he lie to me? I feel something's not right.

> **Axe:** *U still there?*
> **Baylee:** *Yeah. Packing up. Done with work.*
> **Axe:** *Club is sponsoring charity bike rally tomorrow. Want to go?*
> **Baylee:** *Yeah. Is it in town?*
> **Axe:** *Ya. In Lakeside Valley.*
> **Baylee:** *K. What time tonight?*
> **Axe:** *7:30. I'll pick u up.*
> **Baylee:** *K. See u.*

She massaged the back of her neck, trying to rub out the kinks. Even though Axe said his uncle's actions were innocent, she didn't believe it for a moment. He was probably just biased because it was his uncle. She switched off the office light, happy the work day was over.

"ARE YOU SURE he's telling you the whole story?" Dean asked as he adjusted the fan in his hot office.

Axe wiped his palms on his jeans. "Yeah. I have a way of getting people to tell me the truth."

The private investigator glanced sideways in surprise. "Your own family? Damn, that's cold."

Axe's gaze was flat and hard. "So, we set to go next Tuesday?"

"Sure. Shit!" He jumped back, shook his hand, then placed his bleeding thumb in his mouth. "This damn fan is a pain in the ass."

"Why don't you fix the AC? I know you can afford it, I paid you enough fuckin' money."

A nervous laugh bubbled from him as he turned around, wiping his perspiring forehead. "It's a goner. I'm going to have to buy a new fan."

Axe only stared at him.

Clearing his throat, Dean sat behind his desk, took out a monthly calendar, and jotted something down. "This Tuesday. Does Ms. Peters know anything?"

Axe shook his head. "It's gotta stay that way. I can't risk her knowing."

Dean held his water bottle against his neck. "Damn, can't wait for the summer to end. It'll be soon. Have you noticed some of the leaves are starting to change? Can't come soon enough."

Axe sat, stone-faced.

"And you're right about not telling her. The average person can't hide fear or nervousness too well. It takes a steely SOB to not crack. Make sure you don't weaken and spill your guts to her. I've seen that happen too many times." He set the water bottle on the desk. "Women have a way of making us tell them shit we don't want to."

Pulling himself up, Axe's lips curled into a cynical smile. "No worries. I'm a steely sonofabitch."

He left the office, grateful to be out of the sweat box with the sweating PI. The fresh air energized him, and he headed his bike to the clubhouse. He wanted to tell Chas, Jerry, Rock, and Jax they were set for Tuesday. The PI had accomplished what Axe wanted, creating a buffer to throw the killer off. When the PI discovered Baylee's old room had been bugged, Axe wasn't surprised. He wanted the killer to conclude that Axe had turned over the investigation to the investigator, so Axe could be free to track things down behind the scenes.

He turned into the club's lot and nodded to Puck who was in the back, scrubbing trashcans. Axe entered through the back, the scent of hickory surrounding him. In the kitchen, he watched Doris, Marlene, Cherri, and Addie talking and laughing as they prepared the food for the dinner after the rally.

The club sponsored three rallies a year: the big one in the fall at Cooper Peak, and two smaller ones at Lakewood Valley. The one set for the following day was to benefit a charity that helped bikers out with their children who'd been diagnosed with cancer. It killed Axe every time he'd see the kids at the rally. They were all in various stages, and the ones in the later stages saw the rally on their DVD player when their dads brought them the recording after the event. *Fuck. Life doesn't make sense.*

"Smells good," he said as he neared the stove. "Whatcha makin'?"

"Beef ribs and honey-baked hams," Addie replied as she stirred the glaze on the stovetop.

"Make a lot, we're expecting a big crowd tomorrow night."

"Chas told me, and he also wanted extra to bring home." Addie laughed.

"See you, ladies."

Axe made his way to the great room where he saw Chas, Jax, and Jerry sitting at a table, drinking beers. He headed over to them.

"Saw your old ladies cooking up a storm in the kitchen. Smells good," he said to Chas and Jax.

"She's cooking, and I'm babysitting." Jax pointed to Paisley, who ran around the great room, squealing in delight.

"Me, too." Chas pointed to his daughter, Hope, sleeping in a yellow car seat, a green blanket with giraffes on it tucked snug under her chin.

Axe shook his head. "Fuck. What the hell's happened to us?"

"Loving a woman," Chas replied.

Jax and Axe nodded.

"So, what's the word?" Jerry asked. "We doing this on Tuesday?"

"Yeah. I had to verify some shit with my uncle, which took longer than I'd have liked. He didn't cooperate in the beginning." Axe threw back the shot of Jack the prospect set in front of him.

"Is he gonna snitch?" Jax questioned.

"Nah. He's stupid, but he's not crazy. He likes living too much."

They chuckled then grew quiet as Axe explained the plans for the following Tuesday night.

CHAPTER TWENTY-EIGHT

EXCITEMENT WAS IN the air as bikers, their families, and citizens milled around the rally, checking out a few of the stands dotting the area. The maple and oak trees provided shade from the rays of a late August sun, and the breezes off the lake cooled the area.

Baylee had never seen so many people in leather. Women, men, and children donned leather boots, vests, and jackets, even though the temperature hovered around ninety degrees. A boy around eight years old with dark hair ran up to her and Axe.

"Uncle Axe, have you seen my mom and dad?"

"They were by the stage listening to the band. Come on, let's go look for them."

The boy looked up at Baylee, then back at Axe. "Is this your girlfriend Mom and Dad keep talking about?"

Red brushstrokes painted her cheeks, and she swatted Axe's arm when he laughed deeply.

"Yeah. Jack, this is Baylee. Baylee, this is Jack. He's Chas's son."

"Nice meeting you," Baylee greeted before following the two.

After reuniting Jack with his parents, Axe grasped her hand and led her over to the Harleys on display.

"I didn't know Addie and Chas had a son," she said.

"They have a daughter together. Jack is Chas's son from another marriage. His ex was such a bitch. Since they got hitched, Addie's been in the process of adopting Jack."

"What about his mom?"

"She doesn't give a shit. She signed the papers. Not sure how it works. Cara's helping them with that."

"Addie seems like she'd be great mom."

"She is. Jack's crazy about her. You want kids?"

Baylee sputtered then coughed. "Where did that come from?"

"We were talking 'bout kids. Just wondered. Do you?"

"Someday, it'd be nice, but I'm not even thinking about it now." She swallowed. "How about you?"

"Yeah. Someday."

They stopped in front of fifty Harleys gleaming in the sun. As Axe whistled and admired them, Baylee mulled over Axe's question. Why had he asked if she wanted kids? Did he plan on spending his future with her? Even though he'd told her she was his forever, the fact remained that she lived in Denver and he lived there. How were they ever going to resolve that problem?

Axe spoke with a few guys in leather, and Baylee noticed several women in short skirts and shorts wearing halter tops stood at a distance, giggling and pointing at Axe. Soon, a few of them came over and spoke with them, a blonde one constantly touching his upper arm. Clenching her teeth, Baylee's hands curled into fists as she watched Axe laugh and talk with the women.

"Hi, Baylee. I thought I might run into you" Palmer greeted.

"Palmer. How are you?"

"Good." His gaze slowly moved up her body. "You're looking hot."

Ignoring his comment, she pulled down her crop top in a vain effort to cover her belly button.

"What've you been up to? You haven't returned any of my phone calls," he said.

"Busy with work."

"And with me." Axe's arm hooked around her waist.

A dark scowl replaced Palmer's smile. "I wasn't talking to you," he spat.

Axe walked away with Baylee close to his side.

"You have a real attitude problem, jerk," Palmer called after him.

Axe continued walking, but Baylee winced as his hand tightened around hers. Turning sideways, she noticed his jaw was clenched.

"I can't believe my dad married your trashy mom."

Before Baylee could think, Axe dropped her hand and marched toward Palmer.

"Fuck off. Stay away from my woman," Axe hissed.

Palmer snorted. "You *wish* she were your woman. She's not the type of woman who goes out with trash."

Baylee blanched, the tension around the two men thicker than fog on a rainy day. She spotted Banger, Hawk, and Chas watching them. She moved forward but a hand held her back; looking up, she recognized Jax, relief washing over her. Palmer took a step back and Axe took one forward.

"Aren't you guys going to stop this?" she asked.

Jax replied, "Axe can take care of himself real good. This isn't our business."

Palmer then turned to her and questioned, "Are you this guy's woman?"

Everything stopped for her. It was like she was looking down on the scene from above: Palmer tight-lipped and staring at her, Axe's fists clenched with hatred in his eyes.

"Turn the fuck around. We've been gunning for this day for a long time."

Baylee knew who would win this fight. If she didn't do something, Palmer would leave on a gurney and Axe in a squad car. She couldn't let it happen.

She ran between the two men.

"Baylee, get the fuck out of the way," Axe commanded, his voice sharp like a whip.

"No." Axe's predatory growl sent shivers down her back, and her pulse pounded in her ears. Sucking in a deep breath, she turned to Palmer. "Yes, I'm Axe's woman. I love him, and I don't appreciate you calling him trash. He's a wonderful man."

If a pin dropped, she could've sworn she'd be able to hear it. Palmer stood before her, lips parted and brows together, as if the reality of her choosing a foul-mouthed, leather-clad outlaw over him was incomprehensible.

Axe came up behind her, his hands on her shoulders, moving her to the side. "That was sweet, babe. Now, stand away."

In one fluid move, he punched Palmer right in the jaw. The blow knocked his opponent on the dirt. Shaking his head, Palmer jumped up and turned away. "Neither of you are worth it."

"Stay the fuck away from me and Baylee," Axe said in an icy voice.

Palmer walked away, disappearing into the crowd. The group of people who had stood around waiting to see a fight broke apart, wandering off in many directions. Baylee gazed downward, watching the tufts of grass shiver in the breeze.

"Get over here." Axe gripped her wrist, yanking her against him.

Baylee nuzzled his neck, kissing him, her tongue flicking his earlobe. "I love you," she whispered in his ear.

He placed both hands on the side of her face, her gaze latching onto his. "You are everything to me." Then he kissed her savagely with his hot mouth, sending spirals of pleasure through her.

With his arm wrapped around her, Baylee leaned her head against his shoulder as they walked around the rally. Several women waved to Axe and, to his credit, he either ignored them or gave them a curt nod. When they sat at one of the tables under the oak tree, enjoying the coolness of the shade, Baylee took Axe's hand in hers.

"You seem to know a lot of women," she said, her heart pounding.

"I do."

"It kind of bothers me," she admitted.

"I get that. It'd bother me if you had a bunch of guys you knew flirting and waving at you. You gotta understand they don't mean anything to me. We were only having fun. You're the one who means something to me. We're gonna run into chicks who fucked me. I can't change that. It doesn't have anything to do with us."

"I know it's your past, but there are so many. I guess I don't like seeing the women you screwed because I know they've had the same things I do with you."

His eyes bored into her. "Not true. What I had with them was just fucking. You and I make love. I hold you all night, and when you're not awake, I fuckin' watch you sleep. Don't ever think I gave what we have to other women. I never have. You're my woman. My love."

Baylee jumped up and plopped in his lap, feathering kisses all over his face and neck. She wriggled against him, giggling when he blew against her ear. He captured her neck's soft flesh, biting and sucking it while he caressed her thigh. She squirmed as shivers of pleasure zinged through her. As she jiggled her butt, she felt the bulge between his legs grow long and thick against her ass.

"You better stop all your fidgeting unless you wanna fuck against a tree again." His thick voice caressed her from head to toe.

As he rubbed her thigh, her pulsing sex ached for him to touch her, enter her, and bring her over the top.

"I'm horny for you," she whispered.

"What are we waiting for? Let's go back to the clubhouse. I can show you my room."

"Won't there be people there?"

"They're all here. We'll be alone for a few hours. Later, there's a barbecue then the club party. That'll be wild. Can't wait to show you off to the visiting members." He sucked her bottom lip while his hand slipped under her thigh.

Catching his glance, a sensual thrill rode her spine as she saw hunger blazing in his dark eyes. "What are we waiting for?" she rasped.

He scooped Baylee up then set her on her feet, tugging her along as they went to his Harley. Pressed against his back, the cool, early evening breeze rolled around her as they drove to the clubhouse.

The great room seemed different without the usual chatter of the brothers. Blade was behind the bar, making sure the liquor was in order for the club party that night. A few of the old ladies had also come back early from the rally to finish last-minute preparations for the family barbecue.

"The food smells fantastic," she said as Axe led her by the hand to his room. "How many are coming to the party?"

Axe peeled off his t-shirt and kicked off his boots. "A lot, like a hundred, but that includes the women."

Baylee looked around his room. It was simple with just a queen-sized bed, two tables, one desk lamp, a computer, one desk chair, one recliner, and a forty-two-inch flat-screen TV. The room did not show any markings of a home; the white walls were bare, and cheap plastic blinds covered the large garden-level window.

"How do you like my place?"

"It seems convenient."

"It serves its purpose. Now, get your sweet ass over to the bed."

"There must be mostly men at the party, since there's only a handful of women in the club," she said as she shuffled to the bed.

Seizing her hand, he pulled her on the bed, and Baylee landed half on him and half on the mattress.

Tugging her top up with urgency, Axe answered, "The barbecue is for the family, brothers, charter and affiliate members. After the dinner, the women clean up, go home, and the party starts. The women who come to the parties are the club whores and the hoodrats. You know what they are?"

"I remember reading about them in my research. I didn't think it was real."

"It's real. It's the way the club works. The old ladies know it, and they're cool with it as long as their men don't stick their cocks in another chick's pussy." He twisted her top over her breasts. "Damn, babe, help with this."

Baylee flung off her top. "Am I going to the party?"

"Yeah. You'll be with me, but you gotta stay with me so there isn't any problem." He pulled her shorts down, taking her sheer panties with them.

"Don't worry. I won't leave your side."

Hovering over her naked body, Axe bent forward so his face was inches from hers. "Good girl. Now, give your man some love."

She yanked him on top of her, his hard dick flat against her belly, and covered his mouth with hers.

CHAPTER TWENTY-NINE

Tuesday

"YOU WANT TO meet for lunch?" Baylee asked as she snuggled in Axe's arms.

"Today isn't good. I got stuff to do. We can go out to dinner, though."

In a soft voice, she said, "I'll be going back to Denver soon."

"I know, babe." Axe squeezed her tighter.

After holding on to each other, and Baylee hitting the *snooze* button several times, she groaned as she untangled herself from Axe's arms then rolled out of bed. She padded to the bathroom so she could get ready to start her day.

When she arrived at her office, there was a new floral arrangement on her desk. She opened the card, and the brief "Can you forgive me? Let's have dinner" note from Palmer turned her stomach. *Doesn't this guy ever give up?* She picked it up and marched over to Tina's desk, setting the bouquet of carnations and roses on her desk.

Tina smiled widely. "Thank you, Ms. Peters. I'm sorry you're allergic to flowers."

"I'm very allergic, especially to these. Enjoy."

When she went back to her office, she was surprised to find Gary sitting in it, since he'd gone back to Denver the past weekend.

"Hi, Gary. What brings you back to Pinewood Springs?"

Gary looked up from the document he was reading. To her, he looked tired—weary, really. He was probably over-worked since the firm had taken on more projects than they should have. Baylee was going crazy juggling several jobs they'd given her in addition to the strip mall gig. The newest assignments were all in Denver, so at least being back in the city would help make her workload more manageable. Her stomach lurched, as it always did, when she thought of leaving Axe.

She knew he wanted her to stay in Pinewood Springs, but how could she give up her career, something she'd worked so hard for? It'd be like her asking him to leave the Insurgents. He'd told her it wasn't the same since the club was his family, not a job, but there was a Denver chapter he could be part of. For the past two weeks, she'd been musing over possible ways for them to make their relationship work long-term, but it looked like nothing would help. They'd decided on taking turns visiting each other, but Baylee knew from a past relationship with a fellow architect she met on a project in Cheyenne, Wyoming, that it would only work for a while. Then life came up and one or the other party couldn't get away until the whole relationship fizzled out.

For her, the difference with Axe was that she adored him. She loved him more than she'd ever loved any other man, so she'd try hard to make a go of it. She worried Axe would grow restless. Without her around, would he succumb to the advances of the women who seem to always make a play for him? *He is very sexual, and he* is *a man.* She shook her head, not wanting to think about *that.* What were they going to do?

"Baylee?" Gary's voice transported her back to her office.

"I'm sorry, Gary. I was thinking about the projects I'm working on. Is there something wrong with the strip mall?"

Gary darted his eyes around, as if to avoid her gaze. Baylee sensed something was wrong. He seemed more nervous than usual, and he wouldn't look her in the eye. *Maybe he's come to tell me I didn't make partner.*

"What is it?"

"Stop asking me that," he snapped.

Taken aback, Baylee leaned back in her chair, the sting of his comment weaving its way through her. She'd not say anything more and let him take the lead, since he obviously wanted to tell her something. They sat in awkward silence which seemed like hours to Baylee, but was only a few minutes before Gary, locking his fingers together, leaned forward.

"You've been a great employee, Baylee. A real asset to the firm, and we've been impressed with your fresh, creative designs. You have your pulse on the look for the future." He paused. "I've enjoyed watching you grow as an architect. Your mother would've been very proud of you." His voice caught.

Is he leaving the firm? Is he sick? What's going on?

"Thanks, Gary. I love working for the firm, and I'm happy you and Bob gave me a chance."

"Your mother was a lovely woman. She was so creative. You remind me of her. She was also very ethical—sometimes too much." He muttered the last part of the sentence so she had to lean in to pick up his words.

"It makes me happy to hear you compare me to my mom."

Okay, this is getting weird. Why does he keep talking about Mom?

"Is your biker friend still in the picture?"

"Yes."

Gary nodded then stared at her with piercing eyes, the tenderness of the past few minutes gone in a flash. "Is he going to pick you up after work tonight?"

"I'm not sure. Why?"

"I noticed your bodyguard is gone."

"Yes. I haven't had any more problems. I guess it was just some loony who got his kicks scaring me. He was probably doing the same type of things with other women. Some people are very strange."

"You see, I told you there wasn't anything to worry about." He smiled thinly at her.

For a split second, an icy fear froze her as she looked at him. Then it melted away, leaving a sense of confusion in its wake.

Gary rose to his feet and walked to the doorway.

"You'll have to work late tonight. I have some things I need to go over with you, but I don't have time now."

"On the strip mall?"

"Yes."

"I thought everything was on target."

"Well, it's not. Are you questioning me?" he asked tersely.

"No. Sorry. I'll see you at seven-thirty."

"Okay."

Then he stalked away.

That was weird as hell. I wonder what he's talking about. Too strange.

She walked down the hall to Logan's office. He was staring at his computer screen intently, so she knocked on the door frame. He pivoted to the door, a smile crossing his face when he saw her.

"Baylee, come on in. What's on your mind?"

"Gary's back in town."

"I know, I just saw him."

"Did he tell you about the meeting tonight?"

Slowly shaking his head, a frown crossed his brow. "No, he didn't mention any meeting. When did he tell you that?"

"Just a few minutes ago. That's strange."

"It is." Logan tapped his pen against the desk.

"Maybe he forgot to mention it to you. He seemed a little out of sorts," she offered.

"Yes, that's probably it. You're right, he didn't seem like his normal self."

Pushing up from the chair, she said, "I'll let you get back to work. I was just checking. Are you excited to be going back to Denver?"

"Hell yes. Small-town living isn't for me. It's been a long summer."

Baylee ambled toward the door when she heard Logan call out.

"Baylee, thanks for the heads-up about the meeting. What time?"

"Seven-thirty."

"I'll be there. See you."

"Later."

Back in her office, dread pricked at her, and as hard as she tried to shake it, it persisted. She chalked it up to her anxiety about leaving Axe and going back to Denver. She was tired and over-anxious, and the strange visit from Gary didn't help. Why hadn't he told Logan about the meeting? Her hands shook as she brought her lukewarm coffee to her lips.

What if I'm going to be fired? I bet that's it. That's why Gary was so weird, and didn't tell Logan. There is no strip mall meeting, the firm is letting me go because I dated Axe—a client. It all made sense. Gary probably felt guilty about the firm's decision to terminate her, so that was why he was reminiscing about her mom.

Her eyes stung and her stomach churned. How could she have been that stupid to think they would keep her after Gary warned her about getting too friendly with Axe? She'd known she was taking a huge risk with her job by seeing him, but she hadn't cared. But it was all coming crashing down. She pulled out her phone and dialed Axe, needing to hear his voice.

"The firm's letting me go because we went out," she blurted out when he answered.

"Whoa, babe. What the fuck? Who told you that?"

"Gary. He wants to meet with me tonight. I know he's going to fire me. He was acting so off this morning."

"Gary's in town? Good."

"Good? Why the hell is that good? He's going to can me. Do you understand what I'm saying?"

"He's not going to do that. Why would he come all the way up here to do that when you'll be back in Denver in a few days? It doesn't make sense, babe."

"I know something's wrong. There're no loose ends with the strip mall project. No reason for a meeting. Plus, I have this feeling…"

"Calm down, sweetheart. Breathe deeply. No reason to get yourself all worked up until you know for sure what's going on."

"I *do* know. Gary's going to fire me. I'm not going to the meeting."

Baylee waited for Axe's response, but when it didn't come she thought her phone had disconnected.

"Axe? Are you there?"

After a long pause, she heard him breathe out forcefully.

"I'm here."

"Are you doing something else?"

"No. You have to go to the meeting tonight. You're jumping to conclusions. Maybe he's going to tell you that you made partner."

"From the way he talked earlier, I doubt it. At first, I thought he was leaving the firm or that he'd been diagnosed with an illness, you know? He definitely acted like he was indirectly saying goodbye to me. Now, I get it. He's canning me."

"Go to the meeting."

"Why do you care if I go or not?"

"I know you. You'll obsess about it for weeks if you don't know for sure. Just go, and we can talk about it when I pick you up after."

She sighed. "You're right. I'll go, but if I'm going to the slaughter-house, I'm going to treat myself to a helluva shopping spree."

Axe chuckled. "That's my woman. Call me when the meeting's done, and I'll come by."

"Thanks. Love you."

"Me, too."

The heaviness in her heart lifted after she'd spoken to Axe. He was her elixir, and she couldn't imagine him out of her life. *Don't go there, Baylee. Stop it. Right now.*

She grabbed her purse and sunglasses and headed down the hallway. When she passed Tina's desk, she said, "I'll be out for a couple of hours. I have something very important I have to do." With cash and credit cards in her purse, Baylee left the building to do some serious shopping.

THE GREEN-EYED MAN stretched his arms over his head as he looked out the window. In less than three hours, he'd do what he should've done seventeen years before—kill Baylee Peters. He'd let his spineless cohort talk him out of it too many times. He'd tried to do it again by saying Baylee would never be able to positively identify the killer with the green eyes, but as long as she lived, the green-eyed man had no peace. Against his better judgment, the killer had left a mess for all these years, but later that night, he'd rectify it once and for all.

He smiled as he watched the clear blue sky slowly take on tinges of gold. Having the Insurgents involved in all this had given him some anxiety, but he depended on their stupidity, and he wasn't disappointed. Not able to figure out squat, they'd hired a private investigator to track the murderer down. He laughed. The inept PI bungled his way around town trying to track down clues, and all the while, he—the man of Baylee's nightmares—sat back and watched, enjoying the farce.

The nice-looking man went over to his desk, opened the drawer, and stared at his Glock 20 semi-automatic pistol. He loved the power of the gun; it was a pistol on steroids, and it'd make his job a lot easier. He closed the drawer then glanced at the clock. The man figured he'd have time for a prime steak dinner before he met up with Baylee and his partner. By the end of the night, the killer would have struck again, but this time, there would be no loose ends.

CHAPTER THIRTY

A FTER DROPPING OFF numerous shopping bags at her hotel, Baylee drove back to the office with a heavy heart. Not knowing for certain what the meeting was about drove her crazy. Even though Axe thought it was about making her partner, she'd seen how dejected Gary was, and her instincts told her something was amiss. She'd known Gary since she was born, and she'd never seen him as downhearted as he was that afternoon.

As she pulled into a parking space, she knew that if she did lose her job over her relationship with Axe, so be it. If she had to do it over, she would in a heartbeat. Falling in love with Axe had been one of the few highlights in her life since her mother died.

When she got to the office, no one was there. It was eerie. Usually a couple of the engineers worked late, but they were gone. Even the cleaning crew had come and gone. She checked out Logan's office on the off chance he may be there, but he was gone, as well. It was seven o'clock—not enough time for her to run back to the hotel or even do an errand. No, she'd pull up a game of Yahtzee on her computer to pass the time before the chopping block fell.

When she caught a shadow in her doorway from the corner of her eye, her breath hitched, her heartbeat pounding erratically until she recognized Gary.

"Oh, it's you. I didn't hear you come in. You startled me."

He lowered his head and walked in, his shoulders rounded. He fell into the chair opposite her desk, rubbing his eyes. Gary sat quietly, staring at the floor. Baylee shifted uncomfortably in her chair. *He seems so sad. I am totally getting canned.*

She cleared her voice. "Gary, I know why you wanted to talk to me."

He lifted his head and gazed at her, his eyebrows raised. "You do?"

"Yes, and I know this is hard for you. I mean, you've known me since I was born."

His eyes glistened.

Oh, my God. It looks like he's going to cry. He must really not want to fire me.

"But it's okay. I understand."

Gary's eyes widened. "You do?"

She nodded. "I screwed up. I knew the firm's policy, and I got involved with Axe anyway. I know you can't make an exception because you and my mom went back a long way, and I wouldn't want you to. I take full responsibility. I only ask that you, Bob, and Warner give me a good recommendation."

Tilting his head to the side, Gary said uncertainly, "You think we're firing you? That's crazy. You're one of our best employees. We decided to make you partner." His smile faded. "Isn't it ironic?"

"Wait, you mean I *still* have my job *and* I'm a partner?"

He nodded. She squealed then jumped out of her chair, her thoughts scattered.

"This is awesome, Gary. Oh, thank you!"

She hugged his stiff body and gave him a peck on the cheek. Pulling back, she placed her hand on his wet cheek.

"You're crying. Why?"

He opened his mouth, but nothing came out. He lowered his head again.

"Gary, talk to me. Are you sick, or something?"

"I'm sorry," he choked out.

"For what?"

"For being a coward," a cold voice said.

Baylee spun around. "What are you doing here?" she asked Stephen Rodgers, then gasped as she stared into his flinty green eyes.

Eyes she'd seen before. In her dreams.

Her *nightmares.*

Baylee's limbs went weak and she fell back, hitting the corner of the desk. Looking at Gary, she noticed he avoided her gaze.

"Gary? What's going on?" she asked weakly.

Gary lowered his head while shaking it.

Stephen Rodgers loomed over the crumpled man. "You empathetic piece of shit. I should've taken care of you years ago."

As reality began to sink in, icy shivers weaved through her, and she pressed her fists to the side of her face. Black spots moved in front of her eyes and she gasped for breath. *I can't pass out. I'm in danger!* Holding onto the desk, she steadied herself right before Logan burst into the office.

"Sorry I'm late." He smiled broadly at the group.

"Who the fuck is he, and why is he here?" Stephen snarled.

"He's an employee. I don't know why he's here," Gary said in a monotone voice.

"I'm here for the meeting." Logan looked at Baylee, confusion evident on his face.

"There's no meeting. Too bad you came," Stephen Rodgers snarled.

Before Logan could utter another word, a shot filled the room. As Logan fell back, blood oozing from his chest, Baylee placed her hands over her ears, her screams drowned out by the deafening gunfire. She leapt toward the door, stepping over Logan's motionless body. A strong arm yanked her hair, dragging her back into the room.

"Our meeting isn't over, Baylee," Stephen sneered.

Baylee twisted out of his hold, her eyes landing on a large, angry scar running up his forearm. She clutched her throat as the sound of her heartbeat thrashed in her ears.

"You! You killed my mother! Why? She didn't know you. You're fucking crazy!"

"You're wrong. She knew me very well. She was always teasing me with her low-cut blouses. She had nice breasts. Just like you." His finger traced right above her camisole's neckline.

She forced the bile down. "You sick bastard."

"Maybe, but I didn't kill her for that. I killed her because she couldn't keep her mouth shut. Gary warned her, too, but she was so high and mighty. She was going to turn us in to the police. If she would've kept her nose out of our business, we wouldn't be here now. But…"

It was as if someone had sucker-punched her. She stared at Gary. "You were responsible for my mother's murder? You were her friend. She was so close to you. How could you let her die? You sonofabitch!"

She flew at him with outstretched hands, clawing and hitting him as hard as she could. Gary didn't budge as she attacked him. From behind her, the killer's deep laugh sickened her.

Baylee whirled around and raised her hand, but Stephen caught it before she struck him.

"You don't want to do that." He spoke harshly, his eyes narrowed to slits.

"How did you know my mother?" she asked softly.

"I worked closely with the firm, passing zoning permits through. I was head of the department for the city. She was a beautiful woman."

Baylee's stomach churned.

"He took bribes. Our firm wasn't the only one who had him on payroll."

"My mom went along with this?"

Gary shook his head slowly. "No. I didn't involve her or Bob. I was the one responsible for securing the permits. Our firm was just starting, and we had to compete with the larger, more prestigious ones on 17th Street. If we hadn't been able to get the permits, we would've closed our doors long ago."

"And my mom would still be alive," she said bitterly.

"Your mom wanted the firm to move forward," he replied.

"I hardly think she wanted to die for it." Baylee wiped her wet cheeks. "So, Mom found out."

Gary nodded. "I begged her not to go to the police. I told her I'd make it right, but she threatened to tell Bob, to throw me out, report me to the ethics board, and file a charge with the police. Embezzlement and paying bribes. I would've lost everything. I had young kids. I told her I'd pay back the money I took, and I'd sever ties with Stephen, but she was adamant. She was going to destroy me."

"So, you destroyed her instead?"

"I didn't have a choice. I warned her."

"You told him, and you *knew* he'd hurt her. You sent her to be slaughtered. How could you?"

"I didn't know he was going to kill her. He told me he'd talk to her, try and have her see it our way. I didn't know. Please, Baylee, you have to believe me. I did not want your mother killed." He hung his head.

"But you've known who the killer was all along, and you did nothing. You're worse than he is, because you were my mother's friend." Her throat tightened. "And my father's." Her eyes burned with the heat of her tears. "And *mine*."

Stephen butted in. "Gary didn't want to give up his lifestyle. I've paid him well, though, since I needed him around. He kept tabs on you all these years. Even fucked your shrink's nurse to get information on your progress, and that's how I knew your time had come. Your mother wanted to destroy me, and so do you."

Gary shook his head. "It doesn't have to be this way. Baylee, tell him you won't say anything."

"It's a little late for that, isn't it?"

Another deafening blast shook her. Gary crumpled to the floor.

This is it. I'm next. Her legs gave out and she sank to the floor.

"And now, Baylee, it's just you and me."

"You're crazy! Don't you think someone heard the gunshots? You can't actually believe you can get away with this."

"I'll just walk away," he told her with a shrug. "Just like I did before."

He lifted the gun once more. Covering her face with her hands, her body shook like a leaf, and her limbs were so cold. Another blast echoed around her. She waited for death to take her. Something strong pulled her up and pried her fingers off her face. She opened her eyes slowly and stared into Axe's. *What is he doing here? Am I dead?*

"It's okay, babe. I'm here now."

"Stephen Rodgers killed my mom," she said through chattering teeth.

"I know."

"You knew?"

"I had your back the whole time. My uncle Max tipped me off. Rodgers paid him to keep an eye on you, but he didn't know the reason. Whenever money greases my uncle's palms, he doesn't ask any questions."

"He almost killed me."

"We had to get the shit on tape. The PI planted a bug in your office, and the tapes will be turned over to the fuckin' badges anonymously. We wanted to make sure we got enough to close your mom's case." He hugged her. "I was here all along. I had your back. My brothers had a sniper rifle aimed at the fucker's head the whole time—just in case." Axe gestured to the building across the street.

"Logan and Gary, they're dead."

"Casualties of war."

Baylee couldn't grasp it all. She heard his words, but they didn't sink in. She was retreating back into the shadows. Not remembering was her safeguard, and she wanted to forget about what had just happened. Squeezing her eyes shut, she wrapped her arms around her knees and rocked back and forth, her mind retreating to her safe zone.

CHAPTER THIRTY-ONE

One month later
Cherryvale Clinic
Denver

LEANING BACK ON the leather chair in Dr. Scott's office, Baylee folded her hands in her lap. "I can't wait to go home. I thought I'd be here longer—like the last time when I had a breakdown." She shifted her eyes from Dr. Scott's to the window behind him. Outside, sprinkles of red and orange mingling with the hues of summer showcased the arrival of autumn.

"You're much stronger than you think. You've made amazing progress over the summer. There was a time when this would have crushed you and sent you spiraling backward into darkness." Dr. Scott placed his pen down and closed her case file. "I credit your strength on your decision to no longer be a victim of the past, and your love for your young man."

Baylee held her therapist's gaze as warmth curled around her. "He's pretty special. I never would have made it without him. I've been so afraid of a relapse into darkness, but the opposite has happened. After the initial horror of it all, all the shadows have been replaced with clear memories. The clarity was always there. I guess my fear just blocked it from coming out."

"Fear holds so many things back from us in life. In your case, you weren't ready to face what had happened the night your mother was killed. Your guilt of not being able to help your mother overpowered everything. The memories were always there, you just needed to let them in."

"Guilt almost made me slip back again when I started blaming my-self for Gary's death and what happened in my office in Pinewood Springs." She smiled when she spotted a small rabbit scurry across the lawn. In a low voice, she said, "I now understand that I wasn't responsi-ble for anything that had happened—Stephen Rodgers was. I knew something was up with him. My instincts told me he was bad news when I'd met him at Axe's mother's wedding; I just didn't know how to connect the dots at that time."

"Your mind was trying to free you. Our minds can either be our allies or our foes. All the snippets of memory you experienced while in Pinewood Springs were a collage of Rodgers, down to the scent of apples and vinegar. He'd been shaking down a small apple cider business and had collected his pay before he'd come to confront your mother. The smell of fermented apples was so strong that your mind tucked it away, only for it to come forward that night at the restaurant in Pinewood Springs." He smiled warmly at her.

"It's so freeing to be able to remember. It's like I took an eraser and rubbed out a large, black spot from the tapestry of my life. It's wonder-ful."

Baylee had never felt this complete since the night her mother lost her life. She also credited Logan's miraculous survival as playing a role in her recovery. The shot had narrowly missed a major artery, and he'd be returning to the firm in the next three weeks. She'd bet he'd be as ambitious as ever. When she'd spoken to him on the phone the previous week, he hadn't held any animosity toward her, for which she was grateful.

"Is there anything else you'd like to go over?" Dr. Scott said.

Shaking her head, Baylee said, "I want to know when I can go home and return to work."

"By the end of next week."

"Seriously?" Baylee's eyes danced.

Nodding, her therapist smiled.

Baylee leapt up from her chair, rushed over and gave him a big hug.

"Thank you for everything," she said.

"You're welcome. I'm so happy the way things worked out for you. I wish all my cases had a happy ending."

As she left his office, she looked over her shoulder at her doctor who stayed with her through thick and thin. He'd been her life saver for the past two years. It would seem strange not to see him anymore. Their parting was bittersweet. She flashed him a big smile then closed the door behind her.

Not wanting to go back to her room, Baylee walked outside and sucked in the air, enjoying the moistness after the dry summer heat. Scattered around the grounds were oak and maple trees gilded with gold leaves that hadn't yet started to fall. Baylee raised her eyes to the cloudless, blue sky—the licks of amber formed a stark silhouette against it. Sitting on one of the many white, wooden benches around the clinic, Baylee tilted her head back, relishing the warm shafts of sunlight caressing her face as the light breeze tousled her hair.

When coolness replaced the sun's warmth, her eyelids fluttered open to reveal Axe in jeans and a leather jacket standing in front of her. Since she'd been at the clinic, he'd been coming and staying at the charter clubhouse for days just so he could visit and be near her, and whenever he came by to visit her, the thrill of seeing him sent jolts of pleasure through her each and every time. He was her rock, her world, and her love.

"Hey, babe." He sat down next to her and leaned toward her giving her a soft kiss on her lips. "How are you?" Axe pulled back and ran his fingers up her arm.

"Good. Did you bring me something?"

"That's the first thing you ask me?" He scowled, but the smile on his lips told her he wasn't really mad.

She poked his chest lightly. "It is when you have your hand behind your back like you're hiding something from me." She craned her neck as she moved sideways. "What is it?"

Shaking his head, he kissed her again, his dark eyes lit with merriment. He swung his arm in front, and in his hand, he held a red rose and a purple chrysanthemum.

Blinking rapidly, she asked, "Are those for me?"

With a smile tugging at his lips, he nodded.

She took them in her hand, bringing them close to her nose as she breathed in their sweet scent. Her glistening eyes scanned his face. "Thank you," she said as she leaned over and kissed him. "I didn't peg you as a flower type of guy."

"I'm not."

"I know, and that's what makes this even more special." Her lips quivered.

Axe yanked her close to him, crushing the delicate petals of the rose as he slid her top's neckline aside then kissed her shoulder. "I fuckin' miss you. When you getting outta here?"

She pushed him back. "You're ruining my flowers."

He winked at her. "I'll just pick some more for you."

"I want these. They're the first ones you've given me."

Shrugging, he leaned back on the bench. "It's time to come home, babe. I need you."

Tracing her finger over his t-shirt, she smiled. "Dr. Scott said I can go home next week."

"Are you fuckin' with me?"

"No. I'm okay. Actually, I'm better than okay—I'm fantastic."

Axe hugged her tightly. In her ear he whispered, "I can't wait to fuck you all night. I love you more than you know."

She squeezed him closer and whispered back. "I know, because I feel the same way you do. I love you so much."

The two lovers kissed and held each other as the sun's rays slowly gave way to the early evening chill. Baylee shivered against the cold, and Axe took off his jacket and placed it around her shoulders. She snuggled further into it, breathing deep his scent of citrus and the wind. With Axe, she felt safe and cherished.

When the realization hit her that Axe had coerced his uncle to tell

Rodgers and Gary that her memory had come back, she'd been livid that he'd set her up and hadn't warned her that she was meeting with the killers that night. She could've been murdered, and even though Axe had assured her repeatedly that she hadn't been in any danger because he and his brothers had her back, reliving the terror she felt when Rodgers aimed the gun at her, made her body shake.

Through therapy, she'd worked through the anger, the terror, and the hurt which had been consuming her since the incident in her office. She forgave him for not clueing her in on what was going down on that fateful night. Axe was right, she would've been nervous, and Rodgers would've caught on that something wasn't right. Cruel people could always smell fear.

He stroked her hair as she leaned her head against his chest, feeling his heartbeat against her temple, his soft breaths sounded like a gentle summer breeze. In the inky sky, chips of light twinkled and burned, and the faint scent of hickory blended with the musty scent of marigolds and earth.

Axe kissed the top of her head. "I'm here for you, always. Never doubt that."

In the darkness, Baylee smiled as she hugged his waist tighter. "I don't."

The serenity of the night engulfed the couple as they clung to each other, content to be together, sharing the moment.

Chapter Thirty-Two

Six weeks later

BAYLEE REPLACED THE wilting flowers in the two vases framing her mother's tombstone with fresh bouquets of sunflowers—her mother's favorite. Brushing her fingertips over the stone, she said in a soft voice, "You're finally at peace, Mommy. You don't have to worry about me. I'm fine." After all these years, Baylee had finally said goodbye to the fear and darkness.

Leaves scurried across the graves as the wind blew them out toward the horizon. In the distance, the Rocky Mountains had a bluish hue under the late October sun. During the week, there were very few people who paid respect to their loved ones, and it was Baylee's favorite time to come. She loved the solitude.

A roar shattered the peacefulness of the cemetery. She jumped, then smiled when she saw Axe ride up on his Harley. Since she'd left the clinic, he'd been coming down most weekends to see her, unless club business interfered.

She smiled at him as he walked toward her.

"How'd you find me?"

"Bob told me you come here every Wednesday."

"You have club business in Denver?"

"I came to see you. I wanted to talk with you."

"It couldn't wait until the weekend?"

"No. Let's go to your place."

She had him follow her to her condo downtown; it was located in one of the many high-rises which had cropped up all over the city, forever changing its skyline. Inside, the sun shone brightly through the large picture windows. Axe closed the door behind him then swung her into his arms, his lips gently covering hers. A shiver rippled through her, and she drew his tongue into her mouth.

"I've missed you, sweetheart," he said against her lips, his hands roamed over her, a paper bag banging against her thigh.

"Me, too. It's hard living apart. What's in the bag?"

"Something for you, but I want to talk to you 'bout something first."

"Now you have me curious as hell," she said as she led him to the couch. Dropping the bag on the coffee table, he tugged her close to him then held her hands, staring intently into her eyes.

"Babe, this fuckin' sucks, you being three hours away from me. We see each other on weekends, but I want you with me all the time."

"I want that, too, but I live in Denver."

"I'm gonna change that. I love you. You're the only woman who has taken my heart one hundred percent. I can't live without you. Fuck, the brothers are threatening to throw my mopey ass out if I don't bring you back with me."

Baylee laughed and kissed his chin softly.

"Bottom line, I need you with me. This commuting bullshit's got to stop."

"What're you saying?"

"I want you to move to Pinewood Springs and live with me as my old lady. And I'm telling you now, no is not an option."

Joy twinkled in her glistening eyes. "So, I don't really have a choice."

Axe shook his head, "Nope." He brushed his lips against hers. "I need you."

"I need you, too."

"Then it's yes?"

She nodded her agreement. "Yes."

He hugged her then handed her the bag. "Open it. I got it for you before I came."

With shaking hands, she opened the bag and saw a leather vest folded neatly. Taking it out, she shook it out. The back of the leather vest had the words "Property of Axe, Insurgents MC" embroidered in white. She wiped the corner of her eyes.

"Pretty sure of yourself, huh?" she joked.

"Fuck yeah. I found a house. I think you'll like it, but if not, we can get another one. It doesn't matter. All that matters is that you're with me."

Tears rolled down her cheeks, and she peppered his face with kisses as happiness flooded her to the core.

"You happy? 'Cause I'm confused here. You're crying and kissing me, so I don't know if that means you're good with being my old lady or not."

She laughed, her head bobbing up and down. "I'd love to be your old lady. And I have a confession to make. I'd asked Bob about opening a satellite office in Pinewood Springs to serve the different counties around there. There's a ton of building going on in the area, and since I'm a partner now, I'm the logical one to run it. He agreed. I was going to tell you this weekend that I was moving back. Of course, Logan is thrilled to see me go so he can be the shining star in the Denver office."

Joining in on her laughter, Axe shook his head. "Again, fate throwing us together. We gotta listen to it, 'cause it keeps happening."

"We have been, and that's how we found each other. I love you so much."

"So, can you move this weekend?"

"I can't just move. I've got to pack and get my place ready to rent."

"I'll help you pack. We can come down on the weekends and work on your place. You know, I have money. The club does well with our dispensaries, so you don't have to rent your place if you don't want to. It'd be good to have somewhere we can stay when you come back for business."

"Let me think about it. I feel like things are moving a little too fast."

"When I want something, I don't like to wait."

"I noticed that."

"And I want you by my side forever."

Baylee pressed against him and pushed him onto the cushions. "I want that more than anything else." She palmed the bulge in his jeans as she rubbed her breasts against his heaving chest. Caressing the inside of his leg with hers, she whispered in his ear, "And I want this, too."

"Fuck, babe. It's all yours. Always," he rasped as his hand glided under her blouse.

With a devilish grin, she slowly unzipped his jeans.

The End

Make sure you sign up for my newsletter so you can keep up with my new releases, special sales, free short stories, and other treats only available to newsletter readers. When you sign up, you will receive a FREE hot and steamy novella. Sign up at:

http://eepurl.com/bACCL1

Visit me on Facebook
facebook.com/Chiah-Wilder-1625397261063989

Check out my other books at my Author Page
amazon.com/author/chiahwilder

Acknowledgments

I have so many people to thank who have made my writing endeavors a reality. It is the support, hard work, laughs, and love of reading that have made my dreams come true.

Thank you to my editor, Kristin, for all your insightful edits, excitement with the Insurgents MC series, and encouragement during the writing and editing process. I truly value your editorial eyes and suggestions as well as the time you've spent with the series. You're the best!

I also want to thank my other editor, Amber who worked with me and gave good suggestions, and was open to my ideas as to why certain events in the story had to take place.

Editors are invaluable to writers and I am grateful to have Kristin and Amber on my team.

Thank you to my wonderful beta readers, Kolleen, Paula, Sue, and Barb—my final-eyes reader. Your enthusiasm for the Insurgents Motorcycle Club series has pushed me to strive and set the bar higher with each book. Your insights are amazing, and I consider each and every recommendation you offer. Your dedication is amazing!

Thank you to my proofreader, Amber, whose last set of eyes before the last once over I do, is invaluable. I appreciate the time and attention to detail you always give to each book.

Thank you to the bloggers for your support in reading my book, sharing it, reviewing it, and getting my name out there. I so appreciate all your efforts.

Thank you to Carrie from Cheeky Covers. You put up with numerous revisions and panicky late night requests for graphics. You always come through for me! I so appreciate your calmness and your artistic vision. You rock!

Thank you to the readers who continue to support and love these tough Insurgents guys. You are the best! Without your readership and love of a good story, the bad boys of the Insurgents MC wouldn't have a platform. Each one of you has made the hours of typing on the computer and the frustrations that come with the territory of writing books so worth it. You all make it possible for writers to write because without you reading the books, we wouldn't exist. Thank you, thank you!

Axe's Fall: Insurgents Motorcycle Club (Book 4)

Dear Readers,

Thank you for reading my book. I hope you enjoyed the fourth book in the Insurgents MC series as much as I enjoyed writing Baylee and Axe's story. This rough motorcycle club has a lot more to say, so I hope you will look for the upcoming books in the series. Romance makes life so much more colorful, and a rough, sexy bad boy makes life a whole lot more interesting.

If you enjoyed the book, please consider leaving a review on Amazon. I read all of them and appreciate the time taken out of busy schedules to do that.

I love hearing from my fans, so if you have any comments or questions, please email me at chiahwilder@gmail.com or visit my facebook page.

To hear of **new releases, special sales, free short stories**, and **ARC opportunities**, please sign up for my **Newsletter** at http://eepurl.com/bACCL1.

A big thank you to my readers whose love of stories and words enables authors to continue weaving stories. Without the love of words, books wouldn't exist.

Happy Reading,

Chiah

BANGER'S RIDE

Book 5 in the Insurgents MC Series

Coming in April, 2016

Banger, President of the Insurgents MC, isn't looking for a woman to replace his beloved wife. Since she died, he's closed his heart to loving again, only looking for carnal pleasure. It's safer that way.

The President of the national club may have sparkling blue eyes and an infectious smile, but make no mistake, if someone crosses him or his club he'd slit their throat in a heartbeat.

Set in his ways, tough, tattooed, and a no BS-type of man, Banger is doing just fine until he meets the sassy, curly-haired, single mom who can cook the best fried chicken he's ever tasted.

He can't get enough of her cooking…or her.

And for the first time since he's been widowed, he wants a woman in his life who will warm his bed.

His orderly life has just exploded.

Belle Dermot is a widow with two kids whose husband left her penniless. Wanting a fresh start, she moves to Pinewood Springs and takes a job at the local diner cooking tasty, home cooked meals.

After finding out her husband was a cheating louse, the last thing she wants is another man in her life. She has her hands full with a rebellious teenage daughter, paying the bills, and fending off nasty accusations that she poisoned her husband.

Yeah he did her wrong: he spent all their money, and was ready to run off with another woman.

Belle was a woman scorned, and her stepdaughter and a detective think she carried her anger a little too far….

Then she meets Banger, the muscular, handsome, and rugged biker who comes crashing into her life.

If only he wasn't so nice to her and didn't get her all hot and bothered. And why does he have to be so damn good in bed?

As hard as she tries to push him away, he keeps slipping back into her life helping her with her life's problems.

And Banger's not the type to let go once he decides on something. He's decided Belle is the woman for him. Now, he just needs her to agree to be his…

Chiah Wilder's Other Books

Hawk's Property: Insurgents Motorcycle Club Book 1
Jax's Dilemma: Insurgents Motorcycle Club Book 2
Chas's Fervor: Insurgents Motorcycle Club Book 3

I love hearing from my readers. You can email me at chiahwilder@gmail.com.

Sign up for my newsletter to receive updates on new books, special sales, free short stories, and ARC opportunities at http://eepurl.com/bACCL1.

Visit me on facebook at
facebook.com/Chiah-Wilder-1625397261063989

Printed in the USA
CPSIA information can be obtained
at www.ICGtesting.com
LVHW012308250424
778512LV00028B/831